A LITTLE BIT WILD

"What would I like stroked? Oh, let's see. My curiosity, I guess. I'd like to get to know you."

There was a tiny pause. "Get to know me? In what way, Harold?"

"Oh, I want you to tell me what sort of a woman you are." He glanced at his scribbled notes. "Tell me what you like to do for fun, what you read, what movies you like to watch. Talk to me as if I were a new friend instead of a customer."

"Well, let's see." Again, there was a small silence. Her voice was more tentative now, her diction slower.

He guessed she was feeling her way, trying to figure him out.

"I guess you could say I'm a little bit wild, Harold. I always was. I like to take chances, I like to live on the edge. . . ."

Gentleman Caller

BOBBY HUTCHINSON

LOVE SPELL NEW YORK CITY

So many thanks to Lauren, my research assistant.
And with love and gratitude to my agent,
Evan Marshall, who believes all things are possible.

LOVE SPELL®

December 2002

Published by

Dorchester Publishing Co., Inc.
276 Fifth Avenue
New York, NY 10001

ISBN 0-505-52500-3

Printed in the United States of America.

Visit us on the web at www.dorchesterpub.com.

Gentleman Caller

Chapter One

"India, baby doll, it's me, Tom. I've been trying to get you for an hour, but the line's always busy." The male voice was sulky and husky with thwarted passion.

"Tommy, honey, I was just lying here on the bed thinking about you. How are you, big guy?"

Thank goodness it was one of her regulars. Maxine shoved her unruly hair out of the way so she could prop the telephone against her ear and change baby Graham's messy diaper while purring suggestive comments into the receiver.

She caught sight of herself reflected in the bathroom mirror and grinned at the witchlike image. She wasn't wearing a scrap of makeup, she had a zit on her chin, her green cat's eyes

1

were puffy from lack of sleep, and she needed a haircut. She had on a pair of much-washed gray sweats and a pink T-shirt already stained from the apricots she'd fed Graham for breakfast, and contrary to *her* fantasies, the ten pounds she'd gained with Graham hadn't evaporated overnight.

Man, she *really* needed a haircut. Her shaggy auburn mane, thick and impossibly curly, was now well past her shoulders, and any style it had ever had was long gone. She usually braided it, but this morning there hadn't been time.

Graham was cutting a tooth. He'd been awake nearly every hour last night, needing a cuddle or a bottle or a diaper change. Aware that Edna was out in the living room working the night shift, Maxine had put James Taylor on the tape player at one point and danced the baby around the bedroom until he slept again.

A child wailing in the background when you were trying to do phone sex wasn't easy to explain. Maxine—and Edna too—had often told callers the noise was an imaginary poodle named Candy.

Maxine yawned hugely, only half listening. The night had taken its toll. She had been a wreck when she groggily took over the business phone at seven A.M. so Edna could go home, and the calls had been steady ever since. She'd fed Graham his cereal and made a pot of coffee

2

with the receiver clamped to the side of her head.

"I'm not wearing much of anything, darlin'," she said in answer to the usual question. She giggled provocatively. "Just a lace negligee and a teensy pair of black panties, and they're . . ." She lowered her husky voice to an intimate whisper as she described her imagined lingerie.

Her neck bent at an awkward angle, she murmured provocatively into the receiver and tried to keep her wriggling ten-month-old son amused with goofy faces so he'd lie still long enough for her to get the fresh diaper secured and the snaps of his jumpsuit done up. It was a little like trying to contain mercury; Graham was good-natured when he wasn't teething, but he was also determined, and he was getting stronger every day.

He was also trying to talk.

"Mummummmum." He gave up struggling for an instant, grinned up at her, and gabbled again, and she smiled at him, quickly covering the mouthpiece. But Tommy hadn't heard a thing; he was far too busy telling her what he wanted to do to her. She rolled her eyes and silently mouthed every word he said; she'd heard it all so many times before. He was a faithful customer, but like most of the others, he definitely lacked imagination.

Maxine got the last snap fastened and hoisted Graham from the countertop to the floor, where he took off toward the living room and his toy box, using the funny sideways crab walk that was his version of crawling.

She watched him adoringly as she absent-mindedly groaned and panted into the telephone. "Oh, Tommy, I love it when you talk dirty; it makes me so hot. . . ."

Darn, but she needed the portable headset she'd seen advertised on the Shopping Channel. That way her neck wouldn't ache so much by nighttime. She needed to change her sweatpants for clean ones; these had gobs of farina stuck to them, as well as a streak on the leg of something she'd rather not identify.

"Bbbbmmmmmm . . ." Graham rolled a toy bus along the rug and grinned when she waggled her fingers at him.

She needed to launch another career before her son began to understand what she did for a living.

The call ended just then with the usual results. Maxine checked her watch: twenty-three minutes, not bad at all. She felt more than a little proud of how far she'd come with this phone sex thing. At first she'd had a hard time keeping a caller on the line at all. It was a technique she'd learned gradually, and at the beginning it had taken concentration. Now she could do it almost automatically.

Considering the other calls that morning, too, she'd done well, she concluded as she tidied the bathroom and gathered up the soiled laundry.

Even with the hefty amount the telephone company charged for the use of the 900 line they'd installed in her house, she'd be able to pay the rent and the utilities again this month and put a little into her savings.

Guys always wanted to know if telephone sex was as good for her as it was for them, and she could honestly assure them it was. For two months before Graham was born and during the ten months since, it had paid the bills and bought diapers and formula. It had even made it possible—and necessary—to hire an employee; Edna Gimbel had been working for Maxine for only the last seven weeks, and it still seemed a miracle to be able to sleep through the night . . . when Graham cooperated, of course.

Yup, life was hectic, but it was also a triumph to know that she was self-supporting, Maxine mused as she hurried into the bedroom for fresh clothing.

She hastily tied her hair back with a stray shoelace and managed to get a load of laundry tossed into the washer and the stuff from the dryer half folded before the business phone rang again.

"Hi, this is Jerome." The deep voice sounded shy, and Maxine felt sympathetic. Guys were often bashful at first.

"Hi, Jerome. I'm India McBride. It's so nice to hear from you." She automatically pitched her deep voice even lower as she poured herself

a cup of coffee and added a spoonful of sugar.
She needed the energy this morning.

"Where are you calling from, Jerome?"

"Florida. Where are you located, India?"

Sometimes her callers identified their exact
location, but mostly they just named a state or
province. She didn't care; it was the time they
spent on the line that mattered. Every extra
minute they stayed on was more money in her
bank account.

"I live in Vancouver, Canada."

They always wanted to know specifically
where she lived, which was fine with her. They
also wanted to know what she was doing. As
always, she mixed a bit of truth with a lot of
fiction.

"I'm lying on my bed right now, in the bedroom." She glanced around at the beige living
room walls that needed painting, the ugly
brown rug that could use a shampoo. Outside
her front window, her next-door neighbor was
taking his mutt for a walk, and across the street
the macho guy who had the pinup-pretty wife
crouched over his motorcycle with a wrench, a
cigarette clutched in the side of his mouth. The
suburb where she lived was comfortable,
mostly family-oriented, and definitely lower
middle class.

"I have a condo overlooking the ocean. I can
see the sailboats and freighters on the inlet this
morning," she improvised, wondering what it

would feel like to ride on a motorcycle.

"I've never been to Vancouver."

"You'll have to come up and see me some-time." It was an old Mae West line, delivered with all that great lady's innuendo. Maxine loved Mae West, although hardly any of her customers recognized the quotes.

"Maybe I'll just do that. How old are you, India?"

"Twenty-four." Plus four, but most men liked her to be younger.

Jerome apparently did. He made a noise that denoted approval and then said, "So what's the weather like up there in Vancouver, India?"

"It's not bad for April. It's overcast this morning, but yesterday we got a bit of sun. I suppose you're basking in ninety-degree temperatures?"

Maxine had learned to allow the customer to initiate whatever he wanted from the call, and she was still surprised at how many times her callers never got around to sex at all. They talked about their golf game, or football, the stock market, the problems they were having with their wives or girlfriends. They often seemed satisfied just to have her listen.

Jerome wasn't one of those, however.

"I'm lyin' in the sun, all right, honey. Out on my deck." His voice dropped two decibels and took on a certain tension. "With not a stitch on. And Jimbo is just standin' up and salutin' fer you, darlin'."

Chapter Two

Maxine manufactured a little shriek and a provocative giggle. "Oh, you wicked thing. You're getting me all excited. Tell me exactly what you look like, and Jimbo too—don't leave out a single detail." She opened the fridge to check on the milk supply. The gallon jug was nearly empty. She was going to have to make a run to the supermarket before Graham's nap time.

Jerome launched into a detailed description. It was amazing how many of her callers were six-feet-two and a hundred and ninety pounds, with full heads of thick, wavy hair. And virtually all of them were extraordinarily well equipped, which was amazing considering all the media

8

attention lately on the diminishing size of the male penis.

As she wiped the counters off and quietly cleared the table, Maxine slowly and adroitly led Jerome through arousal to fulfillment, with plenty of time spent on fictitious details designed to titillate. Satisfied and euphoric, he promised to call again soon.

The call had lasted eighteen minutes. Not bad, but not good either. Now that she knew his style, she'd be able to slow Jerome down when he called again.

Maxine did mental arithmetic as she forcibly removed Graham from the bathroom. He'd recently discovered the toilet bowl, and his favorite activity was dropping toys in the water. He stiffened and screamed in outrage as she closed the door firmly behind them. It took several moments before she could distract him with the contents of the pots-and-pans cupboard in the kitchen.

When he was quiet again, sitting on the floor happily fitting plastic containers inside one another, Maxine stole a moment to admire him, and pride made her heart swell until it hardly seemed to fit inside her chest.

Her son was a picture-perfect baby—curly golden hair, fair skin, dark brown eyes. Though his eyes were a different color from hers, they were the same shape, triangular and tilted up at the outside corners. He had her thick lashes as well. Her eyes were her best feature, she'd always thought, and she was grateful her son had inherited them instead of her mouth, which she considered too wide for her face.

His mouth wasn't. It was perfect, well shaped and quick to smile. His arms and legs were long, his small body perfectly proportioned. He was going to be tall. He hadn't gotten that gene from her; she was barely five-seven. His tiny chin was already strong and determined, again like hers—which was a good characteristic only if you were male, she'd been told. Being stubborn wasn't admired in a woman's character. Her father had drilled her on that one, not that it had done any good. Being stubborn was all that had gotten her through at times.

Graham's ears were flat against his skull, he had six white teeth, he said *mama* and *doggy* and *woof*, and every day he seemed to learn another new and, to her, amazing accomplishment. She was so proud of him she thought her heart would explode sometimes.

She was also a stay-at-home mom, and not a day passed that she didn't breathe a prayer of gratitude for being able to care for her baby herself and earn a living at the same time.

The business phone rang, and the part of her that was sexy, sultry, dangerous India McBride created a heated fantasy for a businessman in Colorado, while at the same time Maxine Bleckner, who considered herself a shaky six at best on the attractiveness scale, wrote *milk, cereal, bread*, and *teething biscuits* on a shopping list, wiped away a long string of dribble from Graham's chin, and came up with new and resourceful ways to amuse her son and keep him relatively quiet while she yakked on the phone.

Harry Watson had also devised ingenious games to amuse his three-year-old daughter, Sadie, while he talked to editors or did interviews on the telephone, but he'd used up every single one this morning. They'd reached the last resort, which was "Here's Daddy's Watch." Sadie was alternately holding it to her ear and vigorously banging it on the floor as Oscar Sullivan droned on and on.

It was only a Timex, but Harry was fond of it, and he winced each time it hit the wooden floor of his bedroom-*cum*-study. He could only hope that Timex was as good as its advertising claimed.

Sullivan was an all-right guy, but he had a talent for taking the long way around any subject. He'd bought a number of Harry's articles over the past several years. He edited with a light hand and paid promptly, which made Harry a fan as well as a friend; they'd spent a boozy weekend fishing at a mountain lake the previous summer, while Sadie was visiting her maternal grandmother in Seattle.

11

The worst part of business dealings with Oscar was the time it took. There was real danger of dying from old age by the time he got through whatever it was he'd called to say. Harry knew Sullivan had grown up in Saskatchewan on a farm, but he could well have come from Alabama, judging from his torturously slow and circuitous speech patterns.

". . . thought of it when I heard a couple young copyeditors talking about the phone sex trade," Sullivan was finally saying, after a prolonged discussion about the stock market (Harry had no money to invest), Sullivan's golf game (Harry hadn't golfed since before Sadie was born), and which politician would win the upcoming election, a subject Harry could actually discuss knowledgeably because he'd just ghostwritten speeches for two of the leading opposing candidates.

"This phone sex thing is big, Harry. The *Star* has more ads for it than we ever had before, and that must mean that somebody's makin' money doin' it, wouldn't ya say? And the fact that it's safe sex probably adds to its appeal, although I'm still a fan of the old-fashioned kind, dangerous or not." He gave his gurgling laugh which inevitably ended in a coughing fit, wasting still more time. If he didn't stop smoking soon, Harry thought, Oscar wouldn't be having sex much longer—or anything else, either.

Because Oscar was the editor of the *Star*,

12

Vancouver's most popular morning tabloid, Harry had managed so far to keep himself from snarling into the receiver, "Would you, for God's sake, just spit out what you want, Sullivan?"

Restraining his mouth was both a smart career move and a supreme effort to honor the vow he'd made this week that he would never again swear in front of Sadie.

His little redheaded angel had called her elderly baby-sitter, Mrs. Campanato, a muffin two days before, which would have been sweet if she hadn't preceded it with a four-letter sexual expletive she'd heard Harry use when he smashed his finger in the car door. Harry had apologized profusely to the horrified lady, who'd given him a stern but passionate lecture about foul language and innocent little motherless girls and middle-aged men who ought to know better.

Harry, thirty-six for another four months, didn't think he quite qualified as middle-aged, but God forbid he'd ever argue with Maria Campanato.

He *was* contrite, but he was also secretly a little proud of his daughter. It was ingenious of Sadie to put the two words together, but Harry, of course, didn't say that to Mrs. Campanato, and he'd spent a long, frustrating time trying to explain to Sadie why one word was okay to use and the other wasn't. She hadn't bought his reasoning, either. In fact, she was gleefully using the *F*-word right now to punctuate the destruction of his watch.

Harry smacked his palm on the desk to get her attention, which sent cold coffee splashing all over the notes he'd made for the article that was due on smoking for the Vancouver Health Unit. He scowled ferociously at Sadie and shook his head no, but the kid knew when she had him. She gave him a sweet, coy grin and went right on banging and cursing.

"See, Harry, I wanna go at this phone sex thing from a human interest angle, a firsthand encounter, that kind of approach."

Harry figured sex of any sort was definitely interesting to humans, but Sullivan was finally on a roll, and there wasn't any point in interrupting. If he did, he'd be here with his ear glued to the phone for the rest of the day.

"Does this sound like a thing you'd want to explore, Harry?"

Harry assured Sullivan it was. He was interested in exploring any damn thing this side of the law that would bring in a few extra bucks.

"Good. Excellent. Now, I'll tell you how I want to go about this. I want you to find somebody *local* who's in the business, an' I want you to do me an exposé with lots of human interest, plenty of *detail*. Readers are gonna want *detail* about this here subject, you understand, Harry. And I want it from the customer's POV, like it was actually happening. I don't want an interview with some little gal who'll give you a shined-up version of what really goes on in this business. I want it to be authentic; I don't want her to *know* you're doing a story on her. Get as up-close and personal as you can. Readers are gonna wanna know what makes these sorta women tick, if you get my meaning."

Harry thought so. "You want me to be more than just a onetime telephone customer. You want me to develop a personal relationship with the lady?"

"Within reason, Harry. I don't want you to get us sued for slander, or compromise your honor. Or your body, neither, old buddy." Sullivan gurgled and coughed, and Harry waited.

"But yeah, I want you to get to know her away from the job, if you can. I, for one, would like to know just what these women really look like, and if I'm curious, you can bet our readers will be too."

Harry frowned, considering. "That might be tough, Oscar. I'm pretty sure they don't make a habit of meeting their customers face-to-face. It could be dangerous for them, for one thing."

"You're a persuasive guy, Harry. Talk your way in."

Harry broached the other reservation he had about the assignment. "These services charge by the minute, don't they?"

He had no experience with telephone sex. He

preferred the real thing, although lately he'd have taken whatever was offered, in any form available. He'd been celibate, much against his will, for longer than he cared to recall. The combined demands of single parenthood and the stress of earning a living as a writer for hire had practically turned him into a monk. Well, not quite. But closer than he'd ever wanted to come.

"This is going to take time, Oscar—to build up a relationship, get a woman to tell me details about herself and her business, maybe get her to trust me enough to meet me. At God knows what per minute, expenses could get pretty steep."

There was a prolonged and pained silence on the other end, and Harry grinned. The sure way to put a crimp in Sullivan's tongue was to mention expense money. The *Star* paid well, but Oscar had a thing about keeping expense accounts down.

"Daddy, I gotta go potty." Sadie's voice was loud and urgent, and Harry hastily covered the mouthpiece.

"Can you go by yourself, tiger?"

"Unh-unh. I gotta go poo. I *need* you, Daddy."

Sullivan was back, sounding reluctant. "I'll advance you something to cover phone expenses, but don't go hog-wild on me here, buddy. You gotta consider this'll likely be more pleasure than actual work, right? You'll be gettin' paid to have a good time, if you see what I mean?" He laughed. "Maybe we could split expenses on this one?"

Bull. Work was work. Writing was *hard* work, sex or no sex. Harry trailed down the hall after Sadie and tamped down his irritation. "A writer's gotta stay detached if the story's gonna be any good, Oscar; you know that. And in order to do a good job, I've gotta put in the time." He tried to sound reasonable, but his impatience came across anyway.

"Daddy, I can't get these off." Sadie sounded frantic, and Harry tugged at her striped tights, but it was a two-handed job. Why were little girls' tights so damned *tight*? Why was Sadie such a nutcase about what she wore? She'd had these red-and-blue horizontally striped circus things on for three days now, and even by his relaxed standards, they needed to go in the laundry.

"How about I call you back on this, Oscar?"

"Can't be done. See, I'm goin' down to San Diego on a two-week golfing holiday, leavin' today. I want this in the bag before I walk out of here. Let's see, I guess we'll agree to reimburse you . . ." He named a figure that in Harry's estimation was low, but still more than he'd expected Sullivan to cough up.

"Just see you don't go getting addicted to this phone sex stuff, okay, Harry?" Sullivan laughed again as Harry finally managed to get the tights unglued and peeled down.

"Sure, Oscar. And what about the finished piece? How much?"

Again, Sullivan surprised him by naming a figure that was well above what Harry had expected. The editor was obviously thinking of this as a lead story, maybe even a cover item, which might give Harry a little bargaining power. He thought of the negative balance in his checking account, mentally crossed his fingers, and talked fast.

"How about I do some research during the next couple weeks, write you out a general outline of what I figure the story could be, and if it's all that you expected, you pay me half the article fee at that point?"

There was a longer silence than before, and then Sullivan sighed. "You know that ain't the way it goes, but okay, Harry. What the hell, I know you'll do a decent job."

Harry's spirits soared as he hung up and reached out to plop his daughter on the throne. She scowled at him and pointed an imperious finger at the door. "Go 'way, Daddy. I can do it my *own*self."

He grinned and shook his head at her contrariness. "Okay, button. Call me when you're done."

The bathroom was off the kitchen, and he went over to the coffeemaker and poured himself a fresh cup while he waited for Sadie's summons. He sipped and absently scratched his face, which was itchy because he hadn't shaved in three days.

A few weeks before, he'd watched a program about stay-at-home moms on the Women's Television Network, about women who pursued their high-powered careers from home while they raised a family. One of them, a former fashion model turned graphic designer, warned that the first thing to go was personal grooming.

Harry had wanted to call in to the program to confirm how right she was. In his former life as an advertising executive, he wouldn't have dreamed of starting a day without shaving. He would never have worn sweatpants that sagged at the knee and bagged at the ass. But that was before Sadie. Kids changed a guy, all right.

He leaned on the counter that held the grisly remains of last night's supper as well as this morning's breakfast and contemplated his life and the timeliness of this new assignment.

The transmission was going on his old Chevy. His laptop was five years old, and he had nightmares of the hard drive crashing. Three years ago he'd cashed in most of his retirement savings to make the down payment on this house, so Sadie would grow up in a real home, in a family neighborhood. Financially, he was barely making it, which should keep him awake nights but didn't.

The truth was, he was happier with his life

than he'd ever been, apart from not having enough hours in the day. The decision he'd made when Sadie was born—to leave his lucrative job at the agency and start freelancing so he could stay at home with her—had been the smartest thing he'd ever done in terms of personal satisfaction.

There were a few drawbacks besides the financial ones. His conversation with Sullivan had reminded him that he'd like to get laid again before he lost his hair and teeth, but there were also times he longed just to talk to an intelligent female. There were things you could say to a woman that you'd never in this lifetime confide to a guy, old rugby buddy or not. Guys didn't get into emotions much, at least the guys he knew.

There *was* Mrs. Campanato, of course. She lived at the end of the block, she was like a grandmother to Sadie, and God knew she was a lifesaver for those times Harry had to interview someone in person, but she wasn't somebody he could really have a conversation with. At five-ten, she was four inches shorter than he, but at maybe three hundred pounds, she outweighed him by sixty, and he considered her one scary lady. She didn't converse; she pronounced, and because of her size and her attitude, Harry always had to fight the urge to salute and stand at attention.

God knew how tiny Mr. Campanato had survived thirty years of being married to her. No wonder he spent most of his time in the workshop he'd fixed up behind their garage, making some lethal concoction he labeled *vino*.

"Daaaddy, I'm all done now."

"Coming, princess." Harry swigged the last of the coffee and headed for the bathroom, thinking over this latest assignment as he did what was necessary for Sadie and then, at her insistence, wrestled her back into the godforsaken striped tights.

He would look up a few of the telephone sex ads in the paper. He'd never paid any attention to them before and wasn't sure what to expect. Then he'd pick a couple that sounded the most intriguing, and narrow them down to the most likely candidates. And he'd have to make sure she was local, he remembered. He had a contact at the phone company who could probably help with that.

How the hell did you have sex with a person you'd never laid eyes on, over the telephone?

Apparently he was about to find out. It made him just a little nervous, and curious as well.

What were these women like who did phone sex for a living? What were their lives like, how did they spend their days? He had a vivid imagination, but try as he might, he found it impossible to imagine.

Chapter Three

The day had been hectic for Maxine, but there was a lull in business around seven-forty-five, long enough to bathe Graham and rock him to sleep. The lull lasted until Edna arrived to start her ten-hour night shift.

"Want a cup of herbal tea?" Maxine had the kettle on.

"I'd love one, thanks." Edna's slight lisp and little-girl voice were at variance with her ample, motherly shape. Her straight gray hair was cut in a no-nonsense bowl shape around her square jaw, and as usual she wore comfortable black stretch pants and a blue-checked flannel shirt, frayed at the cuffs and neck, that had probably once belonged to one of her sons. She had the most flawless skin Maxine had ever laid eyes on, creamy and unlined.

Her detective novel and her raffia knitting bag were close at hand; she was making a sweater for her younger son's birthday, and she always had a mystery handy to read during the inevitable quiet times that came toward dawn.

Maxine had learned that movies, books, and knitting were Edna's passions. She went to matinees in the afternoon, and she was wonderful at describing them. Maxine almost felt as if she'd seen the latest releases herself by the time Edna told her the story line. It was undoubtedly that ability to inject action into stories that made Edna so good at phone sex.

"Has Graham's tooth come through yet?" Edna sipped her peppermint tea and daintily bit into one of the chocolate brownies Maxine offered.

"Not yet." It was good to have a friend, reassuring to be able to talk about her son and know that Edna sincerely cared about him. "I wish it would pop. He hardly napped at all today, poor little guy."

"Teething's hard on them; I remember what a time Gary had with his eyeteeth. Marshall was easier, or maybe it's just that with the second one you know what to expect."

Edna's sons were in college. It was amazing that she could remember such details as teething. But things probably stuck in your mind

23

when you were doing something you loved, like raising your kids, Maxine thought as she made short work of her brownie.

"Mmmmmmm." Edna was enjoying hers as well. "There're advantages to being overweight," she mused with a wink. "It gives you license to indulge, because it isn't going to show on these hips." She moved her ample bottom from side to side on the chair and laughed.

"When I was an airline hostess," Maxine remarked, "I had to watch every morsel I ate— they wanted us to stay thin."

"When I was married I had to do the same thing," Edna said with a grin. "John always wanted me thinner."

"I saw a program on **PBS** where a woman doctor said studies now prove chocolate is good for women; it has a beneficial effect on their sexuality," Maxine declared. "So have another— they're just what we need."

They giggled and munched until the phone interrupted.

Edna glanced up at the clock and then picked up; it was close enough to ten to be her call.

"Lilith here, how are you tonight? Oh, Walter, hello there. I'm so glad it's you."

It was one of Edna's regular clients.

"Oh, me too, honey. What is it about rainy evenings that makes a girl horny?" Edna held up the remnants of her brownie and rolled her

24

eyes at Maxine as she cooed and giggled into the receiver.

Edna had come a long way in the weeks since she'd answered the ad Maxine had put in the newspaper under "Help Wanted, Female."

Do you like to talk on the phone? Seeking woman with feminine voice for romantic discussions, it had read. To Maxine's amazement, there had been twenty-six applicants, some of them with previous experience.

She'd chosen Edna mostly because the older woman had the perfect voice, one that was vastly different from her own but equally as provocative. She'd also hired her because Edna had been painfully open and honest about her circumstances.

"My husband, John, left me for a bimbo after twenty-two years of marriage," Edna had explained at that first meeting. "I'm forty-six and I've been a housewife all my married life. The only job I've done in years besides housework was volunteering at the library, reading books to kids on Saturday mornings."

She'd gone on to say that no one would hire her, and she was getting desperate.

"For the first few months after it happened, I went into a depression," she related. "I wanted to die, and I didn't give a hoot about anything. John divorced me as fast as the law allowed, and when he told me one day that he'd sold the house, I acted like a wimp. I took my clothes and some furniture and moved into the first apartment I looked at. I was your classic stupid hausfrau," she admitted, her beautiful gray eyes rueful.

She'd never bothered about business affairs; John had taken care of all that, Edna recounted with a bitter smile. He'd done a good job of hiding whatever assets there were.

She'd gotten a share of the sale of the house, but it was minute, and legal bills had already eaten up most of it. John had taken out a large mortgage on the house the year before they separated, supposedly to buy out a partner at the law firm, but the money had somehow disappeared.

"I have a lawyer, but he doesn't seem to be doing much except billing me," Edna had said with a sigh.

"I'll introduce you to my lawyer, Polly Kelville," Maxine had offered. Within a matter of days, Edna had fired her lawyer and hired Polly.

Edna had admitted readily that she wasn't any expert at sex; John had been anything but adventurous in that regard. But she'd read widely, and she had a good imagination and no inhibitions, and she was eager to learn, she'd assured Maxine.

Maxine hired her on the spot. She knew all too well what it felt like to be dumped and duped by a man. She knew how betrayal felt, and the self-doubt that came with it. She'd taught Edna everything she herself had learned about giving good sex on the telephone.

Edna was a quick study. Her distinctive voice and what proved to be a wicked and bawdy imagination stood her in good stead, as did her sense of humor. No one could do phone sex and be successful without a well-developed sense of the ridiculous.

Edna gathered up her knitting now, phone clamped to her ear, and went to sit in her favorite chair in front of the television. The picture was on, but the sound was off, and the muted clack of knitting needles was soothing to Maxine as she rinsed the teacups and put plastic wrap over the remaining brownies.

"What am I wearing?"

Hearing Edna repeat the familiar question, Maxine peeked around the corner, enjoying the scene. Edna had set down her knitting and picked up a catalog from the table beside her.

"Oh, honey, this little peach camisole with lace up the front. It's satin, and it feels so smooth and sexy against my bare skin," Edna lisped. "It has matching thong panties and a garter belt." Edna picked up her knitting again. "I just love garter belts, don't you? And thongs make me think of . . ."

Maxine shook her head and smiled. Thanks to Polly, she and Edna always had the latest Victoria's Secret catalog on hand so they could vary their imaginary lingerie.

Polly actually ordered from the catalogs. Maxine and Edna figured at least half of their sexy lawyer's wardrobe came from Victoria's Secret. Tall and leggy, she could have modeled for the catalogs, although Maxine suspected Polly's IQ qualified her for Mensa.

She'd told them that the pastel suits with the teensy skirts and low cut jackets had helped her win many a case; males underestimated the keen intelligence and wily mind underneath the fall of long blond hair. Even other female lawyers tended at first to think she was a lightweight, until she nailed them on some point of law and won the case.

Polly had also become a good friend. Maxine had known her now for more than a year. Polly worked for the Family Law Clinic, and Maxine had first gone to her in an unsuccessful effort to locate Ricky Shwartz, the louse who unfortunately was Graham's father. So far Polly hadn't been able to locate him, but Maxine was positive she would eventually.

She didn't want to think about Ricky Shwartz now. She wanted to have a hot bath and go to bed. Maxine yawned, waggled her fingers at Edna, and headed down the hall.

She tiptoed into Graham's room. He was sleeping soundly, bottom in the air, thumb plugged into his mouth. She gently pulled the quilt up over him, praying he'd sleep through the night so she could too.

With luck, tomorrow would be as busy as today, she thought as she ran a tub of hot water, stripped off her grubby clothes, and climbed in, sighing at the sheer pleasure of being alone with no phone clamped to her ear.

But busy was good. Busy didn't leave any time to think about how long it had been since she'd talked to a man about something besides sex, or held anyone close except her son. Her clientele might be totally male, but she hadn't had a real date since long before Graham was born. The truth was, she never met any men suitable for dating.

There *was* Leonard, the produce manager at Safeway, she reminded herself with a wry grin, sinking deep into the bubbles. He always made a point of telling her how fresh the broccoli was while his eyes lingered on her breasts.

She did have quite nice breasts, she decided, admiring them as they bobbled in the water.

But it wasn't fresh broccoli she wanted to talk about, and it sure wasn't breasts either. She got more than enough talk of breasts just doing her job.

She wanted to laugh with a man, the same way she did with Polly and Edna. Why couldn't a man and woman have the kind of funny, outrageous conversations that came so easily to her and her female friends?

Maxine thought that over and then chuckled at herself.

It could have something to do with the fact that the conversations she and Polly and Edna enjoyed so much were mostly about men. Polly loved the wicked, funny stories Maxine and Edna told about their customers, and they listened raptly to the outrageous tales Polly told of the men she dated and discarded like used tissues.

The last thing she needed was a man in her personal life, Maxine assured herself, slowly rubbing lavender soap over her belly and arms.

Every man she'd ever known, beginning with her father, had wanted her to be something she wasn't. And she'd tried to change herself into whatever it was they wanted.

She'd become adept at it. Ironically, that adaptability was the very thing that had made her successful at creating illusions on the telephone.

She used that talent to earn a living, but she vowed she'd never again be anyone but plain old Maxine Bleckner in her normal life. No matter how much she wanted a companion along the way, no matter how much she longed for a grown-up male to share the rest of her life, she wouldn't pretend for him. He'd have to take her exactly the way she was.

Well, maybe she'd shave her legs, she amended with a grin. And have something constructive done with her hair. She'd go that far, but no farther.

Gentleman Caller

What are you wearing, Maxine?

Flannel pajamas and sports socks with holes. Vaseline to soften the skin on my heels. Tea tree oil to dry up the zit on my chin. And baby puke, lots of baby puke.

If her callers only knew the truth.

If they did, they'd never call again. Maxine grinned and pulled the plug in the tub.

She was the fifth one he called, and it was her voice that instantly captivated him.

"India McBride, hi, there," she said. "How are you this fine day?"

It was a bedroom voice, husky and sultry, provocative, honey-smooth. It was also, in some complex fashion, innocently friendly and inexplicably filled with joy.

Harry had thought he was getting good at this. The other local numbers had resulted in conversations so blatantly and immediately sexual, he'd felt amused rather than aroused; it had sounded as if the women were reading out of X-rated magazines. He'd cut them short, conscious of his budget restraints and the fact that Sadie was napping and would awaken before long.

He absolutely didn't want her to hear him talking about sex on the phone, and he hadn't wanted to develop any sort of a relationship with the voices on the other end of the line, not even in the interests of research.

31

This voice was different.

He cleared his throat and found his tongue. "I'm fine, thanks." What the hell was there to say next? "You're looking good today, India."

She giggled, a sophisticated giggle, and again the timbre of her voice thrilled him. "And you're a smooth talker, sir. Do you happen to have a name?"

"Harold." He hadn't planned to use his full name, but once he had, it was fine. It made what he was doing less personal, because everyone called him Harry. Harold was a different guy altogether.

"Well, Harold, how do you do? I like that name, Harold. It's dignified, sort of a Volvo name."

"Volvo?" For an instant he'd thought she'd said something else.

"You know, significant. Solid, dependable. Trustworthy."

He'd never thought about his name in those terms. He'd only thought how much he'd rather be called David or Robert. All of a sudden, Harold wasn't bad at all.

This lady definitely had a different slant on sexy than the others he'd called.

"Where are you calling from, Harold?"

Her voice wrapped itself around his name like caramel around an apple, sweet and firm and inviting. It made him smile.

"Vancouver, I live in Vancouver. I travel a lot,

so it's nice to be back; I've been out of town for a while now. And all the daffodils are blooming; I like that." This was pure stream-of-consciousness stuff. He hadn't really planned any of it.

"I love the daffodils too. Where did you go?"

His eyes searched his desk for inspiration. "Pen . . . Pennsylvania. Do you enjoy traveling, India?"

"Not really—I'm sort of a homebody. You travel for work or for pleasure, Harold?"

"Work." *Improvise here, Harry.* "I'm a businessman, corporate stuff. It, ummm, it makes it hard to meet women."

"I guess it would." She sounded sympathetic and understanding. "And what sort of woman would you like to meet, Harold?"

He grinned at that. "You'd do just fine, by the sound of you."

She laughed, a gentle laugh, provocative. "That's so sweet. But you don't really know me yet." That languorous voice caressed each word, and for the first time there was sexual innuendo. "Wouldn't you like to know me lots better, Harold?"

It was the opening he was waiting for. "I would, India. Very much better, but not in the way you think. I know most men who call probably want, ummm, just sex, but I'd like it a lot if you'd just talk to me. I guess I'm a little shy."

Pencil poised over the scratch pad, he started

Bobby Hutchinson

the interview. "You ever get other guys like me who just want to talk, India?"

"Oh, sure." She was so damned accommodating, so easy to talk to. "Lots of people are lonely. And I'm here to satisfy whatever hunger you have, Harold."

The intimacy of her tone, the emphasis she put on the words, relaxed him for a moment, and then he was suddenly irritated with himself for being taken in by her, reminding himself of the number of times a day she must say things just like this to countless other men. *Stay focused on what you're doing, Watson.*

It was far too easy to forget this was just a job to her. She got paid for the number of minutes she kept him on the line, he reminded himself. He'd better get on with the interview, or Sullivan would be billing him instead of the other way around.

"D'you mind my asking how old you are, India?"

"Twenty-four." The answer was prompt, and it certainly sounded honest. He had a powerful mental vision of a long-limbed slender woman in something slinky and black, stretched out on a chaise longue. . . .

Don't be such a jerk, Watson. There's no way of telling age over the phone; she could be sixty-three and four hundred pounds for all you know.

"How about you, Harold? How old are you?"

"Thirty-six." Maybe if he was forthcoming,

she would be as well. "I'm six-two, two-forty, black hair, blue eyes." He rubbed a hand across the stubble on his chin. "I'm pretty ordinary-looking. I'm not in the greatest shape; traveling doesn't leave much time to go to the gym."

Neither did being a single father.

"You sound really attractive to me. I'll bet women find you sexy."

They had, at one time. He grinned and shook his head. She was good at this, and he noticed she hadn't given him a verbal on herself.

"Thanks, but don't feed me a line, okay, India? I'm comfortable with my shortcomings; I don't need my ego stroked."

That teasing little laugh again. "What *would* you like stroked, Harold?"

He wasn't going there, although he was beginning to understand how easy it would be. Her voice was a slide of silk on bare skin. It made the hair on his arms stand up. A certain tension in his groin made him uncomfortably aware that other parts of his anatomy were also erect.

Staying objective was going to be a lot harder than he'd imagined.

Chapter Four

It took all his self-control to sound casually amused.

"What would I like stroked? Oh, let's see. My curiosity, I guess. I'd like to get to know you, like I said before."

There was a tiny pause. "Get to know me? In what way, Harold?"

"Oh, I want you to tell me what sort of a woman you are." He glanced at his scribbled notes. "Tell me what you like to do for fun, what you read, what movies you like to watch. Talk to me as if I were a new friend instead of a customer."

"Well, let's see." Again there was a small silence. Her voice was more tentative now, her diction slower.

He guessed she was feeling her way, trying to figure him out.

"I guess you could say I'm a little bit wild, Harold. I always was. I like to take chances; I like to live on the edge. I like, ummm, motorcycles. I like . . . oh, to dance by myself in the middle of the night. I read erotic poetry, nonsense rhymes, traditional verse. I like romantic movies that have an edge to them, like *The Thomas Crown Affair*."

"I didn't see it." He'd gotten rather fond of *Teletubbies*. It was Sadie's favorite show. He scribbled furiously, wondering how much of this was fabrication. It sounded a lot more literate than he'd expected from a phone sex worker.

"Daddy?"

Harry was so involved in the phone call he hadn't heard Sadie waking up or coming along the hall. She stood in the doorway of the study, her acorn brown eyes still heavy from sleep, strands of silky red-gold hair caught on her eyelashes. She had her tattered blanket over her shoulder and her toy rabbit under her arm, and her face was creased from the pillow.

"Daddy? I needs a love."

He clamped a hand over the receiver and beckoned her over to him. She always needed cuddling after her nap. She snuggled her face into his chest, and he spoke hurriedly into the phone. "I'm terribly sorry, but something urgent's just come up and I have to go now. Can I call you back this evening, say about, oh, nine?"

"Eight-thirty would be better," she murmured suggestively, as if they were planning an intimate liaison.

"Eight-thirty it is." He hung up and wrapped his daughter in his arms, wondering why it had been such an unsettling call. He thought it over and came to the conclusion that for some obscure reason, he didn't like misleading the invisible woman behind that beguiling voice.

Maxine thought she'd heard a female voice in the background. Well, it was nothing to her; whoever he really was, he must have a life that included women.

When the line went dead abruptly she shrugged and thought about the call. She'd assumed that she and Edna must have heard every kind of call imaginable, but this one had been in a class of its own.

Harold had sounded polite, hesitant, a little shy, but certainly not the type of shy she was most familiar with. That kind was usually into domination and submission, and she was willing to bet that Harold wasn't one of them.

He was intelligent, not that some of her other

38

callers weren't; the difference was that they were just intelligently single-minded, intent on having their needs satisfied. They certainly weren't interested in what she was like, beyond the standard stuff such as what she was wearing and how excited she was by them and was she enjoying their encounter.

Would he call back?

She went over the conversation in her head, puzzling over it, wondering who Harold really was. There had to be more to it than just wanting to get to know her. He must have some obscure fetish that she'd never come across, she decided.

There wasn't time to think much about it. She could hear Graham, awake from his nap and wanting to be picked up, and the business phone was sure to ring again at any moment.

Maxine dismissed Harold from her mind and hurried off down the hall to rescue her son.

That evening, however, she knew instantly who it was when the call came at precisely eight-thirty. Graham had had his bath and gone down forty minutes before, and Maxine was curled in an easy chair with the newspaper. The radio was turned low, tuned to an FM station that played hits from the seventies.

She turned the volume down still further and used her most languorous business voice.

"Hello, there, India here."

"Hello again, India. It's Harold"—there was the tiniest of pauses—"Walters."

"Well, Harold Walters, how nice to hear from you." It was only then that she was aware she'd been waiting for his call. Now why would she do a thing like that?

Her heartbeat picked up. She had to work at keeping her voice normal. "Are you having an enjoyable evening, Harold?"

Too late, she realized that wasn't a question she'd normally ask a client; the fact that they were calling her meant that they *hoped* to have an enjoyable evening.

She wasn't on the ball tonight.

Snap out of it, Bleckner. This is business.

"Actually, I'm having a great evening," he said in the deep baritone that Maxine recalled so well from their earlier conversation. It was sexy, understated, a quiet, assured voice that hinted at a man who knew who he was and accepted it.

"I have a glass of red wine going, Bob Dylan on the sound system, and now you on the telephone." He gave a deep sigh that made her smile. "It doesn't get much better, India."

"Glad to hear it. I like Dylan, too." She could hear the music playing softly in the background. "I've got the radio on—they're playing Rod Stewart. What other music do you listen to, besides Dylan?" If this guy was going to pay her just to chat, why not talk about things that were interesting to her?

"Tom Waits, ever heard of him?"

She never had.

"Funky blues," he explained, adding that if she liked Dylan, she'd probably like Waits as well. "I used to play blues guitar in college, a long time ago."

"Do you still play?"

"Once in a while. To amuse myself, when I have the time." He turned the conversation back to her.

"What do you read besides poetry, India?"

"Mystery." Thank God Edna was as good at reviewing books as she was at relating the plots of movies. "How about you, Harold?"

"Oh, bits of everything. I like science fiction, mystery, biography. I enjoy reading about how other people live their lives, what motivates them to make the choices they make."

She might enjoy that, too, if she ever got the time, Maxine thought a little wistfully.

She heard Edna's key in the lock. The older woman came in and gave her a wave and a smile as she hung her raincoat in the closet. She pretended to tip a teacup to her lips and Maxine nodded hearty agreement. She'd love a cup of tea. She also wouldn't mind finishing this conversation in private, which was weird; she'd never had any qualms before about having Edna hear her business patter.

41

"You never told me where you live, Maxine. I assume you're also from Vancouver?"

"How did you guess?"

He chuckled, a warm and intimate sound that brought an answering smile to her lips. "Daffodils. When I said I liked daffodils, you said you did, too. And I just assumed from that that you lived here."

"It's a great city; I love Vancouver." She did, even though she lived in a suburb outside it.

Edna had come back into the living room while she waited for the kettle to boil, and Maxine suddenly felt duty-bound to add some spice to this strange call.

"It rains a lot here, but I don't mind it. One of the things I most enjoy doing is walking in the rain with just a raincoat on; it's such a delicious feeling, the coolness against the thin material, being naked underneath."

Edna pursed her lips and raised an eyebrow, then nodded hearty approval. It was a new line, one neither of them had used before.

Harold was less enthusiastic. "I've never tried it—don't think I will, either. I've heard that guys in raincoats with no pants get arrested and thrown in the slammer. I guess gals are different, but aren't you afraid of getting in an accident?" He laughed. He had a nice laugh, deep and hearty and spontaneous. "Didn't your mother ever give you that old lecture about wearing clean underwear in case you had to go to the hospital?"

Maxine had to laugh too. "Come to think of it, she did, Harold. I guess everyone's mother used that line."

"Are you close to your mother, India?" The question was sincere and unexpected, and she hesitated before she answered, taken aback. No one except her female friends had ever asked her that before.

"I was, but my mother died when I was sixteen." Now, what had possessed her to be truthful? And why would such old news make her feel a sudden new pang of loss?

Edna stopped on her way into the kitchen and turned, giving Maxine a puzzled look. She was talking to a client about her *mother*?

Maxine rolled her eyes and shrugged, indicating that she had a really strange one on the line.

"I'm sorry. That must have been tough for you, losing your mom when you were so young." His voice was thoughtful. "Think it's hard for a girl, growing up without a mother?"

Of course, Maxine instantly thought about Graham not having a father. "I'd say it depends a lot on the other parent. Kids definitely need one person who loves them, don't you think?" It was a subject she'd spent a lot of time mulling over. "They need one person who loves them unconditionally, who lets them find out who they really are without trying to make them into"—she hesitated, because this was an area she had strong feelings and fears about—"into something society thinks is acceptable." She couldn't seem to stop talking, now that she'd started. "I think at a certain stage parents should ask kids, 'What is it you really want?' And then listen hard to what they say, and respect it, whatever it is."

"Hmmm." He was considering her answer. "That's pretty perceptive, India. I definitely agree with you. So did you have that when you were growing up? Somebody who let you just be you, who asked you what you really wanted?"

This guy was just way too peculiar. "Not really." *Not at all.* "My father was the type who had strict ideas about what his daughter should be and how she should act. Nobody ever asked me what *I* wanted." Maxine bit her lip. She was being much too candid here. Besides, she tried not to think too much about her father. She wondered again how the heck a business call had turned so personal.

"So who has a totally happy childhood, Harold?" She made her voice deliberately upbeat. She really didn't want to go any deeper into her family problems. "How about you? What kind of parents did you have?"

"Oh, normal, I guess. If there is such a thing. My family was nomadic; my dad was in the army, so we moved constantly. How about you, India? Did you grow up moving, or did you stay in one place?"

He was too adroit at turning the tables. "A small town in the Rockies until I left home," she said, and before he could pursue the topic she hurried on. Two could play this game. "You said you travel a lot with your job, Harold. Ever thought about settling down? Marriage, kids, the whole nine yards?" This call was going where no call had gone before, so she might as well just let it roll. He was paying, after all.

There was a tiny pause, and then he said, "I was married once. I think that's about all I can handle."

"Bad memories?" She knew all about those, the times in the middle of the night when there was no way to get off the treadmill of "what if" and "I should have." She'd learned by now just to go through the scenes, counting them off like beads on a string. Even now, when she was wide-awake, thinking about Ricky gave her the familiar tight knot in her gut.

"Some bad memories, yeah," he said slowly. "She wasn't any better than I was at marriage. It takes two to make it, and it takes two to wreck it, and looking back I did my share," he said in a rueful tone.

"Sounds like the words of a country-western tune."

He grunted, and then to her surprise went on

explaining. "See, my childhood left me with wanderlust, India. I'm just not much good at everyday, mundane living, I'm afraid. I like, ohh, nice hotels and room service and executive-class seating. I want to be able to take off to Europe or Asia or Africa at a moment's notice, no strings, no responsibilities."

"That's my motto too, no responsibilities." The idea had only superficial appeal. Graham was her anchor, and she liked it that way, although there were times . . . Maxine glanced at the stack of bills that had arrived that morning. She'd put them on the top of the bookcase so Graham wouldn't tear them up or try to eat them.

"So it sounds as if you enjoy your work, Harold."

Edna set a mug of tea on the chair's armrest. She took a seat on the sofa, propped her reading glasses on her nose, and opened a paperback, sipping her tea, but Maxine knew she was listening avidly to this unusual conversation.

"Yeah, I do enjoy it, most of it." He sounded more relaxed than when he'd talked about his marriage. "A little less pressure would be good, but basically I'm pretty happy. How about you, India? You enjoy what you do?"

"Absolutely." There was nothing like making enough to pay those pesky bills. "I was born for this job. Where else could I be myself, be outrageous and naughty and scandalous, and get paid for it? I'm sensual and adventurous, but not indiscriminate, Harold. This is an ideal way for a lady like me to enjoy safe sex, wouldn't you say?"

Edna gave a thumbs-up sign, and Maxine winked at her.

Harold gave a little grunt that might or might not be agreement. "Maybe I shouldn't ask, but how did you get into this line of work in the first place?"

She filtered quickly through truth and fantasy to find a suitable middle ground. "I was a stewardess, and I developed a phobia about flying." Combining fact with fiction wasn't too hard. "I didn't have any other career, and it was tough to find a job that paid as well as this, and was one that I enjoy."

One that she'd been able to do as her belly expanded to monumental proportions, one that she could resume within days of Graham's birth, one that she could manage while she sat and nursed him.

"So you were a stew, huh? You must have traveled the globe at one point?"

"Maybe not the entire globe, but a fair portion of it," she lied in a world-weary tone, thinking about all the small towns in B.C. she'd grown familiar with. She'd had only one job after her initial training. The regional airline she'd worked for had been too cash-starved even to buy uniforms for the employees; she'd worn her own dark slacks and white shirt. In-flight refreshments had been bulk peanuts and small tins of tomato juice. She'd thought that first job would be only a stepping-stone, experience until she got hired with a major airline.

"Doing this is a great way to make money." She glanced across at Edna and suddenly had a disturbing mental vision of them both as really old women, still gasping and moaning into a phone. Maxine shuddered.

She was all too aware that she had to find another job before Graham began to understand sentences.

"This job's great while I upgrade my skills and train for a career," she added on impulse.

Again, Edna gave her a startled look and raised her eyebrows.

"And what career have you decided on, India?"

Maxine was stumped. Her gaze fell on the radio and inspiration struck. "Broadcasting," she blurted. "I'd like a career in radio broadcasting."

"Great idea," Harold said enthusiastically. "You've really got the voice for it."

Maxine barely heard him. She was astonished at what had just come out of her mouth. *Would* she like to be a radio announcer? She'd never given it a thought until right now.

She regained her composure and remembered that this was supposed to be a business call. "How about you, Harold? Is there something you want to do besides this business you're in?"

There was a lengthy silence, and she imagined him staring into the distance, thinking it over.

"I always had a yen to write a book," he said after a minute. "I'd like to try to write a murder mystery."

"Well, don't wait too long," Maxine advised. "One thing my father used to say made sense." Her father again? What was it about this Harold that brought up things she'd thought well buried?

She forced her voice to sound gravelly and stern. " 'Life has a way of passing while we're busy with something else.' " *Remember that, daughter*.

Harold laughed, and she did as well. His laughter didn't sound as forced as hers felt.

"Good advice. I'll keep it in mind."

They'd been talking an awfully long time, Maxine realized suddenly. She glanced at her watch and realized that the call was lasting well into Edna's shift, which wasn't fair; Edna was paid for the amount of time clients stayed on the line, just as Maxine was. Business was business, and she didn't want to be an unfair employer.

She also didn't want to end this call, and it had nothing to do with dollars and cents.

"I'm sorry to have to do this, Harold, but I have to go now. I have a previous engagement. I do hope you'll call again?" She realized she meant it and was amazed at herself.

"Absolutely, India." The tone of his voice told her he was sincere. "Tomorrow night, same time?"

"Same time, same place." She was smiling as she agreed. She knew the smile was evident in her voice.

"I hope you have a pleasant evening, India. Good night, now."

Maxine was still smiling as she hung up, and Edna gave her a long, curious look.

"What the heck was that all about? Harold sure doesn't sound like a regular customer. Is he some kind of perv?"

They occasionally got calls from people who were very twisted, and the rule was to be polite and firm and hang up quickly.

Maxine took a gulp of her tea and shook her head.

She felt warmer than usual, and lighthearted. A little light-headed as well? "Not a perv at all. He's just really . . . really different."

"Sounded like it."

Maxine told Edna a little about the two calls and the conversations she'd had with Harold. "I know it's crazy," she added, aware that she was blushing, "but he sounds like . . . ummm, a *gentleman*, this guy."

50

It even *felt* crazy to say such a thing.

She hadn't considered any man a gentleman for a long, long time, and certainly she'd never had a caller before who even remotely fit that description.

Chapter Five

"A gentleman caller, now there's a new one to tell Polly about." Edna pursed her lips and whistled soundlessly.

Maxine smiled and agreed, although a small part of her was reluctant. She didn't want to turn Harold into one of their flaky characters. She wanted him to be exactly what he seemed; a nice, worldly man who was truly interested in her life and her opinions.

Now how sick was that?

Harold was a customer, and there were strict rules about customers; she'd carefully related every one of them to Edna and had her promise she'd abide by them.

There could be no personal contact whatsoever with a customer apart from the phone conversations. Such a thing could be dangerous—there were all sorts of fruitcakes out there. The very nature of this business invited fruitcakes. And there was something else as well.

They couldn't ever forget that this job was a game, a charade, a way of spinning the voices they'd been born with, the wicked imaginations they'd developed, and their rather twisted senses of humor into pure gold.

India McBride didn't exist outside of Maxine's head, any more than did Lilith Stone, Edna's nom de plume. The women she and Edna pretended to be were fantasies, dream women, illusions so far from reality as to be ludicrous. There was danger in allowing the game to become real in any sense except the financial.

The phone rang and Edna answered.

"This is Lilith. Hello, there, honey."

Edna was soon involved in a familiar and predictable conversation, and Maxine tuned it out. She'd do well to remember her own rules, she decided as she gathered up the teacups and made her way into the kitchen.

Harold might sound like a gentleman, but there was no way of knowing who or what he really was. She needed to be a lot more careful about what she told him in the future. She had to guard against thinking there was any more to his calls than just business. The next time, she had to be a lot more India and a lot less Maxine.

She didn't know why she was so certain he'd call again, but she was. She also didn't want to admit to herself how much she was looking forward to that next call.

Harold did call, the next night and the two nights after that, and as soon as she heard his voice she promptly forgot all about the rules.

Maxine wasn't certain, afterward, exactly what they talked about. Conversation just seemed to flow, and he made her laugh, made her think. He had a way with words.

Something else happened that amazed her.

For the first time in her entire career as a telephone sex worker, Maxine was feeling turned on by a caller. She and Harold didn't even talk about sex; her excitement had to do with the timbre of his voice and the attention he paid to whatever she was saying.

Between business calls, she sang "Love Me Tender."

Graham's tooth came through and he began sleeping through the night. The phone rang steadily. She made plans to take Graham to a local play school. The scale said that somehow she'd lost four pounds in the past week, and she was in a generally euphoric mood when Polly Kelville dropped by late Friday afternoon, bringing half a dozen beers, the local kind she knew Maxine liked, as well as a huge bouquet of daffodils.

"Polly, these are gorgeous, thanks." Maxine put them in several vases on top of the fireplace mantel, where Graham couldn't overturn them. Then she unplugged the business phone and uncapped a beer, pouring it into a mug.

Polly always refused a glass. She took a hearty slug straight from the bottle.

Maxine sighed blissfully. "I deserve a break. That phone's been ringing all day."

"Yeah, I heard things were going great. I called Edna this afternoon, and she told me business was booming."

"It is." Maxine sank onto an armchair, glass in hand, and sighed with satisfaction.

"Edna said there's some dude named Harold who's been calling you every single night?" Polly's cornflower-blue eyes were alight with curiosity. "And Edna says this Harold character doesn't even want to get off; he just wants to talk?" She blew a raspberry with lush lips that rivaled those of Julia Roberts. "What's wrong with this picture? Any guy who calls a number that advertises erotic conversation doesn't just want to know what *books* you read."

Maxine felt irritated and tried not to show it. "Well, you're wrong. So far that's exactly what's happened." She was more than a little annoyed with Edna for telling Polly all about Harold.

"He's called five, six times now, and all he's done is talk about everyday things."

"Yeah? What sort of everyday things?" Polly looked and sounded skeptical.

They'd discussed smoking—Maxine had never started, and he'd stopped four years ago. They'd talked about poetry; he liked Robert Service and Lawrence Housman. He'd asked her opinion on Internet sex. She'd admitted she didn't have a computer and didn't know anything about it. He'd said that in his opinion computers weren't very comfortable to snuggle up with in the middle of the night, and her stomach had tensed as she'd waited for him to get further into that fantasy and destroy the illusions she'd built about him, but he hadn't.

Instead he'd started talking about art, asking what kind of art she enjoyed. She didn't know. She'd just hung framed posters on the walls for color, but after that call she'd asked Edna for the names of some books on famous artists.

"He just sounds like a nice, ordinary guy," she told Polly, smiling at Graham as he came crab-walking across the carpet to where they were sitting.

"I thought we agreed a long time ago that there ain't no such animal," Polly said, smiling at Graham as he grabbed the edge of the coffee table and pulled himself to his feet.

"But if by some aberration there happened to be one last living member of that endangered species," she went on, "he sure as heck wouldn't be calling a number for phone sex, now would he? He'd be out volunteering as a Big Brother or reading to his blind grandma in the rest home." Polly's sarcasm disappeared entirely as she cooed at Graham, "C'mon, snookie, you can do it. One big step and you're home."

She held out a finger to him. He was hanging onto the coffee table with one hand and trying to work up enough nerve to let go and take the step it would require to reach her. "C'mon, sugar, take that big first step over here to your auntie Polly."

Graham pumped up and down as if he were doing calisthenics and grinned at Polly adoringly, drool running off his chin.

"Watch out for your suit," Maxine warned. "His hands are none too clean. He's been on the floor since he got up from his nap."

But the warning came too late. Graham hurled himself across the great divide and Polly scooped him up in her arms and held him close, cooing into his ear.

"I'm on my way to the gym; this suit's headed for the cleaner's anyhow," she declared. "Besides, I need a cuddle, and with this guy there're no strings, right, darlin'? Your cuddles are still free."

Graham rubbed his face against the lapel of the silky shell-pink garment, leaving a trail of goop. He reached a hand up and touched Polly's face, and then babbled out a long, indecipherable string of adoring syllables as he stared into her eyes from a distance of six inches.

"You have the most amazing effect on him. He can be cranky as all get out and you walk in the door and he acts like he's a kitten and you're catnip." Even though she, too, loved Polly, Maxine couldn't help feeling just a little jealous.

"It's probably this pheromone stuff I ordered from the back of *Vegetarian Times*," Polly confided, gently unhooking Graham's fingers from her shiny blond hair. "It's supposed to increase your attractiveness to any male in the vicinity, regardless of age." Polly rubbed noses with Graham and giggled when he tried to put a finger up her nostril. "You can add it to your perfume, or just use it alone in a base of witch hazel."

"And it works?" The way Polly looked, Maxine figured any male in the vicinity wouldn't give a damn if she smelled like cow manure. They'd be after her regardless.

"I can't believe you think you need it." She shook her head in amazement. "Even without pheromones you've got guys drooling over you; witness my son."

And grown men as well. Since Maxine had known her, the pretty lawyer had dated and rejected so many guys, they could form their own support group.

"A woman can never be too attractive," Polly declared, nuzzling Graham's neck and making him giggle and writhe with delight. "Besides, I figured it might work on that crusty old Judge Barkoff. I'm trying to get him to sign an order freezing all John Gimbel's assets until I can get an actuarial service to do an analysis. Edna's gonna be one wealthy woman when I get this all sorted out; it's just gonna take me some time." Polly scowled. "And a little cooperation from that mastodon of a judge. I swear, they drag their feet when it's a lawyer they know." She narrowed her eyes and shook her head in disgust. "Old boy club, that's what it is. I've asked for an order for copies of Gimbel's telephone and credit card records for the purpose of confirming what he spends. He's got money socked away somewhere, and I'm gonna find it."

"If Edna gets rich, I'll lose a great employee." The thought made Maxine sad, even though she wanted her friend to get what was legally hers.

"Sometimes I feel like confronting that ex-husband of hers and saying to him, 'You know what you've forced your wife to do for a living, you piece of human'"—Polly glanced at Graham, who was staring curiously up into her face, and substituted—"piece of human garbage?"

Polly's language tended to be explicit and graphic. Maxine had been shocked when she'd first met her, because the visual image didn't match the audio. It hadn't taken long to understand that Polly would go to any lengths for her clients, and that her heart was as soft as her mouth was tough. But she also had decided ideas about what was right and what wasn't.

Maxine, on the other hand, suspected there were gray areas. "You know you can't tell Gimbel what Edna does," she warned. "Edna'd die of shame if her sons ever found out she does phone sex. They think she takes care of an elderly invalid during the night."

Polly snorted. "Edna's way too softhearted. She should lay it out on the table to those boys, exactly how their father snookered their mother into that travesty of a settlement."

Maxine shook her head. "Edna doesn't want the boys involved."

"Boys, hell. They're adults, they're nineteen and twenty-one. And I don't exactly see either of them standing up for her against that creep of an ex."

"It's because he's the one with the bank account," Maxine reminded her. "Money inspires loyalty, especially when it pays for your university fees and a snappy sports car to drive instead of taking the bus."

"It makes my blood boil for both of you when I think about the rotten deal you got from guys you trusted." Polly sighed. "And I still can't get a single line on where Slippery Shwartzie is, either. Sometimes I feel like a bloody failure."

Maxine couldn't help feeling disappointed.

"No news from Costa Rica yet, huh?"

Polly shook her head. "The lawyer I contacted down there is still doing inquiries, but so far nothing. Don't despair, Maxine. I'll find that slimeball if it's the last thing I do." Her eyes narrowed and her voice took on a steely note. "And when I do, I'll nail his sorry ass to the wall and sell it, if that's what it takes to get your money back and the support legally due this little tiger."

Ricky Shwartz, the swashbuckling pilot Maxine had once loved and been engaged to, had talked her into loaning him twenty-three thousand dollars, her entire life's savings, supposedly to help save Eagle Airlines, the small regional company they'd both worked for.

Ricky was supposedly a part owner of Eagle. She'd been crazy in love with him, and she'd emptied her bank account for him. She'd been smart enough, though, in spite of being lovestruck, to get a promissory note for the money.

That was just before she found out she was pregnant. When she broke that news, Ricky had casually suggested abortion. He'd changed his mind about marriage, he announced. He wanted adventure instead of matrimony. He was going to Costa Rica to start a business with an old friend.

When she asked for her money back, he said he didn't have it. He'd repay it the moment his new business took off.

But Ricky took off instead, and Maxine had never seen him again. She'd also found out that the friend he was going to Costa Rica with was female and gorgeous.

Things had gotten very bad after he left. No one would hire a pregnant stewardess, and when she grew desperate enough to try to pawn the diamond engagement ring he'd given her, she found it was a zircon.

That was the day she'd found Polly in the phone book, under "Legal Aid." She'd gone through an entire box of tissues in Polly's office that morning, explaining her predicament.

But disasters are really opportunities in disguise, Maxine reminded herself now. That had been the beginning of her business; totally destitute, she'd answered an ad that same week and been hired on the spot by a company that sold phone sex. They didn't care that she was pregnant; she had the right voice for the job, they assured her.

At first she'd been shamed, shocked, and horrified at what she was doing. Somewhere deep inside, she was still the daughter of the town minister, Zacharias Bleckner.

But the job paid her rent and bought her food and vitamins, and she got better and better at it.

Within a few weeks, Maxine had realized that she was exceptionally good at the job, and that her ability might be the key to earning a living while staying at home with her baby.

She'd saved every cent she could, enough to pay the first and last months' rent on this house, get a 900 line installed, and run a few ads. At first calls were sparse, but when she began to attract regular clients, the pace quickly became frantic. She'd hardly slept for months on end, between caring for Graham and answering the phone twenty-four hours a day. And through the haze of exhaustion one thing stayed clear in her mind: she was going to get back the money that she'd loaned Ricky, plus interest. He owed it to her.

And, Polly insisted, Shwartz also had a financial obligation to support Graham. At first Maxine had objected, saying she wanted nothing more from Ricky than what he owed her, but Polly had explained that it wasn't Maxine's choice; it was Graham's birthright.

"I'm gonna insist on a DNA test that'll prove to the court that Graham's his. Then we'll hit him with expenses and support payments extending back to Graham's birth."

Polly made it sound as if it was only a matter of time before it all happened. Although Maxine would never tell Polly so, she privately believed that finding Ricky Shwartz was about as likely as winning the lottery.

Graham was squirming to get down, and Polly reluctantly set him on the floor. "So what's the score here, Maxine, you in *looooove* with this dude who's calling you all the time?"

"Oh, gee, yeah, totally. All it takes is a little sweet talk and I fall head over heels." Maxine simpered, crossing her eyes and assuming a half-witted expression. "Next thing you know, I'll be loaning him money."

"*Not,*" they chorused in unison, laughing at their own nonsense.

Polly left, and Maxine gave Graham his supper and then bathed him and put him to bed. When she switched the phone back on, it rang almost instantly, and she caught herself watching the clock as she impatiently dealt with favorite positions and imaginary sex toys.

She very much wanted the line free at eight-thirty, because she was sure Harold would call again, and in spite of what she'd said to Polly, there was *something* going on with him.

With her, she corrected, making the appropriate moaning sounds into the receiver.

With both of them?

If only she knew.

Chapter Six

Harry was getting restless because Sadie wouldn't settle. He read her favorite books to her, twice each: *Where the Wild Things Are* and *I'll Love You Forever*. He sang "You Are My Sunshine," four repetitions, with an encore of "Closing Time." He rubbed her back and tried to curb his impatience, and at last—at last—she slept.

He bent over and kissed her head. Her hair smelled of the fragrant fruity shampoo she'd seen on a TV ad and insisted he buy. She was already so *female*, this child of his. It was frightening, because there were some things he knew about females, but there were also mysteries he had no idea about. He doubted any man did.

He pulled the duvet up over Sadie and glanced at his watch. It was after nine-thirty. He swore under his breath and hurried into his office to dial the now familiar number.

"Lilith here, hello."

The girlish voice with the slight lisp caught him off guard, and he didn't answer immediately.

"Don't be shy, sweetie. I don't bite unless you want me to."

"I'm not . . . I mean, actually, I wanted to speak to India. Please. Is she there?"

"She's not available just now. Are you sure you don't want to talk to me?" A little girl giggle. "I'm really quite entertaining when you get to know me."

Damn, blast, double, triple damn. The disappointment he felt was way out of proportion, and that troubled him.

This is an assignment, Watson, he reminded himself. Why should it matter whether he talked to India tonight or tomorrow or next week? The questions he'd wanted to ask would wait. There wasn't a single valid reason for feeling so let down.

Except that he'd come to rely heavily on these nightly conversations, he admitted reluctantly.

"If you should hear from India, would you tell her Harold called, please?"

There was a pause, and then Lilith said carefully, "Is there a number where *she* could reach *you?* If I should just happen to hear from her?"

"Yeah." He recited his number without much hope. India was paid on the basis of incoming calls. No way in hell would she call him.

He hung up and tried to work on the newsletter an insurance agency had hired him to write, but after five minutes he knew it was hopeless. Frustrated and unable to concentrate, he got up and went to the kitchen, opened the fridge, and scanned the contents for something to fill the sudden void in his gut. He settled on a slab of cold pizza and cracked a beer, taking both back to his office.

His mouth was full of cheese and mushrooms when the phone rang. He swigged a gulp of beer, swallowed hard, and snatched it up.

"Harold, I heard you were trying to reach me." The deep, honeyed voice was like soothing balm to his nerves.

"India." His spirits went straight from dismal to exuberant. "I'm so glad it's you. Want me to call you back on your business number?"

"No, that's not necessary." There was a moment's pause. "Actually, I'm calling you from my private line."

Harry understood that her admission subtly altered their relationship. This was the moment to try to push it even further, to do what Sullivan had suggested and try to arrange an actual meeting. He was about to go where he hadn't ventured before, but there were some things he had to know first. He didn't relish the thought of getting his head bashed in by some hulk of a jealous boyfriend.

"India, is there someone special in your life?" That sounded nosy, so he quickly qualified it. "I mean, do you have a husband or a live-in lover or a guy you date regularly?"

"Not anyone special. At the moment." After a moment's hesitation she said a little defensively, "I *do* date, of course."

He was filled with relief. "Of course."

"But there's nobody special. Not in that sense."

He didn't ask her what she meant. He was too busy trying to figure out the logistics of what he was going to suggest next.

"India, I wondered . . . That is, I know this is a long shot, but . . . would you consider going out with me?" His heart was hammering and his throat was dry. "Dinner, dancing, maybe a show, anything, whatever you'd enjoy the most . . ."

His hands were sweating. He hadn't taken anyone on a date for so long, it made him horribly nervous even to ask, and the long silence that followed didn't help at all. She was going to refuse; he just knew it. His heart plummeted.

"Gee whiz, I don't know, Harold."

He had to grin, because he hadn't heard anyone say *gee whiz* in a long time, and it was so unlike her usual sexy sophistication, it caught him off guard. And he was also grinning because she hadn't outright refused, had she?

"I know there are probably all sorts of rules about not dating customers," he said in the most reasonable tone he could manage. "I can see how necessary that would be, but I think you can tell that I'm not an ax murderer or a rapist or anyone who'd hurt you in any way. I just want to get to know you, India. I want us to get to know each other better. And we can't do that over the telephone."

His voice was rueful, and it wasn't all an act. "I only wish there were some way to give you a character reference, but there isn't."

Certainly not when he'd fed her such a bloody big pack of lies, he thought with a stab of guilt. Maybe over dinner, they could start over?

Sure, Watson. You can spill the beans about the article and admit you've been lying through your teeth just to get a story. Now that'll get you brownie points, Romeo. And she's gonna be thrilled to hear you're a single, stay-at-home dad who scribbles insurance company ads for a living in between doing the laundry.

"India, how do you usually meet the guys you date?"

There was a short silence, and he wondered if she was finally going to blast him for being too nosy. "Oh, ummm, I guess mostly friends. I have friends who introduce us."

She must have better friends than he did, he

thought glumly. None of the guys he knew ever set him up with anybody. They were too busy trying to get laid themselves to worry about him, the selfish bastards.

"Could you maybe just pretend I'm somebody one of your friends introduced you to, then?"

This time there was a long, thoughtful silence. "I suppose I could do that," she finally said, and Harry realized he'd been holding his breath. He let it out with a whoosh and then realized he'd done it in her ear.

"Sorry. I'm just relieved. That's wonderful, India." He had to glance at the calendar to figure out what day it was. Wednesday? Yeah, Wednesday.

"How about Saturday evening?" He crossed his fingers, praying that Mrs. Campanato would be able to sit for Sadie. "Around seven?"

"Eight would be better for me."

For him as well. Sadie would be ready for bed by then. "Eight it is." He was elated. He hadn't dared believe he'd pull this off.

"Tell me where we're having dinner, and I'll meet you there, Harold."

"Absolutely." She was being cautious, and he admired her for it. Trouble was, he had no idea where to take her for dinner.

"I'll call you tomorrow afternoon and give you the details. Will that be okay?"

"That'll be fine."

He detected a bit of strain in her voice. This

70

was a stretch for her, too. Or at least, he hoped it was. Surely she didn't date every weirdo who called for sex?

"Good night, Harold."

"Night, India. And thanks."

Elation filled him as he hung up. He couldn't wait to see what she looked like. He'd been careful not to ask her, because he'd guessed that what she'd say would be exactly what she told her other callers. His hunch had paid off now, because if the description was a fantasy, it would have made her refuse to see him.

And what about you, super stud? You're supposed to be a big time sophisticated businessman. How the hell are you gonna pull that one off?

With a sense of trepidation, Harry walked into the bathroom and really looked at himself in the mirror.

His heart sank. He was a real prize, all right, but it wasn't first prize. His blue eyes were bloodshot because he'd worked until two in the morning meeting the deadline on the golf article. His thick black hair badly needed cutting. And of course he'd have to shave off the stubble; even Sadie had complained that his whiskers scratched when he had kissed her tonight. There was nothing to do about the crooked nose, a keepsake from long-ago rugby games. There was that cleft in his chin that women had seemed to like, back when he was a player in

71

the dating game. Was it still there under the whiskers?

Would it come to kissing Saturday? God, he hoped so. He was sadly out of practice, but surely it would come back to him; it had to be like riding a bike.

He'd have to get his sports jacket and his gray slacks cleaned. Did he have a decent shirt?

Did guys still wear sports jackets on dates, or had the whole men's clothing scene changed drastically since he'd last taken a woman out? He tried to figure out how long that had been.

Six, no, seven months ago, it must be. He'd asked that ER nurse out, the one who'd been so nice when Sadie had had the ear infection. Janice? Jasmine? Jackie. It had been a pleasant enough evening, he remembered, but it hadn't taken long to figure out that they weren't on the same page when it came to what they wanted out of life. She talked about traveling to exotic locations, living in a town house on the water, owning a boat. He thought in terms of paying down his mortgage and investing in mutual funds that would put Sadie through college.

He hadn't called her again.

The memory started him wondering what he and India would talk about. Would she tell him her real name, for instance? He knew India was her working title. He ought to go over the notes he'd made during their conversations, find out what else he needed in order to make the article personal and powerful. Right after he met her, he'd do the outline for Sullivan, get the advance, and hire Joe at the garage to put a rebuilt transmission in the car.

And what the hell was he going to do if the evening worked out beyond his wildest dreams, and she gave him signals about wanting to go way beyond dinner and dancing?

He frowned and rubbed a hand through his hair. He'd buy some condoms, but he couldn't very well bring India home, introduce her to Mrs. Campanato, and then ask her not to make any noise while they were doing it, in case Sadie woke up.

He didn't know any good old boys with a nice vacant apartment. He worried over the possibility while he finished his beer and studied the latest copy of *Vancouver* magazine, which he wrote for occasionally.

There were, as always, reviews of Vancouver's better eateries. One, highly recommended, was located in the Hotel Vancouver, and he had a flash of inspiration.

He'd take her there and he'd book a room for the night, just in case. He'd never told her where he stayed when he was in Vancouver, and obviously Harold was the type of high roller who'd keep a room at the Hotel Vancouver.

He called and made reservations, pleased that his credit card wasn't maxed out. It was going to be an expensive evening, and it was unlikely

Sullivan would pick up the tab for dinner, never mind the room, but Harry realized he didn't give a damn.

He was looking forward to being with India. He wanted to see the face and figure that matched that velvet voice.

He wanted to be Harold Walters for just one evening, a worldly sophisticate with pots of money who knew nothing of potty training and temper tantrums and Teletubbies, a man familiar with luxurious surroundings and gourmet food and beautiful women.

He just hoped he could make it through the evening without making a fatal error, like reaching over and cutting up India's meat, or automatically wiping food stains from her mouth.

Chapter Seven

Maxine confided in Edna, and Edna, bless her generous heart, didn't say a single word about breaking the rules by dating a customer. Instead she turned immediately to practical matters.

"I'll come over early and baby-sit Graham for you, I'll just unplug the business phone if he needs me. But what are you going to wear?"

"I don't know." Maxine had worried about that all day. Her wardrobe didn't warrant the title. "I'm gonna have to look like India, I guess. But I don't know what she'd wear out to dinner—she's always in her underwear."

Edna nodded. It was a major problem.

"I couldn't concentrate today, just thinking

about it," Maxine admitted. "None of the things I have from before Graham fit me," she said dolefully. "And since he was born, I've only bought practical stuff to wear around here." And most of it from Goodwill.

Edna frowned and thought about it. "I have plenty of expensive clothes from when I was married, but I doubt anything would be suitable. And my things wouldn't fit you anyhow. Besides, they're not sexy. John always said he preferred the classic look." She rolled her eyes. "Classic Lolita, I guess he meant. Maybe we oughta ask Polly for advice? You haven't got a whole lot of time."

Judging from the conversation they'd already had about Harold, Maxine figured Polly was going to go ballistic when she found out about the date. But Maxine's rising sense of panic over the clothing issue made her reluctantly agree, and Edna called immediately. She explained what was going on, and Polly insisted on talking to Maxine.

"You're nuts, you know that?" Her tone was chastising. "This is a crazy, irresponsible thing you're doing, and Edna and I oughta tie you up until the urge goes away."

"I've made up my mind, I want to go out with him, Polly."

"Then the only way I'll help is if you let me come over and baby-sit Graham."

Maxine grinned and shook her head. Polly

had a weird way of bargaining. "Edna's offered, but she's working, so it might not be a bad idea. If you haven't got anything else planned?" Polly always had a date on Saturday night.

"Oh, drinks with some dork from work. I'll cancel. He's not a guy I want interested, believe me. What the hell are you gonna wear? You've got to look like India, right?"

"Right." Maxine's heart sank all over again. It was impossible to be India, except on the telephone. "Maybe *I'll* just cancel."

"Don't jump the gun, I've got a few things that would look great on you. And you need your hair done anyway—you know that."

Maxine did know. She also needed to lose another eight pounds in two days and see if there was a plastic surgeon who could restyle her lips. "Your clothes wouldn't fit me; I'm way bigger than you."

"Haven't you heard about Lycra, honey? I've got this one-piece undergarment that'll work miracles, and a suit and a couple dresses that will fit; trust me. First thing in the morning, make an appointment to get your hair styled with somebody decent."

"I don't know a good stylist," Maxine admitted in a small voice. "I always go to that chain place in the mall." And she hadn't even been there for at least three months.

Polly groaned. "God spare me. I'll make you an emergency appointment with the guy who does my hair. He owes me a favor—I did a prenup freebie for him and his partner. I'll drive you over and take care of Graham while Terry works on you. And then we're gonna buy you a pair of shoes. You need something outrageously high with straps. New underwear, too. Thong panties."

"Thong panties?" Maxine was really alarmed. "But I'm not going to—"

"Damned straight you're not. They're for you, not him. They'll make you feel sexy."

Maxine had looked at them in Victoria's Secret and thought they'd make her feel squirmy. But Polly knew about these things.

"Okay." There must be some instruction book that she'd never seen, Maxine decided, that gave all the directions for this stuff. Then she remembered what else Polly had said.

"Shoes with high heels? Maybe that's not such a good idea. What if he's short?"

"Didn't you ask how tall he was?"

"He told me six-two, but they always lie about it."

Maxine was getting more and more nervous about this whole thing, but there was also a part of her that was excited. She hadn't been out with anyone since Ricky, and in spite of the butterflies in her gut, she wanted to do this. She wanted to do it right. She wanted to meet Harold. She wanted, just for one evening, to sit across from a man and smile and drink wine and talk about something other than his erection.

By seven on Saturday, however, she wasn't so sure.

There was a feeling of excitement in the house. Edna had come early to take over the business calls, and Polly had arrived just past noon with two enormous suitcases and a makeup case that was bigger than Graham's diaper bag.

She'd given Maxine a manicure and then insisted she try on every last item in the suitcases.

"I think this ice-blue suit with the longer jacket is the one that does the most for you," Polly finally declared, patting and tugging it into place. "What do ya think, Edna?"

"She looks beautiful." Edna had said exactly that about everything Maxine had tried on. Edna was loyal, Maxine concluded, but unreliable when it came to decisions about wardrobe.

"Your hair's good," Polly conceded, giving it an assessing glance.

Terry had gone into raptures over the color, and declared that Maxine's long hair suited her, but not the way it was. With scissors and a drier and something he called "product," plus a dose of utter genius, he'd somehow turned Maxine's bushy head into a jumble of sexy, tousled curls that dipped and swirled around her ears and chin. It felt light and natural, and he'd shown her how to use her fingers when her hair was wet to get the right effect. She kept sneaking looks in every mirror she passed.

If only getting dressed were as easy.

"This skirt's too tight at the waist," Maxine complained. She felt like a stuffed sausage in the Lycra tube that Polly had ordered her to wear in lieu of a slip. "It's fastened right now, but if I eat anything, it's gonna burst." She sucked in her belly a little more. "But I'm way too nervous to eat anyhow, so maybe it'll be okay."

"Don't be crazy. Order everything your heart desires—he's paying the bill," Polly said. "Just don't fasten the button. Here, loop this elastic band through the buttonhole and hook it like this." Polly demonstrated, and then gave Maxine a narrow-eyed stare. "It doesn't look tight because the jacket skims down right over your hips."

"Yeah, it almost covers the hem of the skirt." Maxine frowned down at the shocking spectacle of her legs, bared to midthigh by the scrap of silky fabric. "You don't think the skirt's a little short, Polly? And these heels too high?"

Maxine felt naked in spite of the panty hose she was wearing. And she hadn't worn heels for so long she was sure she'd fall on her face when she tried to walk in these.

"Look, honey, you've got killer legs; use 'em. And the portrait neckline looks lovely."

Edna murmured agreement. "I wish I had that long neck and firm jawline."

"To say nothing of cleavage. God, it never dawned on me that you were hiding that pair under those baggy sweatshirts you wear. That underwire bra was worth every penny," Polly purred.

Maxine fingered the fragile gold chains Polly had fastened around her throat. "I hope I don't lose these."

"So you lose 'em. They're not heirlooms or anything. I can't even remember which guy gave 'em to me. Now, perfume—this is the stuff with the pheromones in it. Might as well see if they work for you the way they do for me."

Polly dabbed scent liberally behind Maxine's ears, on her upper lip, at the base of her throat, on her wrists. "That oughta do the trick."

She scooped Graham up in her arms and gave Maxine one last critical perusal. "It's not raining, so you don't need a coat. Just loop this cashmere shawl over your shoulders. Here, don't forget your handbag."

It was Edna's handbag, actually, black, made of eelskin.

"There, you look like a million bucks," Polly declared. "You've got Edna's car keys?"

Edna had insisted that Maxine take her car as well as her purse. Maxine's battered and rusty old green Toyota didn't have the right image, and if she took a cab, there could be awkward suggestions that Harold drive her home.

"Wave bye-bye to Mommy, punkin; then we'll go give you a nice bath and Auntie Polly will feed you your bottle."

Polly's tone was proprietary.

Maxine had sort of hoped that her son might scream when she left, but instead he gave her a lackadaisical wave and buried his nose contentedly in Polly's neck.

So much for masculine loyalty, Maxine thought sourly as she tottered out to Edna's clean and shining little car. All she could hope for now was that she'd be able to hold her stomach in for the duration of the evening.

The room key was safely in his jacket pocket, and Harry's heart was hammering. He'd told India he'd be wearing a gray sports jacket and a white shirt, waiting for her in the lobby of the hotel. He could have skipped the fashion plug and just said he was Occidental; a huge group of Asian tourists were checking in, and Harry stood out in the crowd—head and shoulders above them, in fact.

He'd been peering over their dark heads for fifteen minutes now, watching the revolving doors, looking for someone with auburn hair— anyone with auburn hair.

"Harold?"

The sultry voice behind him was unmistakable, and he whirled around. He'd overlooked the fact that she might come up in the elevator from the parking level.

"India?" His voice felt as if it were coming from somewhere deep in his gut instead of his throat. He'd tried to imagine what she would look like, and now he was trying not to gape.

He'd never have guessed freckles, was his first idiotic reaction, or a face that was round and country-girl healthy. She had a strong, straight nose under the freckles, delicately flushed cheeks, and amazing grass-green eyes—intelligent eyes, framed by thick dark lashes. She also had the sexiest mouth he'd seen off of a television screen, wide and full-lipped and tremulous.

She was doing her best to smile, but it wasn't quite working. She looked decidedly nervous, which immediately made him feel more confident.

Her hair, rich and thick and the color of mahogany, had the bedroom-tousled look that he'd noticed attractive women wearing lately. Strands of it curled around her jaw and clung to the soft navy shawl draped around her shoulders.

She looked classy. She smelled delicious. And he knew all too well how she sounded.

"India. India, I'm so glad to meet you. In person, I mean." He held out a hand and she hesitated and then reached out and took his fingers, giving them a slight squeeze before pulling her hand away.

He'd imagined her tall and languorous, bone slender, sensually arrogant, with chiseled features and mysterious eyes and a one-sided smile. He'd thought she'd be wearing leopard skin, maybe.

She wasn't tall at all. She was wearing heels, but without them he'd guess her to be five-six, maybe five-seven. And she wasn't bone slender. She wasn't heavy either, not at all. *Voluptuous* was the word that came to mind. *Zaftig.* Under the shawl she had on something slippery and blue and breathtakingly short, and he didn't want to get caught staring at her legs or examining what was visible of her marvelous boobs, so with extreme self-discipline he gazed straight into those keen green eyes and said, "The dining room is along this way. Are you hungry?"

Great opener, Watson. He was obviously far too accustomed to making dinner conversation with a three-year-old.

She gave him another slight, quizzical smile and nodded. "I am, yes."

"Good. Great. So am I, starving." Jesus, now he sounded like a fast-food commercial. He guided her out of the crowded lobby and past the wine bar, where the weekend crowd stood three deep to sample the restaurant's famous cellar.

She stumbled once, and he reached an arm

to steady her, but released her again as they arrived at the entrance to the restaurant.

There were two couples ahead of them, and as they waited, Harry couldn't, to save his soul, think of anything to say. She was gazing around, and he sneaked the opportunity to glance at her legs.

Damn, they were spectacular: narrow ankles, shapely calves, gorgeous knees, thighs that . . . It must be her perfume that was making him think of hot, musky sex.

The maître d' greeted them at last.

Harry gave his name, mindful that he'd used Walters instead of Watson. They were led to a secluded table by the window, and an attentive waiter lit the candle and asked if they wanted a drink.

"India? What would you like?" He'd like to skip the damned dinner and drag her upstairs to the room he'd rented. He'd like to strip her naked and . . .

He'd been without a woman for too long. He should have taken a double dose of saltpeter before leaving home.

Her smell was making him crazy. What the hell was the matter with him? He had a massive erection, and he hadn't been around her longer than ten minutes, for cripes' sake. Thank God they were sitting down.

"Nothing just now, thank you." Maxine shook her head.

"Wine, perhaps?" Harry asked. "White, red?" She looked undecided. "White, please."

Harry glanced at the wine list and ordered, thankful that he'd written some of the press releases for the place and knew which vintages were highly recommended.

"It's a nice evening," Harry began, feeling like a dork. *A dork with a very persistent hard-on*. "The sunset on English Bay was spectacular tonight. Did you see it?"

The only reason he had was because Mrs. Campanato had arrived forty minutes early, and Harry was forced to either vacate the house or listen to one of her lectures on child rearing. She was fixated on the fact that Sadie didn't have enough contact with other kids, and she went on about it until Harry was dizzy.

It seemed her daughter, Rosalie, ran something called Motoring Munchkins at the community center, not ten minutes' drive from Harry's door. Mrs. Campanato was on a mission to get Sadie enrolled, and Harry suspected it had more to do with Rosalie's recent divorce than with Sadie's social development.

Mrs. Campanato started in again the minute she came through the door, so he left early and spent the time sitting in his car in an English Bay parking lot, watching the sun disappear into the ocean.

"I missed the sunset, but the sky was still beautiful when I got to the hotel," she replied.

He was having a tough time connecting the voice from the telephone, with the demure and unbearably sensual flesh-and-blood lady across from him.

It was a tough connection to make; if he'd met her under other circumstances, not knowing what she did for a living, he'd have guessed teaching or maybe nursing. She had the open countenance and healthy looks that should go with those jobs.

The waiter brought the wine. Harry gave it his stamp of approval, and when they each had some in a fragile glass, he lifted his in a toast.

"To friendship," he said, "and an enjoyable evening."

She smiled at him and sipped.

He watched her lips, marveled at the soft roundness of her face, and at last met her eyes. She was watching him.

"You're beautiful, India." He hadn't planned to say it; it just spontaneously came out, and to his amazement she blushed and ducked her head.

"Thank you." She looked at him and for the first time he saw a hint of flirtatiousness. "You're not bad yourself, Harold."

Her sexy voice made the compliment erotic, and, delighted, he laughed. "Thanks." Her words made the trip to the men's stylist and the new shirt worthwhile. And the sample of men's cologne that had come in the mail must be potent. "And now that we've got a mutual admiration society going for us, we can both relax and have fun, okay?"

"Okay." She sipped her wine again, and he saw a dimple come and go in her right cheek. "Are you about to go out of town again on business, Harold?"

Was he? He was flustered. He tried to remember the last lie he'd told her about his mythical business and couldn't.

"It depends," he temporized. "There are a couple of deals pending. I may have to go and complete them."

"Exactly what kind of business are you in?"

He wished to hell he knew. He understood that she was just trying her best to make conversation. She had no idea that she was making him miserably uncomfortable.

"Mergers," he lied, wondering if his nose was growing the way his penis had a moment before. "I'm a freelance adviser, sort of a peacemaker. I go in when two companies merge and I make the situation as smooth and painless as possible." He hadn't realized how rotten it was going to make him feel, looking across at her and outright lying to her. She had the kind of face that really shouldn't be lied to, damn it.

"Harry, you old son of a gun, how are you anyway?"

The jovial voice, the pudgy hand that landed

on his shoulder, made Harry's stomach clench and his heart skip a beat.

"I haven't seen you in a dog's age, I was over at the wine bar and I thought I'd come and say hello."

God help him, the game was up. His cover was about to be blown, and he'd be lucky if she'd ever speak to him again.

Chapter Eight

Harry made a monumental effort to hide his aggravation as he turned and smiled at the short, stocky man behind his chair. "Hello, George."

George Joost was the owner of a small software company for whom Harry had written an overview and business plan when the company filed for a listing on the stock market a year ago. George, whose wife in Toronto refused to move west with their two children, had spent several evenings at Harry's house, and he'd made a huge fuss over Sadie, even bringing her a Barbie doll with a wardrobe of clothes.

"Good to see you out and about, you old hermit, you." But George's spectacled gaze wasn't on Harry. His eyes were feasting on India.

Harry knew the other man was waiting for an introduction.

Harry couldn't chance it. George, affable and talkative, would undoubtedly say something about Sadie, or ask what Harry was writing these days.

"I'll call you, George. We'll get together for lunch," Harry said in the most dismissive tone he could muster.

"Sure, Harry." George took the hint, good-natured as always. "Enjoy your dinner. Oh, and give Sadie my love and tell her I said hi." He gave them a small salute and then walked away.

"Business acquaintance," Harry managed to croak through a throat that was suddenly parched. "Sadie's my, er, secretary."

India's expression told him nothing, and he could only pray that she bought this new addition to his fat folder of lies.

He was relieved that the waiter brought the menus just then. They studied them in silence for a while.

"It all looks wonderful," she said, and he breathed a sigh of relief. He'd been afraid she'd ask him more about George—or worse, about Sadie. But obviously she'd bought his explanation.

He studied the menu. Now that the crisis was over, he was starving. Lunch had been baked beans on toast. Since Sadie, he'd mastered some of the absolute basics of cooking, but his menus ran strongly to stews and soups and Kraft dinners, because he'd learned there was little possibility of going too far wrong.

India, undoubtedly, was accustomed to far more sophisticated fare.

He was convinced of it when she ordered mustard herb-basted free-range chicken and some complicated salad he'd never heard of.

Harry had a steak.

Awkward silences filled the interval between ordering and the arrival of their food. India wasn't as talkative as he'd imagined she'd be, and there was a strain between them that hadn't been there when they had talked on the phone.

It might have something to do with the powerful sense of attraction he felt every time he looked over at her. He kept thinking about kissing those lush lips and forgetting that this was really just an interview. The neckline of her suit dipped low enough to show the swell of creamy breasts, and he kept breathing in her seductive perfume.

When the food arrived, they ate for a while in silence. Harry was having a hard time remembering the list of questions he'd compiled. He finally came up with a couple that needed answering.

"You mentioned that your mother had died. Is your father still alive, India?"

She paused with a forkful of food halfway to her mouth. She set it down and picked up her wineglass instead, taking a hearty gulp before she answered.

"Yes, he is."

He could sense this wasn't a subject she was comfortable with, but it would make a difference to the article to know about her family.

"What does he do?" As he pursued the subject, Harry realized it wasn't just the article that made him want to know about her; she fascinated him. She had interested him when they'd had only a telephone relationship, but now that he'd met her in person, the attraction was even more powerful . . . and disturbing.

She was still toying with her wineglass.

"My father's a minister in the small town where I grew up." Her words were emotionless, but when he looked at her face, he could see strain there. Those full lips were compressed, and a tiny frown came and went between her eyebrows.

A minister's daughter? He couldn't have imagined a more ironic scenario, or one more perfect for his article. He should have dropped the topic; he knew by her expression he should have. But some demon made him go on. "Does he know what you do for a living?"

Her voice was brittle. "Not to my knowledge. I haven't spoken to him in seven years. He didn't exactly approve of me then; I doubt he would now." She smeared butter on a piece of roll and then abandoned it on her butter plate. She pinned him with those green eyes and his breath caught.

"Did you get along with your father, Harold?" There was a subtle challenge in her tone.

Here, at least, he could be honest. "I wasn't close to him, but we got along fine. He was a colonel in the Canadian army, and he was strict but fair. He died five years ago."

She nodded, and he thought she might be trying to imagine what his childhood had been like. He was doing the same thing about her.

"Being a minister's daughter must have been tough. I guess you'd have to be sort of a model for the community?"

She smiled, an ironic twist of her mouth. "Can you imagine me as the perfect minister's daughter?" Her voice changed, and he knew she was mimicking her father. "Ladies don't walk that way. A proper young woman doesn't wear makeup. That dress is too short; it's a disgrace. You're a disappointment to me, Ma—India McBride."

She'd caught herself quickly, but he now had a clue to her real name. "Ma" what? Mary, Matilda, Maureen?

"After Mom died, when I was sixteen, I quit school and came to Vancouver. I stayed with an aunt for four years. She was sick and I took care of her until she died. She was my mother's only sister—they both died really young."

"And after that?" He had an insatiable need

to know about her, to know what path had led her to where she was, to what she did.

He didn't want her to be someone who did phone sex. That sudden realization shocked him, surprised him. Scared him, too. There was no way he should be having opinions about what she did. He shouldn't care.

She gave him a quizzical look, and he wondered what his face revealed about his thoughts. He cleared his throat, tried to assume an interested but bland expression, and repeated his question. "What did you do after that, India?"

"After that I worked as a waitress, went to night school, got my high school diploma. Then I applied for and was accepted for training as a stewardess with a regional airline."

He nodded. "I remember your telling me that you developed a fear of flying. Isn't there help for that? I remember reading—"

"I didn't go for help," she interrupted.

The waiter arrived, collected their plates, and asked about dessert. She declined, but Harry ordered Grand Marnier chocolate cake and amaretto ice cream, with two forks. "You'll share, I hope?"

She didn't reply. Instead she gave him a long, considering look that made him apprehensive. He knew he'd been clumsy about questioning her. He shouldn't have asked so many questions. She'd guessed that he was interviewing her. For an instant relief poured through him. He'd welcome a chance to be truthful, whatever the cost. They could start all over again, on different footing.

"It bothers you that I do phone sex, doesn't it, Harold?" Her voice was unemotional, but her eyes weren't. They shot green sparks.

It caught him totally off guard. In some uncanny fashion, she'd picked up on his unspoken thoughts.

"Not at all, India." His denial was too quick and too formal, and it sounded phony. He did his best to repair the damage. "Hell, no. Why should I mind? It's the way we met, isn't it?"

Even to him it sounded overly earnest, less than honest. He saw a flash of hurt in her eyes. She looked away, and he silently cursed himself.

"I should have realized it would bother you. I guess I'm not exactly someone you could introduce to your friends. Especially not when they know your wife."

"My wife?" He felt stunned. "I haven't got a wife, India." Harry cursed his own stupidity. She was hurt because he hadn't introduced her to George, and she'd gotten the wrong slant on Sadie. He should have guessed that she'd misunderstand his reasons for not introducing her.

"And as far as George goes . . ." he began, but she was getting to her feet. It wasn't until she tossed her shawl around her shoulders that he realized she was planning to walk out on him.

"India, please sit down. I'll explain. . . ." He got up and reached toward her, but she moved sharply away.

"Thank you for dinner, Harold. Please don't follow me out." She snatched up her purse and moved quickly toward the doorway to the dining room.

He tried to catch her, but there was the bill to deal with, and by the time he finally managed to race out of the restaurant, she was gone, and the room key in his pocket felt like hot lead.

It took Maxine a long, frantic time to find Edna's car. She was shaking, on the verge of tears, and her brain wouldn't work properly. There seemed to be dozens of sleek black cars in the parking lot, and she'd foolishly forgotten to mark down the exact location where she'd parked—or Edna's license number, for that matter.

By the time she finally located the car, her feet hurt in the high heels, and her heart felt scalded by the way the evening had gone.

Trembling, forcing herself to concentrate only on driving, she made her way home through the heavy Saturday-evening traffic. She parked the car in front of her house and sat for a moment, trying to control her runaway emotions before she ventured inside.

Polly and Edna were seated at the kitchen table having coffee and cookies, and they both looked surprised when Maxine walked in the door.

"You're back early." Polly got a glimpse of Maxine's face and scowled. "Okay, what'd that jerk do to you?"

She got up and put her arm around Maxine's shoulders, and Edna quietly got another cup from the cupboard and poured her some coffee.

Their warmth and concern were more than Maxine could bear. The tears she'd been fighting all the way home began to pour down her cheeks, and sobs made her gulp and snort. She sank down in a chair and put her face in her hands.

"Did that dickhead attack you?" Polly's voice was fierce. "Because I'll have him up on charges so fast . . ."

Maxine shook her head and blew her nose on the tissues Edna tucked into her hand.

"You were . . . right, Polly. I . . . I should ne-never have gone out with him," Maxine managed to choke out. "He's . . . he's way out of . . . out of my league."

"Don't even start with that rot," Polly snapped. "Just for God's sake tell us what happened. What's this dork like?"

Maxine got control of herself. "He's . . . he's tall, and he's got thick black hair that curls a little around his ears. And clear, sky-blue eyes, and I liked his smile. He's got good teeth and a strong jaw. He's got a cleft in his chin, and sort of a crooked nose. He's not really handsome; he's more, I guess. . . . I'd say rugged-looking. And he's confident, but also a little shy, and . . . and I really liked him. I liked him right away."

"Okay, so he didn't make you scream and up-chuck on sight. So what's the story?" Polly shoved the plate of chocolate cookies over, but food was the last thing Maxine wanted.

Her throat tightened and she had to clear it. "He was ashamed to be seen with me," she said in a tight voice. "At first I tried—" She suppressed another sob at the memory. "I tried really hard to pretend to myself that I was wrong, but he kept asking me these questions, like how my fa—" Her voice broke. She bit her lip and Edna patted her back until she could get hold of herself again.

"How my father felt about my doing phone sex. And it didn't take a genius to figure out Harold was embarrassed about being seen with me. A friend of his came by and Harold nearly passed out. He didn't introduce us or anything, and then the guy asked about someone named Sadie." She swallowed. "Harold's married; I'm sure of it."

"The bastard. The low-down, dirty—" Polly swore fluently, a long string of curses, graphic and, Maxine thought, very satisfying.

They didn't ease the hurt, though.

"I should have guessed. I thought I heard a

woman's voice once when he was talking to me; then his voice changed and he hung up fast."

"Lots of our clients are married," Edna said matter-of-factly.

"Which doesn't matter as long as they stay just clients," Maxine agreed. "But I thought he was an honest guy," she added bleakly.

"It's just like I always say—their brains are wired differently. There's no sense in expecting logic or reason or especially honesty from them," Polly concluded. "They're men."

The business phone rang and Edna went to answer it.

"I'm sorry, but she's not available," Maxine heard her say.

Edna made a face and gestured at the receiver, and with a sick feeling in her stomach, Maxine knew it was Harold. She was going to have to deal with him, and she might as well do it right now and get it over with.

"I'll take that." With trembling fingers, Maxine reached for the phone.

"Don't you let him charm you," Polly said in a hiss. "Give him hell. He deserves it."

"India here." Her voice shook a little.

"India, it's Harold," he began, as if she didn't already know. "Listen, please don't hang up on me. I'm sorry for what happened tonight. You got the wrong impression of me, and—"

"*I* got the wrong impression? I don't think so."

Maxine was very aware of her friends, one on either side of her, both listening avidly. Her heart was hammering, but her pride wouldn't allow her to reveal in any way the confusing muddle of emotions she felt just hearing his voice. "What I got tonight was a hard dose of reality, Harold."

He tried to interrupt, but she raised her voice and talked right over him. "You lied to me, and I hate being lied to. You and I have nothing in common, absolutely nothing."

Polly gave a thumbs-up sign.

"I don't want you to call me ever again. If you do, I'll simply hang up the moment I recognize your voice. If you persist, I'll make a complaint to the police, that you're . . . that you're—"

"Harassing," Polly whispered.

"That you're harassing me." Maxine felt as if she were choking. Before he could say another word, she slammed the phone down and tried to get her breath.

"*Yes!*" Polly exclaimed, smacking one fist into the other palm. "Way to go, Maxine."

"Good for you," Edna echoed. "I wish I'd said something like that to John. All I ever did was start to cry." Edna shook her head. "I was so pitiful."

The phone rang again, and they all looked at one another.

"If that's Harold, hang up," Maxine instructed, but when Edna answered, it was one of her regulars.

Maxine and Polly left her to it. They went back to the kitchen and their coffee.

"Graham went to sleep like the little angel he is," Polly reported. "I rocked him and sang to him, and then when I put him down I rubbed his back."

"Don't you ever think about having a baby of your own?" Maxine said. "You're so good with Graham." Talking about babies took her mind off Harold, which Polly probably realized.

"I'd love to have a baby," Polly said wistfully. "But I've never met anybody I'd even consider as a genetic donor."

"Don't you believe in love at all, Polly?" In spite of Ricky, in spite of everything, Maxine always had. But tonight she wasn't sure.

"I'd like to," Polly said slowly. "I just don't see much of it around, particularly in my work."

"Did you always want to be a lawyer?" Maxine needed to talk, to keep her mind off the evening's events.

"I actually took a teaching degree first," Polly said. "I wanted to be a primary school teacher, but when I graduated there weren't any jobs, so I went back to college and got my law degree. I figured there's always a need for lawyers."

"And you enjoy it?" Maxine thought of Harold, asking her whether she enjoyed what she did.

102

Polly shrugged. "Sometimes. When I can make a difference, when I see that some woman's life is improved because I've managed to get decent maintenance. But you don't hear a lot of happy stories in this job."

"So what would you do if you weren't a lawyer?" She was borrowing all her lines from Harold, but she couldn't seem to help herself.

Polly frowned. "Y'know, I've thought about that sometimes. Something to do with babies. Maybe a midwife?"

"A *midwife*?" That was surprising enough to make Maxine forget all about Harold—for a moment or two. "That's pretty messy, Polly." Maxine could not imagine the stylish Polly dealing with amniotic fluid. "And you don't make much money at it. Plus you don't get to meet any single guys, either."

"So? We're only playing make believe here. It's not as if I'm gonna give up a job that's finally paying me some real money for one where all the perks are in the product." Polly studied a perfectly manicured nail and tried to look nonchalant. "How about you, Maxine? What do you want to be when you grow up?"

Harold had asked her that same question. He'd asked a great many questions. He'd seemed sincerely interested in the answers, too. It went to show how wrong a girl could be.

"A radio announcer." She'd thought a lot more about it, and she'd even ordered a book from the library that would tell her what the requirements were to attend broadcasting school.

"No kidding?" Polly thought it over and nodded her head. "You'd be really good at it. You've got that fantastic voice, and you're quick with answers. Yup, Maxine, you've gotta do it."

"There's this little problem called money. It would mean no income for quite a while, and there's Graham to think about."

Polly was a realist, and she nodded again. "Yeah, but don't give up on the idea. Where there's a will, there's a way."

Maxine had to smile. "My father used to say that. He knew every old saw in the book."

"My grandpa did too; that's where I heard the phrase." Polly studied Maxine intently for several moments. "You ever think of calling your father? Telling him he's got a beautiful grandson?"

"Nope." Maxine shook her head. "In his opinion, I'd be a fallen woman, having a baby without the benefit of marriage. To say nothing of what I do for a living. Lordie, he'd have a stroke if he knew."

"You never know. People change as they get older."

"Yeah," Maxine said in a sarcastic tone. "They get more like themselves, and when it comes to my father, that's not an improvement."

"Well, you'd know." Polly yawned and

stretched her arms over her head. "I'd better get going. Tomorrow's my big chance to sleep late, and I don't want to waste it."

"I've still got your clothes on." Maxine started to get up, but Polly restrained her.

"Relax. I'll get them some other time. I've got plenty to wear without those."

Maxine had thanked her for caring for Graham, and after saying good night to Edna, who was still on the phone, Polly made her way out to her little red sports car, the first thing she'd bought herself after getting the job at the clinic.

As she drove through the quiet suburban streets and then maneuvered impatiently through heavy downtown traffic, the conversation she'd had with Maxine kept replaying inside her head.

For the past year Polly had been aware of a deep dissatisfaction with her job. She tried to smother the feeling by taking on more cases, fighting more strenuously for her clients, being more aggressive and outrageous, dating more guys, but underneath the brassy surface she presented to the world was an emptiness, an ever-increasing sense of *Is this all there is?*

The men she'd dated added to her discontent. They were lawyers, stockbrokers, businessmen, a few athletes. She tried to get below the surface with each of them, find the man who lived and breathed beneath the *GQ* clothing and the manicured fingernails and the gold MasterCard.

Almost invariably she found a belief that the one who died with the most toys won the game. They wanted huge stock portfolios, yachts, expensive cars, big contracts. They wanted a happening woman on their arm, wearing something silk and very short, to reaffirm their value to themselves and their colleagues, and when she asked about their sense of themselves in relation to the world, they answered in terms of power.

It sickened her. These were the same men, she suspected, who phoned Maxine and Edna for a "quickie," and probably snickered about it in the locker room.

That thought made Polly almost homicidal, and she swore and stepped hard on the gas, changing lanes to avoid a long string of cars making left turns at a light.

Lately, the only time she relaxed and felt totally at peace was when she was visiting Maxine and holding Graham. She'd watched Maxine, with sheer guts and tenacity, keep herself off the welfare rolls and even hire Edna. Polly had the most profound respect and admiration for the two women, and as a lawyer, she vowed she'd get justice for them or die trying.

Now the driver ahead was inching along as if there were all the time in the world to get through the next intersection. *Some people shouldn't have driver's licenses.*

Polly swung the wheel an instant before she glanced in the rearview, and something hit the passenger side of her car with a force that stunned her.

A pain larger than anything she'd ever dreamed possible began in her leg and traveled up her thigh. The last sound she heard as her head smashed down on the steering wheel was that of a car horn blaring.

Chapter Nine

"Ms. Kelville, can you hear me?" The voice was female and insistent. "Can you open your eyes? I'm Dr. Duncan; I'm the ER physician."

It was freezing cold. Some idiotic lamebrain was shining a flashlight right into Polly's face. It was giving her the worst headache. She had to wake up in order to stop it. And she needed blankets, lots of them. She was shivering, icy cold.

"Ms. Kelville, Polly Kelville, can you hear me? You're in St. Joseph's Hospital, in Emergency." That same damn woman, nagging at her again. Couldn't she give it a rest?

"Can you open your eyes, Polly? That's it;

that's good. Try to stay with me now; you've had an accident."

Accident? That couldn't be right. She'd remember something like that.

"You've fractured your left leg. Just stay calm, stay still, help us out here. We're going to do some X rays to determine the extent of the damage." The doctor's voice became authoritative, talking to someone else. "Lorna, we need a CAT scan here. And where's X ray?" The voice became reassuring again as she spoke to Polly. "You bonked your head pretty hard. The scan will tell us if there's anything to be concerned about."

Long moments with activity all around her, and then the doctor's voice again: "Okay, let's get her transferred, on three, here we go . . ."

"My leg, oh, Jesus, my leg, do something, do something, please. . . ." Was that her hollering like that?

"Sorry, sorry, Ms. Kelville." Dr. Duncan again. "I know it hurts. We're going to give you something for the pain in just a little bit, but first we have to make certain you have no other injuries." Then, obviously speaking to someone else, "How's Bruce doing?"

A new male voice. "He's fine. All he got was a cut on the forehead. Greg dug out a chunk of glass and stitched him up. No concussion."

"That's good news. Was he on his way over here?"

"Nope, going home after a delivery."

Was Bruce a pizza driver? Polly must have moved a little, because a pain to end all pains went through her body like an electric shock. It was going to make her sick; it was the kind of pain that made her want to vomit. She screamed instead, and tried to pass out.

It didn't work.

"Ms. Kelville." Duncan's voice. "Can you hear me? We're going to be taking you up to Surgery in a few minutes. Is there someone we can call for you, family, friends?"

There were tubes in her arms, and the pain had receded enough to be bearable. This time she remembered the crash, awful, agonizing flashes of ambulance attendants lifting her out of her car, of agony, of feeling certain she was dying.

"How . . . Where . . . Who . . ." She couldn't seem to put things into a sentence. There were medical staff all around her. She was lying flat on a hard gurney, she seemed to have a sheet over her and not a scrap of clothing on under it, and she didn't care.

She was scared. She hated being scared. She hated hospitals and doctors and anesthetic. They were about to operate on her, the doctor had said, and her entire family was back in Winnipeg, which wasn't a damned bit of use to her right now.

Not that they'd be much use if they were here either. Her brothers weren't that good in any emergency, unless it involved rugby or football. Anything else, they'd argue among themselves, cause a whole lot of commotion, do just what the doctor said, and then haul her kicking and screaming back to Winnipeg with them.

She hated Winnipeg almost as much as she hated hospitals. But at the moment she hated operations most of all.

"Maxine Bleckner," she croaked. "I want someone to call Maxine for me." She tried to remember Maxine's phone number, and after a moment came up with what she hoped was right. Polly repeated it. "Call her *right now*," she ordered in her best lawyer voice.

All of a sudden it was imperative that Maxine know what had happened. Polly wanted someone she trusted to know that she was heading into surgery.

"The nurse'll make the call in a moment," Duncan promised.

Polly wondered if she could trust the nurse to do it. Agony consumed her, and after an interval that seemed to last forever, in which she was subjected to jolting and prodding and tubes and needles, Polly slid gratefully down into a dazed half doze.

The next time she awakened, there was motion. Something green overhead was rushing by at a rapid pace. It took a moment for her to realize it was ceiling tiles. Although there was still pain, it had lessened. The gurney stopped at a nursing station, and a man's voice, obscenely cheerful, came from somewhere behind her. "Hey, Ms. Kelville. How's it going?"

He came alongside the gurney and looked down at her, a blond man with a wide white bandage stuck to his forehead. He had a bony face, dark eyes, and a wide white grin. Looking up at him from this angle was weird.

What big teeth you have, Mr. Wolf. . . .

"I'm Bruce Turner, the guy you hit? You'll be glad to know that apart from a little bump on the head, I wasn't injured at all. I wanted to reassure you about that—I figured you'd be worried."

She wasn't. She hadn't given him a single thought. Why would she, when she was probably dying?

"Our cars, now," he went on, still smiling as if it were the biggest joke in the world, "well, they looked pretty messed up when I last saw them, but what the heck, cars are replaceable, right?"

What is this joker doing here, anyway?

As if he'd read her mind, he went on in that irritatingly cheerful tone: "They just finished treating me in the ER. I wanted to say, 'hi there,' but they were already taking you to surgery. I work here, upstairs on Maternity. I'm OB-GYN. So I was able to track you down pretty easily."

His eyes were dark brown, nearly black, with laugh lines around them. His lashes were blond and long. She could see the light through them.

"Anyhow," he went on, "I'm pleased to meet you, Ms. Kelville. You didn't have to ram into me to get my attention, though. Pretty lady like you, a simple hello would have done the trick."

He thought she'd done it on purpose? Was this guy a stand-up comedian or a doctor?

Polly opened her mouth to ask him that, and a bolt of pain made her cry out.

"Sorry, sorry, don't try to talk. I'll be around. We can get to know each other after they patch you up." At least he sounded compassionate this time. "Hey, Linda, who's doing her?"

Doing her?

A female voice came from behind the desk. "Dr. Bellamy's on call. That's quite a Band-Aid you've got there, Bruce. What happened?"

"Little MVA a while ago. Ms. Kelville here smacked into me down on Broadway. There you go, Ms. Kelville, Bellamy's the best. Just relax and enjoy. You'll be in and out in no time and as good as new."

He had a beard, Polly noted. She hated beards. It was a blond beard. She didn't like blond men, because she was blond herself. Blondes showed up better against dark men.

"Be careful what you say about the accident,"

she warned him. "I'm a lawyer. Don't think you'll get away with telling everyone it was my fault."

He laughed. "I'm a doctor, so just make sure you think good thoughts as you go into surgery. Studies have proven attitude is important." He laughed again. He had a big, hearty laugh, and she hated it.

She hated him. He was obviously a buffoon. Polly wanted to smack him. She opened her mouth to tell him so and some slight movement made her gasp.

"Don't try to talk. I'll pop by and see you after surgery. Oh, and you might as well call me Bruce. I can tell we're gonna be great friends. Your name's Polly, right? I heard them read it off your ID. Here's your team now. Everything's going to be fine, Polly; don't worry about a thing. You're in good hands with Dr. Bellamy."

Polly felt utter terror consume her, and suddenly she didn't want him to leave. *Better the devil you know . . .*

"Could you phone my friend for me? They said they would, but I don't know if they did it." She feared she'd given them the wrong number, and Maxine's private number was unlisted.

"By all means. What's the number? Linda will call right away for you, won't you, Linda?"

"Sure, Dr. Turner, I'd be happy to."

Polly was sick of people here passing the

buck. "I don't see any piano tied to your ass, Turner," she snapped.

His eyebrows shot up and then he laughed that big, hearty guffaw again. He snapped off a salute, making certain not to bump his bandage or her gurney. "Okay, Sergeant. Just give me the number. I'll make the call myself right now."

"I don't know the number offhand; look in the phone book under Yakkety Yak."

"Your friend's name is Yakkety Yak?" He wasn't laughing now. He obviously thought she was hallucinating from the head injury.

"Her business is called Yakkety Yak. Just call the damned number and ask for Maxine."

Polly heard him riffling the pages just as a new group of green-gowned people briskly wheeled her through a doorway and then began doing things to her body that were uncomfortable and frightening.

Really scared now, Polly thought of Graham, of how soft and sweet he felt in her arms. She imagined rocking him, burying her nose in his sweet baby hair. . . .

"Can you count backward for me from a hundred?"

". . . ninety four, ninety three . . ."

Maxine, please be here when I wake up, please . . .

And . . . nothing.

Chapter Ten

"Maxine?"

At first Maxine thought Edna's voice was part of the dream she was having.

"Maxine? Maxine, honey, are you awake?"

She wasn't. Her head was stuffy from crying; her eyes felt glued shut. She forced them open and saw Edna standing beside the bed, the portable business phone in her hand.

Maxine reached over and switched on the bedside light. The clock radio said three-fifteen. She'd been asleep only a little over an hour.

She'd gone to bed right after Polly left, but she couldn't sleep. Instead she'd pulled the blanket up over her head and let the shame, the disappointment, and the betrayal of the evening roll over her in hot, sickening waves.

She hadn't tried to stop the sobs that racked her, or the tears that soaked her pillow. It had taken a long time before she slid into sleep.

"Maxine, sorry to wake you, honey, but there's this guy on the phone who swears he's a doctor. He keeps saying Polly asked him to give you a message. I thought at first he was saying *massage*."

"Polly?" Maxine tried to make sense out of it and couldn't. "But how does he know Polly?"

Edna shook her head. "You got me, but he knew your name. He asked for Maxine, not India. Will you talk to him? He's pretty insistent."

Maxine sat up and stuck a pillow behind her, and Edna handed her the phone.

"Hello?" Her voice was croaky from sleep and crying, and she cleared her throat and tried again.

"Hello?"

"Is this Maxine?"

The voice was pleasant, and he sounded amused.

"Speaking."

"This is Bruce Turner, Ms. Bleckner. Dr. Bruce Turner. I'm calling for Polly Kelville. She and I had a little car accident earlier this evening, and she expressly asked that I call and tell you so."

The message registered and Maxine was suddenly wide-awake. "My God. Oh, my God, is she . . . is Polly okay?"

"I'm sure she's going to be fine. She's heading into the operating room just now, where the surgeons will repair a compound fracture of her left leg. I believe that and a pretty good bang on the head is really all the damage she sustained. I understand she had a slight concussion."

"Are . . . are you her doctor?"

"Nope, I'm the guy she hit with her car." He sounded so cheerful about it that Maxine relaxed a little.

"I'm a doctor, though, OB-GYN. I was heading home after a delivery," he went on, adding, "I do better with contractions than with fractured legs."

"Were you hurt in the accident, Dr. uh, Turner?"

"Call me Bruce. They dug a little piece of glass out of my forehead, but that's all. I'm absolutely fine."

"I'm glad. What . . . what happened? The accident, I mean."

"Oh, Ms. Kelville made a turn into the left lane and drove her car into the side of mine." Again he sounded surprisingly lighthearted about it.

"I'll be right there. Tell Polly I'll be there as soon as I can."

"Don't rush; it'll likely be several hours before

she's conscious." He paused a moment and added in a thoughtful tone, "Although if she happens to come to and you're not here, she's not going to be impressed with either you or me. The lady does have a way with words."

"I'm coming right away. I don't want her to wake up alone."

"Right you are. Oh, and tell your friend— Lily? Lilith, that's it. Tell Lilith I greatly enjoyed our conversation. If things ever get boring here at St. Joe's I'll be sure to call again." He chuckled and hung up.

"What's happened to Polly? Who was that?" Edna's forehead was creased with worry.

Maxine explained as she scrambled out of bed and hurriedly pulled on jeans and a sweatshirt. "It sounds as if Polly's the one who got the worst of it. This Dr. Turner also said he'd enjoyed the conversation he had with you. What's that all about?"

"Oh, he called on the business line," Edna said apologetically. "I thought he was one of those nutsos who are into medical fantasies when he said he was a doctor, and I just went along with it. I'm afraid it took me a while to figure out that he actually was a doctor."

Under other circumstances, it would have been funny, but both of them were too concerned about Polly to be amused.

"Don't worry about Graham, I'll stay until you get back, of course," Edna said. "Just be sure to call me and let me know how she's doing."

"Thanks, Edna. You're such a good friend." Maxine put her arms around Edna and hugged her. "I probably don't tell you that often enough."

It felt strange to drive through the city's quiet streets for the second time that night. She was exhausted, and everything seemed overwhelming. Inside her head the entire evening replayed all over again, from the moment she'd spied Harold, tall and so sexy, waiting for her in the lobby of the hotel.

She'd been terrified. Her mouth and her knees were both trembling when she first spoke to him.

She'd built up an illusion about Harold, a crazy idea that he'd be the man she'd imagined Ricky was in the beginning, the man she'd dreamed of since she was a little girl longing for a Barbie doll.

Her father wouldn't allow Barbie in the house. Zacharias felt the doll was indecent, not a suitable toy for the daughter of a minister. Over the years he'd also criticized Maxine's clothing, her hair, and her personality. The one thing he hadn't been able to touch was her fantasy life.

And that was the beginning of India, Maxine thought, turning up Burrard Street to get to St. Joseph's Hospital.

As a girl growing up she'd imagined herself

beautiful, sensual, untamed. And she'd envisioned the man who'd be her lover. Of course, he'd be the total opposite of her father. He'd be a man who laughed and loved with an open heart, a confident man who celebrated all the things her father deplored in her.

And as she grew, so did the longing to be loved. She'd blinded herself to things that should have warned her what kind of man Ricky was. She'd gone on loving him long after some part of her knew he was dishonest and a cheat.

And now she'd gone and done it again.

Harold had made her feel special. She'd been seduced into believing he was different, that he saw beyond the facade of India to Maxine.

What a gullible fool she was, she thought, turning in to the parking lot at St. Joe's. *Well, no more.* She slammed the car door to punctuate the vow.

Inside, a man at the information desk directed her up to the surgical floor.

"Ms. Kelville is still in surgery," the tall nurse at the desk informed her. "You can wait just along the hall there, and as soon as the operation's over I'll have Dr. Bellamy come and speak to you."

Maxine bought a cup of coffee from the machine and settled down to wait. Even though it was the middle of the night, there was activity, nurses bustling up and down the hallway, a telephone ringing.

"Ms. Bleckner? I'm Dr. Bellamy." A tall, stork-thin man still wearing operating room garb came into the room.

"Ms. Kelville is in recovery. The operation was a total success, and her leg will be as good as ever once it heals. She'll have to do some therapy, of course. You'll be able to see her in a short while."

Maxine found a telephone and called Edna, filling her in on what the doctor had said.

"Graham's just waking up. I'll unplug the business phone while I change him and give him his cereal."

"Thanks, Edna. I want to talk to Polly before I go. The doctor said it shouldn't be too long before she's conscious."

But it was the better part of an hour before a nurse came to take her to Polly. She had intravenous tubes in her arms and a cast on her lower leg. Her forehead had a huge blue lump, and her eyes had shocking purple smudges under them. She seemed to be sleeping, and Maxine didn't want to disturb her, but the nurse had no such reservations. She said in a loud voice, "Ms. Kelville? Ms. Kelville, wake up. Your friend is here."

Polly's eyes reluctantly opened, and when she saw Maxine, recognition slowly dawned and her face crumpled.

"Maxine, I'm so glad you came," she said in a thick, slow tone. "Jesus, Maxine, I smashed into a dumb doctor's car. He's probably gonna sue the ass off me."

It was so typically Polly, Maxine had to laugh. And any sign of vulnerability quickly faded as Polly got her bearings. "Did you meet that idiot ass of a doctor they allowed to practice surgery on me?"

"He's nice, Pol. I'm sure he did a good job. He said the operation went perfectly, that you'd be absolutely fine as soon as your leg heals."

"I'll believe that when I get a good look at what he did to my leg. Did he say when I could go home?" Polly's voice was anxious. "I hate doctors and hospitals. I want to go home."

Maxine had thought about that while she was waiting to see Polly. Polly's apartment was downtown, on the fifteenth floor of an impressive building, with a magnificent view of Stanley Park, but the stairs in the lobby weren't designed for someone in a wheelchair. Or on crutches, either.

Maxine's house, on the other hand, was all on one level. She could move Graham's crib into her own room.

"I think you'll have to stay here for a couple days."

Polly groaned and cursed in a steady stream.

"And when they release you, you're gonna come home with me for a while," Maxine said

123

firmly. "At least until you can get around on crutches."

Polly argued a little, but Maxine could tell that she was relieved. It was the first time she'd ever seen Polly vulnerable.

"Only if you let me baby-sit Graham for you," was Polly's final concession.

Of course Maxine agreed, and then Polly complained that she was cold, and the nurse went for a spare blanket. But before she got back, Polly fell asleep in the middle of a sentence and started to snore.

The nurse came with the blanket, tucked it around Polly, and told Maxine she should leave.

"She's probably going to sleep most of the morning; we'll be moving her to the surgical ward in a little while."

"Please tell her that I'll come back tonight. Is there anything she needs?"

"Is there anything you want your friend to bring you, Ms. Kelville?" The nurse gently shook Polly's arm. "Ms. Kelville, wake up. Is there anything you need?"

Polly stopped snoring and opened bleary eyes. "I need to sleep, for heaven's sake. Is there some bloody law against a person sleeping in this damned place?"

Maxine apologized. The intrepid nurse simply asked again if there was anything Polly needed.

Polly took a sulky moment to think about it.

"My makeup, and some decent pajamas, and some good underwear," she recited. "And something that'll go over this obscene thing on my leg, sweatpants I guess. There are a couple of sweat suits in my drawers at home. I want the pink set and the yellow. My keys must be around here somewhere. God knows what they've done with my purse." She gave the nurse an accusing glare. "Where's my purse?"

"We have it at the desk," the nurse said in a patient tone. "As soon as you're moved to the surgical floor, we'll bring all your things and put them in the locker in your room."

"Well, be sure to give Maxine my ring of keys," Polly ordered. She turned her head to Maxine. "Don't take any snot from the nursing staff, either. This is why we pay medical."

Maxine felt her face redden with embarrassment. The nurse sniffed and walked away. Polly was not going to make friends here in the mood she was in, but Maxine wasn't brave enough to tell her so. Obviously Polly wasn't in any mood to be reasoned with.

"Hold it," Polly ordered in an imperious tone as Maxine started to leave. "That's not all. Call Judd at the clinic and tell him what happened. His number's in my address book at home. Oh, and I'm gonna need some of my files. Tell Judd to get Shirley to bring them; she'll know which ones. And tell him he's gonna have to do that frigging motion for discovery on Monday, the Smith thing."

As she left, Maxine felt guilty about feeling relieved.

The friendly nurse at the station had Maxine sign a form and then let her take the keys to Polly's apartment.

It was only a short drive from St. Joe's, and at this hour of the morning there was street parking.

Maxine made her way through the elegant lobby and up to the fifteenth floor.

She'd been in Polly's apartment only once before, for lunch on a Sunday, with some of Polly's other female clients. It had been Christmas, and Maxine had worried about what to wear, expecting sleek sophistication and cool elegance. She'd been taken aback by the cluttered, casual apartment, and by Polly's total unconcern for dust and litter.

That hadn't changed. Books, magazines, and the pages of several different newspapers were scattered across the floor in the spacious living room. The coffee table held a stack of file folders and several thick books on law. In the kitchen, dirty dishes and the dried remains of at least three meals were strewn over the table and the counters.

Maxine shook her head. Polly, who always looked as if she'd been put together by a fashion coordinator, was a slob at housekeeping.

She found the address book and called Polly's associate at his office number. It was too early for him to be there. She left a lengthy and detailed message on his answering machine.

Then she called Edna to update her on what was happening. "I should be home in about an hour. I'll just bundle up the stuff Polly needs and pop it back to the hospital first."

"Don't rush," Edna said comfortably. "We're getting along just fine here."

Maxine heard Graham babbling in the background, and Edna held the phone to his ear so Maxine could talk to him for a moment.

In startling contrast to the untidiness everywhere else, Polly's closets and drawers were arranged with military neatness and precision, her dresses and suits color coordinated. Maxine found a bag and loaded it with the things Polly had requested.

In the kitchen she wrinkled her nose and then threw away leftovers and loaded the dishwasher, scouring the sink and counter. She tidied the books and newspapers in the living room into neat stacks, and when she was finished she wandered over to the sliding patio doors and stepped outside.

The small rooftop deck had a breathtaking view, overlooking the park, Lost Lagoon, and the towering snowcapped North Shore Mountains. This was the view that Maxine described when her clients wanted to know where she

127

lived; it was a perfect setting for a fantasy.

Did Harold live in an apartment like this?

The thought of him brought back the tumult of feelings she'd had the night before. She had to forget about him. The way to do that was to keep busy.

She hurried back inside and grabbed the things she'd packed. Between her business, her son, and now Polly's accident, staying too busy to think shouldn't be a problem.

Her gaze fell on the law books and file folders, mute testimony to Polly's devotion to her work.

It was too bad her own job didn't use her brain a little more, Maxine thought. She remembered the books she'd borrowed about radio broadcasting. There were night-school courses offered at a local college, weren't there?

With Polly staying at the house, there was no reason she couldn't be away for a few hours one or two nights a week. And after Polly left, maybe she could hire Edna to come a few hours early and baby-sit.

She hated the thought of being away from Graham at bedtime. And it was a scary idea, going back to school.

For a while she did her best to talk herself out of it, but as she drove back to the hospital, dropped Polly's things at the nursing station, and then hurried home, the idea just wouldn't go away.

Chapter Eleven

"Daddy? Wake up, Daddy. Today is my *school*; you promised."

Sadie's persistent nagging finally penetrated the dream he was having about a boat and a naked woman. Harry groaned, rolled over, and managed to come to enough to squint at the clock.

Eight-fifteen.

Eight-fifteen?

He threw the covers aside and leaped out of bed. He had a fuzzy memory of turning off the alarm earlier, and he groaned. The week before, he'd crumpled under Mrs. Campanato's relentless campaign, and Sadie had been attending the program ever since. She was due at Motoring Munchkins in fifteen minutes.

At least Sadie was dressed, after a fashion—her own fashion. She'd put on the costume he'd bought her last Halloween, a floor-length, silver-spangled, Cinderella-at-the-ball number. She had her magic wand under her arm and her yellow rubber boots on her feet.

Tugging on the jeans and sweatshirt he'd worn all week, he raced into the bathroom and splashed his face with cold water.

No time to shave; he had to get Sadie fed.

He solved that dilemma by putting Cheerios in a Ziploc bag and slapping jam between two slices of bread.

"You can have a breakfast picnic in the car," he declared, hauling her out the door.

Damn, he'd forgotten to brush her hair—and his own, he realized, glimpsing his unshaven face, bed-head hair, and glum expression in the rearview mirror.

What the hell. His looking like a crazed street person would convince Mrs. Campanato's daughter Rosalie he was a bad prospect as a future husband and maybe put a stop to the coy glances she shot his way during the juice break. He could only hope.

"Are you pissed off, Daddy? You look pissed off, Daddy."

"No, I'm not pissed off, and I told you not to use that word."

"Why, Daddy? You say it on the phone; I heard you say it *lots*."

Damn. He must have been talking to the software company who'd owed him money for two months now.

"It's a man word; language like that isn't for little girls. Eat your picnic, kid."

He stopped at a light and noted that the strawberry jam he'd smeared on her bread was now decorating the front of her white Cinderella ball gown. He was gonna get those scathing looks again from the European mother whose little Elsa looked as if she'd been bathed in bleach and dipped in flour.

His spirits were at an all-time low. It had been two weeks since his disastrous date with India. After the first several calls, he'd given up trying to contact her; she'd obviously put out the word with her colleague that if he called, the rule was to hang up.

He'd written the outline for Sullivan, but he'd felt like a traitor doing it. And then when Sullivan said it was good stuff, and to go ahead, and "This here telephone sex broad sounds like a real firecracker," and "Here's the money, Harry," he'd wanted to punch Sullivan in the chops and tell him where to stuff the check.

Except he needed the money. The washing machine had packed it in, and Joe at the garage had found out the car needed brakes as well as a transmission. So he sold India to pay for it, God help him.

Meeting her had been shocking, because she wasn't at all as he'd visualized. Not that he'd been disappointed; quite the opposite.

He'd found her incredibly attractive. He'd been captivated by the way she looked.

He'd been prepared for one sort of woman, but India was so far removed from his mental image, her appearance had taken him off guard. And he'd been stupid, insensitive. Dumb. He'd been really dumb.

He wanted to tell her that he wasn't married, that she'd misunderstood his reasons for not introducing bloody George Joost, but the more he thought about it, the more he realized that although her reasoning was all wrong, her conclusions were right; he *was* lying to her. He just wasn't lying about what she thought. Did it matter? A lie was a lie was a lie.

And every time his mind circled like that around the situation and arrived back at the same sorry place where he'd royally screwed up, the sick feeling filled his gut and threatened to eat him.

He liked her. *Harry, for God's sake, be honest— at least with yourself.* He more than liked her: he'd wanted to jump her bones right in the middle of the restaurant, for cripes' sake. She was lush and hot and fleshy, the stuff that erotic dreams were made of. And smart; it was the smart part that did him in.

Each time he told himself it was better this way, that nothing could have come of their relationship anyhow, that he had Sadie to consider, that India was from another world, one that he didn't want his daughter involved with, absolutely not, his gut ached until he wondered if maybe he was getting an ulcer.

His dad had gotten an ulcer, and an uncle, too. Lots of dads had ulcers when he was a kid. Did anybody get ulcers anymore? He hadn't heard of them lately, but if this gnawing in his midsection didn't go away soon, he'd have to pay a visit to the doc.

Maybe he could sell an article on ulcers to somebody. He had to start scrambling for assignments again if he wanted to pay next month's bills.

That depressed him even further.

He pulled into the parking area by the community center and stopped the car. He took his daughter's sticky hand in his, convinced her she had to leave the magic wand in the car, and hurried with her into the controlled, headache-making chaos that was Motoring Munchkins.

Maxine was trying to get Graham to socialize with the other kids the way the pediatrician had suggested, but the thing that he liked best was the purple foam tunnel. It was about four feet long, and Maxine was kneeling at one end, head and shoulders half inside, alternately encouraging her son to crawl through it and trying to pry mouthfuls of foam out of his mouth before he swallowed them. He'd learned that if he put his face into the stuff and bit, he could dislodge chunks. He had some canine tendencies she hadn't noticed until now, Maxine decided.

"C'mon, punkin, give that to Mommy; that's my good boy." She stuck her finger gingerly into Graham's mouth. He had seven teeth, and biting was his favorite hobby.

A small girl with tangled carrot red hair and a heart-shaped face smeared with jam was kneeling at the other end, watching Graham through huge blue eyes.

"He's not 'posed to eat it," she announced in a scandalized tone. "Daddy, this baby's *eating* the tunnel."

Maxine could see long denim-covered legs behind the girl.

"This little girl wants to use the tunnel, Graham. Let's go find that truck you like." She reached out to pry him back toward her, but he resisted, head down, determined to take another bite, and she raised her voice as she hauled on her determined son. "C'mon, demon, foam has no food value. Take my word for it."

"India?" The horrified male voice came from

behind the little girl. "India, is that you?" He'd crouched down on his hands and knees, and he was staring in at her, and she was pretty sure it was Harold.

Chapter Twelve

Maxine froze.

"Harold?" It sounded like him, but the scruffy man giving her the incredulous look didn't resemble the Harold she remembered from the restaurant.

Or did he?

"It can't be you." Maxine backed up and struggled to her feet.

He, too, was now standing, and the dumbstruck look on his face must mirror the one on hers.

His green sweatshirt had a hole in the elbow, and the shoulder seam was coming apart. His jeans fit him well, but they'd had cleaner days. His eyes were bloodshot. The thick, shiny hair she'd imagined running her fingers through was was still shiny, but it was flat on the right side, and it stuck up in a rooster's comb at the back of his head. His strong jaw was unshaven, the cleft invisible under a generous growth of black stubble. It wasn't just from this morning, either. It would take three or four days to cultivate that much beard.

It *was* Harold, but he looked more like a fugitive from justice than a romantic hero.

The incredulous look he was giving her suddenly reminded Maxine that not only had she skipped makeup that morning, but the pimple she got every month with her period was glowing like a neon light smack in the middle of her chin.

She had cramps, and her belly stuck out, although that wasn't very evident, because she was wearing the baggy gray sweatpants that Polly had warned her were hideous and rightfully belonged in the garbage. And although her yellow tee had started out clean this morning, Graham had upchucked prune juice on it when she lifted him out of his car seat.

Harold might look disreputable, but she probably resembled an accident victim.

She certainly felt like one, if shock was any indication.

She had to clear her throat twice before she found her voice. "What . . . who . . . what exactly are you doing here, Harold?"

He could as easily have asked her the same question.

"Daddy? Daddy, this baby won't let me crawl through the tunnel, and he's eating it more." The redheaded girl was urgently tugging at Harold's leg. "It's not for eating, is it, Daddy? Come and take him out."

Looking straight into Maxine's eyes, Harold reached down and put his open palm on the girl's fiery hair. His voice was strained. "This is my daughter, Sadie."

Maxine tore her eyes from him and looked at the child. She had the face of a dreamy angel and the eyes of an imp. She was solid confirmation of what Maxine already knew: Harold was married; he wasn't at all what he'd pretended to be. The fact that he'd forgotten to mention he had a little daughter whose mother didn't fuss much about appearances shouldn't surprise her.

So if she already knew what a lying, no good, devious bastard he was, why did it feel as if her chest were caving in?

She was proud of herself for mustering up something like a smile for the child. "Hello, there, Sadie."

Fortunately Graham started gagging right then, and Maxine bent and dragged him out of the tunnel. She forced her finger deep inside his mouth and dislodged a soggy lump of purple foam.

As soon as it was out he bit her, hard. After that, he gave her an angelic grin, wiped his runny nose on her shirt, and squirmed to get down.

"This is my son, Graham." Maxine felt as if things were happening in slow motion. She jiggled Graham up and down and absentmindedly stuck the wad of foam in the pocket of her pants. "I'm gonna take him over to the toy area now. I'd rather you didn't bother us again."

On rubbery legs she turned and walked away, but from the corner of her eye, she could see that Harold was following close behind.

"India, we have to talk."

"No, we absolutely do *not* have to talk." She set Graham down, rather forcefully, beside a heap of red and yellow blocks. "Your wife wouldn't want us talking any more than we already have, now, would she, Harold? By the way, does she have any idea of how much talking we've already done?"

"I haven't got a wife. I swear on my daughter's life I *haven't got a wife*." His voice was loud, and several parents turned to stare in their direction.

He sounded a bit like a manic Dr. Seuss, Maxine thought hysterically.

"Cheryl died in a car crash when Sadie was six months old," he said in a quieter tone.

He sounded as if he was telling the truth, but

he'd sounded like that before. Did she dare believe him?

"Look, I'll get someone to prove it to you, I'll get my accountant to sign a statement; I'll show you my income-tax returns, I'll get a note from my doctor—whatever it takes."

So maybe he wasn't married. A little bubble of relief rose out of the confused and murky depths of her heart.

"What about you, India?" His voice vibrated with tension. "I didn't know you had a son, either. So who's Graham's father?"

He'd remembered her kid's name the first time around. Another little blip wriggled its way out of the mire of her emotions—not exactly pleasure; more like pleasant surprise.

"I didn't marry him. He left when I was four months pregnant. He doesn't even know he's got a son. I have no idea where he is."

Relief sketched itself across his features, but after a second Harold's eyes narrowed and he gave his head a disgusted shake. "He got you pregnant and then deserted you, huh? Some guys need castrating," he said in a growl.

A woman helping her baby build blocks picked him up and hurried away, giving Harold a shocked glance.

"Castration's not a bad idea." Ricky and his dishonesty reminded Maxine that Harold wasn't exactly blameless in that regard, either. "So what about you, Harold? You're not really

140

an international businessman who travels a lot, are you? Or is this just the nanny's day off?"

The sarcasm in her voice would have made Polly proud.

"Of course I'm not a businessman. I'm a free-lance writer," he said in a contrite tone. "I do advertising slogans and short pieces for different publications. I work at home. I used to be an ad man, but I gave it up and went freelance when Sadie came. I wanted to be able to watch her grow up."

Maxine could identify with that. The similarity to her own situation was amazing.

"I have a house not far from here, on Second Street in New West."

That shocked her. Her house was in Burnaby, one suburb over. She wasn't about to tell him that they were nearly neighbors. She wasn't about to tell him anything at all about herself besides what he already knew.

"So what do you write, Harold?"

"Ms. Bleckner? Maxine?" Rosalie, the buxom supervisor of the program, interrupted before he could answer. Rosalie held out a clipboard and a pen.

"Could I just get your signature on this, Maxine, please?" Rosalie's plump, pretty face was wreathed in smiles. "I need a health record for every child, and I forgot to get you to sign this when you registered Graham the other day. And

I do have the right address, 4709 Empress in Burnaby?"

Maxine could only nod. Harold wasn't even pretending not to listen, the louse.

"So how's Graham liking Motoring Munchkins, Maxine?" Rosalie asked. "This is only his second visit, isn't it?"

Maxine nodded. "He loves it," she said in a croak, wanting to strangle the effusive woman.

"You said Dr. Hawkins referred you. He's my son Aldo's pediatrician. He was so supportive when I told him about the program."

"It's a good idea." Maxine felt like sending good old Dr. Hawkins a letter bomb for suggesting she bring Graham here.

Rosalie turned her attention to Harold, and there was no mistaking the coy flirtatiousness in her voice. Her massive breasts actually heaved, Maxine noted with disgust.

"Hi, there, Harry. It's so great to have Sadie with us. She missed last session; Momma said you forgot. Can't have that, now, can we?" She didn't chuck him under the chin, but it was close. "I hope we'll see you this Sunday. Momma said she invited you and Sadie to Aldo's birthday party."

"Yeah, she did. But I'm just not sure if—"

"Oh, you've got to come," Rosalie cooed. "Momma will be so disappointed if you're not there, she just dotes on Sadie. And my little Aldo loves her, too. He was asking a minute ago

142

where she was. I'll tell Sadie about the party, and then you'll just *have* to come, won't you?"

"Yeah, well, I'll have to see." Obviously Harold was now as uncomfortable as Maxine had been a moment before, and it made her feel better to watch him squirm.

"Rosalie, Lisa forgot the juice boxes again. Should I go out and get some? It's almost snack time." One of the young volunteers plucked at Rosalie's sleeve, and with obvious reluctance she hurried away.

"Maxine, huh?" Harold sounded pleased with himself. "So that's your name. Maxine Bleckner. I like the name Maxine."

She'd always despised her name, but he rolled it around and gave it some sort of an exotic twist that made it sound almost bearable.

"Rosalie's mother, Mrs. Campanato, lives on my street." He sighed, rubbing a hand through hair that was already standing on end. "She baby-sits Sadie for me. I try to stay on her good side, but now I'm not so sure I'll be able to. Listen, Ind—Maxine," he corrected with the grin she remembered so well. "Please let me take you and Graham for lunch. This thing must be almost over. There's so much I want to get straight with you, and this isn't the place to do it." He gave her a beseeching look. "Don't make me beg. I'll feel like an idiot getting down on my knees in front of all these kids and their parents. And Rosalie will be so pissed"—he grimaced and corrected himself quickly—"so upset when she finds out we're friends, she'll likely ban both Sadie and Graham from Munchkins forevermore." He looked around and then leaned close and whispered, "Rosalie's got a terrible temper. Her father says that's why her marriage broke up."

"Daddy, can I go on the jungle gym with Elsa?" Sadie danced over, swishing her long white dress. She shinnied up Harold's leg. "Can I, Daddy, please? I gotta have your 'mission, Elsa's mommy said."

"Yeah, you can, sweetheart. Hurry up, because we're leaving in a few minutes." Harold unhooked her and then waved and nodded an elaborate consent to Elsa's mom, a militant-looking woman in a tweed skirt and a brown twinset. She was wearing pearls.

Sadie squealed with delight and ran over to the woman, who gave Harold a cold stare and ostentatiously used a pristine handkerchief to dab at the jam on Sadie's chin.

"That's one lady who definitely doesn't approve of me," he muttered under his breath. "But don't let her influence you, Maxine, okay? Let's have lunch. Please?"

Maxine was trying to figure out whether she should go. Her head told her to say no, but her heart was sending a different message. In spite of their disastrous dinner date, she liked him. She wanted to talk to him.

It was probably just curiosity, she told herself. She wanted to hear more of his phony excuses for pretending to be someone he wasn't. It was probably good research for her work, right? *Wrong*.

That was a bunch of baloney, she admitted. She just wanted to be with him, fool that she was.

She'd have to call home and see if Edna could work another hour or so. She opened her mouth to tell him she'd come, but her eyes were drawn over to the jungle gym.

Sadie was now hanging upside down, her long white dress flopped over her head, and it was very apparent that she had no panties on. Elsa's mother looked horrified. She snatched at the skirt of Sadie's dress and tried to talk her into coming down, but the child was singing a song, swinging back and forth.

Maxine started to giggle.

Harold turned to look, and he groaned and clapped a hand over his eyes.

"That does it," he exclaimed. "Elsa's mom is gonna phone the authorities; they'll have me charged with being an unfit parent. We've gotta get out of here. *Please* say you'll come with me, Maxine?"

Maxine glanced over at the penned area where Graham was. Her son's face was magenta, and his concentrated expression told her that he was doing a good job of filling his diaper.

"I have to change Graham first. I'll meet you in the parking lot." She hoped she had her cell phone in her purse.

"*Yesss.*" Harold's whiskery face broke into a grin. He put his palms together and rolled his eyes heavenward. "Thank you, Goddess," he intoned. And then he reluctantly made his way toward Elsa's mom to claim his daughter.

They went to McDonald's and turned Graham and Sadie loose in the play area. "Please don't do somersaults, okay, punkin?" Harold begged, and he was gratified to hear Maxine giggling. He liked her laugh.

They sat at a table where they could watch the kids, and he got them coffee and burgers and fries. While he was at the counter, he kept stealing glances at Maxine. She was so natural-looking, so fresh and pretty. He loved her freckles. He loved her with no makeup. He was going to tell her the whole truth about himself, he vowed as he paid for the food.

Yeah, and that'll be the end of this new beginning, Watson. As soon as she finds out you're doing an exposé on her, you think she's gonna want anything more to do with you? Forget it. She'll figure you set her up.

He carried the tray over to the table, and she looked up at him and smiled. She had the

146

greatest smile. She had the greatest teeth. She had the greatest breasts.

He wasn't going to tell her about the article.

"I got cheeseburgers—I hope you like cheese?"

"Sure." She picked up a fry, dunked it in ketchup, and munched it. "So what do you want to talk about, Harold? The fact that you fed me a line of hogwash?"

"Harry. My name's Harry Watson."

"I thought it was Walters." She narrowed her green eyes at him, and after a minute she nodded, as if she were adding this to the long, invisible list of his other lies. But then all of a sudden she shook her head and grinned. She held out her hand. Her eyes twinkled.

"Maxine Bleckner, how do you do, Harry Watson?"

He took her slender hand in his, and the connection was electric. He knew she felt it as well, because her eyes widened.

She pretended nothing was happening. She snatched her hand away and said in that incredible voice that gave him goose bumps, "I guess neither of us was very honest, were we, Harry? My excuse is my job. I can't afford to be honest. Who'd phone again if they knew what my life is really like? So what's your reason?"

The same. Oh, Maxine, my excuse is my job, same as yours. But he had enough sense not to say that. And he knew it was going to be all

147

right. She wasn't mad. She wasn't the kind of woman who held a grudge. There was a faint chance she might even let him take her out again, if he handled this carefully.

And, man, he wanted to do that. He wanted it badly.

"I wanted to impress you," he told her. "I didn't want you to know I was a hopeless slob who didn't shower or shave before taking his bare-assed daughter to Motoring Munchkins."

She laughed, as he'd hoped she might, and he could see her relaxing.

The relief he felt was enormous, and it made him hungry. "Maxine, I'm starving. Mind if I eat before we get into the rest of the gritty details of my life?"

"Okay. I'm hungry too. I missed breakfast."

"Me too. I worked late on an assignment last night and turned off the alarm this morning. Lucky thing Sadie woke me up." He took a huge bite of his burger and a gulp of coffee. Then he looked at her and pitched his voice low and intimate.

"I'm *very* glad Sadie woke me up."

Her throat grew pink, and the blush crept up to her ears. He liked that she blushed. He liked that she ate her food with honest relish. In the distant past he'd dated women who watched their weight with fanatical intensity, and he remembered it wasn't enjoyable to eat with them.

When the burger and fries were gone, he

thought about what he should say, how best to explain his duplicity—without spilling the beans about the article.

"I wanted to tell you the truth that night at the restaurant, but I'd dug myself in too deep with that businessman fantasy," he began. It was close to the truth. "I'd created this savvy, sophisticated monster, this guy I could never live up to, and when I saw you, I was too blown away to do the right thing and just confess."

"Why did you phone me in the first place, Harry?"

Here it was, the crossroads where he either told the truth or lied through his teeth.

He lied. "I was working and I had this feeling that everybody else was out having a hell of a good time somewhere. The paper was on my desk, and my eyes lit on your ad."

She nodded. She believed him. He despised himself for lying, but he needed to see her again.

He leaned toward her, and this time he told her the absolute truth: "I thought you were about the sexiest, most beautiful, woman I'd ever laid eyes on, Maxine. I was so proud to have you with me that night."

Her neck and cheeks got pink again, and she looked down at her tray, but she didn't say anything.

"Then that magpie of a Joost came over," Harry went on, "and I knew that in a minute

Bobby Hutchinson

he'd ruin everything by telling you all about me.
You'd find out I was just an ordinary Joe and
I'd lied to you about everything. And I knew that
he was gonna mention Sadie, because he came
to the house when I was doing an ad campaign
and he fell hard for her."

"I thought Sadie was your wife."

"Yeah. It was a logical mistake."

"I'm not surprised he liked Sadie," Maxine
said, glancing over at the play area. "She's a
great kid. Look how she's taking care of Graham."

Sadie was tossing balls in the air and making
the baby laugh.

"Do you enjoy being a parent, Harry?"

"When I was twenty, if anyone had suggested
I'd spend my thirties raising a kid, I'd have
laughed my head off," Harry said. "But I've
never enjoyed anything as much as I'm enjoying
raising her. She teaches me so much." He gave
Maxine a wry look. "Like checking before we
leave the house to make sure she's wearing underwear. That was my lesson for today, and I
screwed up big-time."

They both laughed, and he added, "There's
nothing like a kid to force you to really take a
look at the things that embarrass you, or that
push your buttons. It's a very humbling experience, being a parent, don't you think?"

Maxine nodded. "Before I had Graham, I'd
have slit my wrists rather than be seen in public

with baby puke on my shirt, wearing my oldest track pants."

"You look beautiful," he said, and meant it.

She rolled her eyes and shook her head. "If you're serious, you obviously need to get out more. Either that or have an eye exam."

He'd been trying to figure out how to ask her for a date she might be inclined to accept, and here was an opening. "How about coming out with me, then? Let's take the kids to the park tomorrow morning. I'll bring snacks."

She shook her head. "I have to work. I really can't afford to take time off like this."

He'd been afraid she'd say that. He thought it over and came up with an idea. "You have a cell phone." He'd seen her using it outside the community center. "Just forward your business calls, and if you have to work, I'll watch the kids and you can go somewhere and talk with a free mind."

He was a lot less than thrilled at the idea of her doing phone sex while they were out together, but he wasn't about to admit that.

What right did he have to feel jealous of the men she dealt with?

He could see she was thinking over his suggestions and he tensed, waiting for her answer.

She sipped her coffee and, to his relief, at last she shrugged and agreed. "All right, but only for an hour."

"Gotcha. One hour. Fantastic." It was. If he played it right, it was a new beginning.

Chapter Thirteen

"So you started up with him again? I can't believe this. Can you believe this, Edna?" Polly had been out of the hospital ten days, and out of the wheelchair two. She'd bitched nonstop since the accident. She hated feeling weak, she loathed the cast on her leg, she was frustrated by how sore her armpits were after just two lousy days on the lousy crutches, and she was mad at the cable company; the connection she'd had installed for her laptop wasn't working the way she thought it should.

"Staying here with you is the one thing about the whole fiasco that's okay," Polly had admitted grudgingly.

Polly had grown up with four brothers, and

being with Maxine and Edna was like having the sisters she'd always longed for, she confided. And having Graham around twenty-four hours a day was aces.

"Maybe now you can really get to know Harry," Edna told Maxine. They were sitting around the kitchen table, drinking tea and watching Maxine feed Graham.

Polly snorted. "Maybe now I should get one of the PIs from the office to run a security check on this dude. He's probably a polygamist looking for yet another wife."

Maxine spooned another mouthful of mashed peas into Graham's mouth. "I'm meeting him for an hour at the park tomorrow, not marrying him, Pol." She grinned at her prickly friend. "Did the good doctor call again today, by any chance?"

"Don't bring him up when we're eating; it makes me nauseous." Polly's face took on a mutinous expression.

Bruce Turner called Polly several times a day on her cell phone, which showed a great deal of perseverance on his part; Polly spent untold hours on the phone talking to her secretary, her colleagues, and her clients, so getting through to her took effort.

Maxine and Edna had quickly deduced that the calls weren't for medical reasons. They also noticed that although Polly was exceptionally rude to the doctor, she didn't hang up on him.

"Don't throw out the baby with the bathwater. He could be the one doctor you'll really like," Edna advised her, munching on one of the raisin-oatmeal cookies she'd brought over. "He seems nice, he's funny, he's got a good paying job, and he's a *hunk*." She'd met Bruce Turner while visiting Polly at the hospital. "I wish someone like that would take a shine to me," she said wistfully. "He spent a lot of time in your room, I thought."

"He's a *doctor*," Polly said, as if that explained everything. "My father was a doctor; I know what that's like. They're never home, their family doesn't get any of their attention because they give it all to patients, and when their wife gets past her prime, they trade her in for a bimbo nurse not much older than their oldest kid."

"You never told us that before," Maxine said. Graham shut his eyes and mouth and shook his head. Maxine took it as a signal that he was finished with the peas and picked up the small jar of applesauce.

"I don't think about it much." Polly tried for nonchalance, but Maxine heard the resentment in her tone.

Polly reached for another cookie. "Anyway, I barely knew the man. I was only five when he jumped ship."

"How old were your brothers?" Edna poured them all more tea.

"Darcy was seven, Rob nine, Matt twelve, and Kevin fourteen." She gave a bitter laugh. "Y'know, I used to think that he left us because I was a girl. I thought if I'd been born a boy he might have stayed."

"Do you ever see him?" Maxine thought of her own father and how long it had been since she'd even spoken to him.

"Nope." Polly dipped her cookie in her tea and quickly transferred it to her mouth. "He moved to Hawaii after he remarried, and he stopped paying support for us. Mom was a secretary for an insurance firm, but it was rough going financially for a while. We had the heat and lights turned off a couple of times. Kevin quit school when he turned sixteen and got a job in construction; that helped a lot." She realized that Maxine and Edna were listening with their mouths open. "No big deal. We survived. I have clients who've had it worse."

"Where's your mother now?" Graham had had enough of the applesauce. His eyes were closing; it was time for a nap.

"In a care home in Winnipeg," Polly said. "She has Alzheimer's, has had for five years now. She doesn't recognize any of us. I go back and visit her as often as I can. All of my brothers still live around Winnipeg, and they keep an eye on her. There's not really much any of us can do."

*   *   *

155

As Maxine changed her son's diapers and settled him in his crib, she thought over what Polly had revealed. It explained so much about her friend, Maxine thought as she smoothed the comforter over her son. What happened in childhood affected a person's entire life. Her own childhood, spent fruitlessly trying to gain her father's approval, had resulted in her falling in love with the first man who showed her some affection, and that was a stupid move if ever there was one.

But what she'd gained from the fiasco was worth every moment of heartache Ricky had caused. Graham was a gift, and she was thankful for him every single day.

She bent over and kissed his small, sweaty head. She wanted him to have the best, most normal childhood she could provide. It was sad that his natural father was not around, but she'd see to it that he had everything else a child needed.

She thought of Harold—Harry, she corrected. He seemed to be a man who took his responsibilities seriously, if the way he was with his daughter was any indication.

She liked his humor. She liked his shoulders. She liked his mouth. She liked the shivery way he made her feel when he looked at her as if he wanted to kiss her.

For God's sake, forget sex, Maxine. She needed to know a lot more about him before she could trust him. All the same, she was looking forward to seeing him in the morning.

It was going to be tough getting Maxine to trust him.

Harry watched her walk toward him across the grass.

She was wearing shorts this morning, and his memory of her legs was dead on; they were long, slender, deliciously curvy below the hem of her modest blue cutoffs. He had a sudden mental image of those bare legs locked around his waist, and he silently and urgently willed his body to behave. This was going to be enough of a challenge without a permanent hard-on to contend with; he didn't want her thinking he was like the men she dealt with on the phone.

He didn't want to think about her dealing with those men on the phone.

"She brunged her baby, Daddy." Sadie sounded ecstatic and relieved. She'd fallen head over heels in love with Graham. She'd talked of nothing else yesterday after they'd come home from McDonald's: *How come he can't talk? How come he wears diapers? How come he's a boy? When will he learn to walk? How come we don't have a baby for me to play with? Where could we buy one?*

By the time he'd gotten her to bed last night, Harry was worn out with explanations. But when he made it to bed himself, he hadn't been able to sleep for thinking of Maxine.

"Morning." She gave him a wide smile that gladdened his heart as she reached the picnic bench where Harry had unloaded the thermos of coffee, the fresh pastries, the juice boxes, and the overflowing cardboard carton of toys that Sadie had insisted they bring for the baby.

"Isn't it a fine day?" She squatted down and set Graham on the grass, and Harry stole a look at her ass.

It was every bit as intriguing as her legs.

Graham squealed with excitement and started to crawl away, and Sadie immediately chased after him.

"The weather's just like I ordered, for once," Harry said. "Want some coffee?" Pretending a nonchalance he was far from feeling, he poured two cups, added cream to hers, and handed it over.

"You remembered how I like my coffee." She shot him a shy, appreciative glance.

"Yup." He felt good about it and couldn't resist adding, "I remember everything about you."

"How do you know I wasn't just making up everything I said to you?" *Like you were*. The words were unspoken, but they were there.

"I'll tell you what I remember, and you can correct me if I'm wrong."

"Okay, go." There was more than a little challenge in her tone.

"You were a shy little girl."

"Did I tell you that? I don't think I told you that."

He shook his head. "Not in so many words, but you said that you were quiet in school, and you liked to read poetry, and play make-believe games by yourself in the woods."

She nodded. "I did. What else?"

"You like rainy days, and you love to dance, and your favorite meal is breakfast. You like pasta with seafood sauce, and the color purple, and if you had all the money in the world, you'd use it first on food for hungry children and then on education, so they'd have a way out of poverty. And then you'd go to California and live like a movie star until the money ran out."

There was surprise on her lovely face. "You have a good memory, Harold. Harry," she corrected.

He thought of the detailed notes he'd scribbled while she talked to him, and guilt gnawed at his gut. He shoved it away; it was too nice a day for guilt. He'd deal with guilt later, on his own time.

"Oh, yeah, one more thing," he added. "You wanted to get into broadcasting."

She was quiet for a moment, and then she seemed to decide it was all right to confide in him after all. "I've enrolled in a broadcasting course at night school," she admitted. "I start next week." Her eyes glowed with excitement.

"Maxine, that's fantastic." He held up his cup

in a toast. "Congratulations. With your voice, you'll be tremendous. You'll be a big star. I can see it all now: first local radio, then television news. . . ." He paused dramatically. "And *then* your own talk show."

"In your dreams." She wrinkled her nose and laughed. "But then I could interview you, couldn't I? You'll be a Pulitzer prize–winning novelist by then." She grew serious and looked straight into his eyes. "You were telling me the truth when you said you were writing a book, weren't you, Harry? You said it was a mystery."

"Yeah." It wasn't something he talked about easily; it was too close to his heart. "I hadn't worked on it much for a long time, but that night, after I told you about it, I got out my notes and started again. I've got six chapters done. I never would have started if we hadn't had that conversation."

She beamed at him. "Hey, I'm glad."

"Me too." He wondered if she had any idea how attractive she was when she got excited.

"What's it about, your book?" She cradled her hands around her cup and leaned toward him eagerly.

He didn't glance at her breasts, but it was a real test of his self-control.

"It's a cross between fiction and fact. Faction, I guess you'd call it. See, I interviewed Joe Murphy, the owner of Park Place, a week before he was murdered." Park Place was a well-known

Vancouver nightclub. "We had a long, boozy lunch, and he told me some stuff that I thought was just his imagination. But then he was gunned down a couple days later, and I realized maybe he'd been telling the truth. So I did a lot of research, and I've turned it into a mystery, part fiction, part fact."

"You're not afraid of whoever did it coming after you?" Her tip-tilted eyes were wide.

Harry shook his head. "I doubt it. The cops have already arrested the guys they think did it, but there's more to it than they know. Also, a lot of what I'm writing is the background stuff, how Joe went from a nice Italian kid to a rich mobster." He grimaced. "Sounds better when I write it than when I try to explain it."

"It sounds great. I'll look forward to reading—"

"Daddy, come quick; that baby's eating *grass*." Sadie was horrified. She watched closely as Maxine extracted the gummy green wad from Graham's mouth after following her to the boy.

"Thank you for watching him for me," Maxine told her, crouching down and smiling at the little girl. "You're a very good baby-sitter, Sadie."

Sadie nodded. "I really *likes* him, even if he does eat grass. I wish we had a baby, but my daddy says you gotta have a mommy to get babies." She handed Graham a red plastic ball.

"My mommy died, see, so we can't get a baby."
She punctuated her words with expressive gestures of her hands.

"I see. That's too bad."

"Daddy says that's life," Sadie said with a Gallic shrug that made Maxine smile.

"Well, that's a good way to look at it."

She was still smiling as she got to her feet and walked back to the table.

Harry had been listening. He told Maxine about the dozens of questions he'd answered the night before about babies in general and Graham in particular.

"I worry about her growing up with just me to pattern herself on," he admitted. "It doesn't seem the ideal way for a little girl to learn how to be a woman."

"She'll be okay," Maxine assured him. There was silence for a few moments as they watched the two children play with the ball.

"How old was she when your wife died?" The question was tentative.

"Six months." He dropped his voice so there was no possibility of Sadie overhearing. He wanted Maxine to know the facts about his marriage. "Cheryl was out with the guy she was living with. She hadn't seen Sadie since the day I took her home from the hospital. We were divorcing."

Maxine gave him a shocked look. "She didn't want her own baby?"

Harry shook his head. "Nope. She was totally honest with me, right from the beginning. She wanted an abortion. I bargained with her to have Sadie. She wanted to go to France and take training at some art school there, and I told her if she had the baby I'd give her the money she needed and pay for the divorce." He met Maxine's curious gaze and shrugged. "I'd never thought much about having a family, but when I found out she was pregnant, I realized I really wanted my kid."

Maxine nodded. Her eyes were still full of questions, and he tried his best to explain before she had to ask.

"I fell hard for Cheryl when I met her. She was a talented artist who was hired by the same ad firm I worked for." He did his best to recall exactly the way it had been. "She was unpredictable and smart and pretty, in an offbeat way. Sadie has her hair, the shape of her face. We eloped a few weeks after we met, before I had a chance to really get to know her, or her me, for that matter. She'd been a foster kid all her life. She never wanted kids, which I didn't think to ask about." He paused, and then added, "I wasn't exactly thinking with my head at that point. She was a sexy lady—I just wanted to take her to bed."

Not as much as I want to take you there, though. He didn't say it. It wasn't the time or place.

163

Maxine was watching Sadie and Graham.

Harry heaved a sigh and said, "Looking back on it, I think Cheryl was so scared, she couldn't be a good mother. She couldn't bring herself even to try with Sadie."

He watched Maxine digesting what he'd said.

"Did she decide not to go to France after all?"

"She got a commission for a piece of art, and she was finishing it when the accident happened. She'd have left the following week."

"Do . . ." Maxine cleared her throat and stared down at the picnic table, her cheeks pink. "Do you ever miss her, Harry?"

It was a question he'd asked himself many times over the years. He thought he had it figured out, and he did his best to put it into words. "I miss having someone to share Sadie with," he admitted. "I miss the parts of marriage that were good." The sex had been good— there was no doubt he missed that. "I found much to my surprise that I liked being married."

He reached out impulsively and took her hand in his, relieved when she didn't pull away. "But I don't miss Cheryl," he said in a positive tone. "We made a mistake, both of us. But out of that came my Sadie, so how could I regret it?" He spread her fingers and laced his own between them, and his treacherous mind wished it were her legs instead that he was spreading.

"Can I take Graym over to the swings?" Sadie

directed her question at Maxine, but Harry answered.

"Let's all go." He scooped Sadie up and plopped her on his shoulders. At least it would take his mind off sex.

Sadie giggled and looped her fingers in his hair. "Give me a horsey ride, Daddy. Graym too."

Maxine had already picked Graham up, but when Harry held out his arms, the baby went readily to him, and both children giggled and squealed as Harry did his best to impersonate a spirited racehorse.

Maxine walked along behind, watching them. Harry was strong. He easily trotted along carrying both children. He lunged and bounced and had no reservations about making horse noises through his nose, rearing and snorting.

Sadie clung to his hair and his ears, laughing uncontrollably, and Graham was chortling, his chubby hands gripping Harry's shirt.

It was the first time a man had ever really played with Graham, she reflected with a pang. In fact, the only men he came in contact with at all were his pediatrician, Dr. Hawkins, and Leonard, the lecherous produce manager at Safeway. Leonard always made a huge fuss over Graham while leering at Maxine's breasts.

She'd thought half the night about meeting Harry, and she'd told herself that it was only for an hour, that she'd be wise to end it once and for all, that there was no future in seeing him again.

But being with him, sharing thoughts about their kids, made her think she'd be a fool to tell him she wouldn't see him again. How many guys really liked kids?

And there was also the lust thing. Every minute she was with him, she had to really concentrate to keep from thinking about having sex with him.

The trouble was, this real Harry was dangerously close to the man she fantasized about when she couldn't sleep at night. He was smart and funny. *And hot, don't forget hot.* He was kind and generous and, from what she could see, a wonderful father to his little girl. And just looking at his hands made her want them on her.

He wasn't just pretending to like Graham, either. Harry was a man who truly enjoyed children; Maxine knew that from the way her son reacted to him. People might be able to fool adults, but no one could make kids like them.

And he had shoulders she wanted to uncover. She wanted to know how he kissed. Was he a little rough, the way she fantasized?

He'd reached the swings now, and he was carefully settling Graham in one of the buckets, then lifting Sadie into another.

Maxine heard the cell phone in her shoulder

bag ringing. Her heart sank; the very last thing she wanted to do right now was her job.

She sighed and stopped and pulled it out, using her professional voice and name as she replied to the male voice on the other end.

She waved at Harry and gestured at the phone, walking away from the swings to a deserted bench under a pine tree, out of earshot of anyone, and for the next while she did what she was an expert at, leading the faceless man on the other end into a fantasy and on to gratification.

But the entire time, she watched Harry.

He swung the two swings back and forth gently, alternating between the children. He turned once and gave her a thumbs-up sign, indicating that everything was under control.

Instead of prolonging the conversation and mentally calculating the effect on her income, Maxine hurried it along. She very much wanted to get back to Harry.

He talked to the kids, the senseless patter that came automatically with little people. He tried hard not to think about what Maxine was doing, but he couldn't manage it. He could see her long, lovely legs crossed, one foot swinging, an arm draped casually across the back of the bench, and in his imagination he could hear her spinning some downright dirty sexual illusion in that thick, rich voice.

167

It drove him crazy. It made him jealous. She made him horny. He didn't want her saying those things to anyone but him. He had to stop himself from racing over, snatching the phone, tossing it as far as he could into the underbrush, and then dragging Maxine into the trees. He'd yank those bloody shorts down around her ankles—

"Daddy, push me higher."

Harry tried his best to concentrate on the kids, but it was a tough task. He tried to take his mind off of what Maxine was doing—verbal sex, with another man—by gulping in deep breaths, and tried to figure out a long-range plan.

He had to do this carefully, gradually, so as not to spook her. He'd arrange dates that included the kids for as long as it was humanly possible, which might be a day or two, considering how aroused he got within ten feet of her. Then he'd see if she'd agree to an evening out, just the two of them.

And if she did, he'd do a total replay.

He'd redo the scenario from that fateful first meeting, including the room key, but this time he'd rewrite the ending.

If, of course, she agreed. Would she agree? Could he feel so attracted to her without any response on her part?

It was possible, but he didn't think it was

probable. If, of course, there was a merciful God.

He gave Sadie's swing a healthy shove and Graham's a much gentler one, swinging the two of them in tandem, listening to their laughter and hoping like hell the electricity between him and Maxine flowed both ways.

Chapter Fourteen

Despite her good intentions of spending only an hour with Harry, it was nearly noon by the time Maxine got home.

Polly took one look at her and shrieked, "You let him kiss you. I can tell by the slutty look in your eyes."

Maxine opened her mouth to deny it and thought, *What the hell?* Good lawyer that she was, Polly had an instinct for the truth.

Besides, she hadn't been able to stop smiling all the way home. And her lips *were* sort of swollen. She'd noticed them in the rearview when she was checking on Graham.

"I didn't let him; it just happened. We were in the parking lot and I was putting Graham in his car seat, and when I straightened up, Harry was right behind me."

He'd taken her by the elbows and drawn her toward him, and the intense look in his eyes was mesmerizing. Still, it had started out as nothing more than a friendly brushing of lips. But somehow that brushing started a burning inside her, and her arms had somehow wound around him, and then he'd groaned and his head had angled differently, and his hand was stroking all down her back, and then his tongue—Oh, God, his tongue. He was definitely inventive with his tongue.

"Polly, he kisses as if it's the last thing in this world he's gonna do before he dies."

"Well, it's no indication that he'd be good in bed, so don't get your hopes up," Polly said, reaching up and taking Graham out of Maxine's arms and onto her lap. "I've kissed some guys and wanted to rape them on the spot, and then when we got down to it, they were hopeless. They'd never gotten past page one in the instruction book. You can't go by just kisses."

Maxine didn't want to argue, but she'd be willing to put this month's mortgage up against the fact that Harry wasn't one of those inept creatures. Just thinking about his kiss made the blood pool hot and heavy in her abdomen.

"So are you going to?" Polly was playing patty-cake with Graham.

"Going to what?"

"Go out with him again. Go to bed with him."

Maxine was glad Polly's attention was on the baby, because she could feel how fiery hot her face was. "We're taking the kids to the petting zoo at Stanley Park."

"Petting, huh? When?"

"Tomorrow."

"The petting zoo. This guy has some warped notion of where to take a date; I'll say that for him. Maybe you'd better bring old Harry by the house so I can meet him, this is getting serious. I want to know who Graham's spending his time with, and I've got a few questions for this dude—like could I have a written outline of what his intentions are toward you and my sweetie here."

Maxine pretended nonchalance. "He's coming to pick us up in the morning; you can grill him then."

"I fully intend to."

The next morning Maxine was sorry she'd ever joked about it. She should have told Harry she'd be out on the curb, and he could just scoop her and Graham up without stopping the car.

When the doorbell rang promptly at nine-fifteen, Edna and Polly were both hovering nearby like Victorian duennas.

Edna, who'd insisted she'd stay on for the morning and take calls for Maxine, must have unplugged the business phone, because it certainly wasn't ringing the way it usually did in the morning. Polly, who was always barking orders or advice into her cell by at least eight-thirty, must have told her secretary to hold her calls. And her laptop was nowhere in sight.

Just before she opened the door, Maxine whispered to them, "Don't you two have something to *do*?"

They both gave her innocent looks and wicked grins, and shook their heads in unison. "We're on a mission," Polly stated, adding, "Harry's toast."

Maxine tried to plaster on a pleasant expression as she swung the door wide, but Polly's threat made her nervous. "Harry, hi come on in. Hello, Sadie, what a pretty sundress; I love hot pink." God, she sounded like a simpering fool.

She made the introductions, wondering if Harry really looked as handsome as she thought, or if it was only her imagination. He was wearing khaki shorts and a white golf shirt; his jaw was clean-shaven, his thick hair neatly brushed. And when he looked at her, she saw the admiration she felt reflected back in his dark blue eyes.

"Hey, Sadie, you want to come in the kitchen and get some snacks for your picnic?" Edna made off with Sadie, and Maxine gave Polly a suspicious look.

The lawyer had schemed to get Harry alone;

Maxine was sure of it. Polly knew Graham had filled his diaper two seconds before Harry arrived. She'd probably put the baby up to it, Maxine thought grimly, taking Graham and racing down the hall, leaving Harry totally at Polly's mercy.

Maxine whipped off the soiled diaper and had a new one in place in record time. She shoved spare clothing and diapers in the bag willy-nilly, then scurried back into the living room, expecting to find Harry being flayed alive by Polly's tongue, or worse yet, having to sign a legal declaration of his intentions.

To her amazement, he was smiling, looking relaxed and comfortable, lounging on the sofa.

"Can you believe this guy knows my brother Rob? They played rugby together," Polly announced.

"On opposing teams," Harry corrected. "I haven't played since Sadie was born, so I haven't seen Rob for a few years. How's he doing?"

"He married a ball breaker of a teacher from Edmonton. You can bet she keeps him in line."

"Rob was one hell of a rugby player. He broke my arm once during a game."

Polly beamed as if it were a compliment. "Rob was never much of a fighter at home; he burned it all off with the rugby team. I could bully him around with no trouble at all."

"I met Darcy a couple times, too. Where is he now?"

"He's a firefighter in Winnipeg; he married right out of high school. He and Lucy have two kids, boys. They're practically grown-up."

Polly actually looked mellow, and Maxine figured it was time she and Harry made their escape, before Polly's protective instincts kicked in and she remembered to give Harry the third degree.

"I'm ready, Harry."

He got to his feet. "Give Rob my best when you talk to him. Tell him if he's ever in town to give me a call."

Edna came out of the kitchen and winked at Maxine. Harry took Graham from Polly, and Maxine grabbed Sadie and the bag of snacks. In a moment they were safely out the door and in the car, heading for the park.

"I like your friends," Harry remarked, reaching across the seat and taking Maxine's hand. He squeezed it and then placed it deliberately on his thigh, sending shivers up her spine.

"Edna's the lawyer, right? And Polly's your employee. God, it's such a coincidence, Rob's sister working for you."

Maxine shot him an incredulous look. "Think again. Polly works for me, but she's my lawyer, and she's a barracuda—a good barracuda, but not someone you ever want on your case. And Edna's a wicked sexy genius at thinking up

175

X-rated scenarios to keep the phone customers happy. You oughta hear her; she's fabulous."

Harry's jaw dropped. "How wrong can a guy get? Edna? Edna does . . . But then, the way she is on the phone isn't really her personality anyhow, any more than India McBride is yours."

A short time ago, Maxine would have agreed with him that India was just a figment of her imagination.

She stole a glance over at her hand, resting on his bare, muscular leg. The thick mat of soft hair tickled her palm, and the heat of his skin seemed to radiate all the way up her arm. She could feel his muscles contract and release as he stopped at lights and accelerated again. She imagined those muscles contracting for a different reason. She envisioned what he'd look like without the shorts, and a shudder ran down her spine.

The daydream made her squirm in her seat. Her breasts ached the way they had when she was feeding Graham, but this feeling was anything but maternal. She felt swollen and hot and damp with desire. She wanted sex. She wanted sex with Harry, the sooner the better. The urge was so powerful that if it hadn't been for the children in the backseat, she'd have made a grab at him right here on Burrard Street.

Harry was dead wrong, she thought with a

secret smile, and when the time came, she'd prove it to him. There was a good deal of succulent, wild India mixed in with good old Maxine, and she couldn't wait to show him.

Chapter Fifteen

"It was great for me, too, lover. It was so powerful I'm still shaking. You're the best, Clarence. Call me again soon, won't you?" Edna was placidly finishing the sleeve of a blue sweater, and the soft click of her needles contrasted with her breathless voice and the sexually graphic scenes she'd just enacted.

The performance had Polly mesmerized, which was a good thing, because her injured leg was itching like fury and any diversion was welcome.

"Edna, you ever get turned on when you're doing that?" she asked after Edna hung up.

"Knitting? Nope." Edna's grin was mischievous.

"Of course not knitting, idiot." Polly stuck her tongue out and rolled her eyes, and Edna laughed.

"Not usually," she said. She thought for a minute and then shot Polly a shy glance over the top of her half-moon glasses. "There is this one guy, though. It must be pure chemistry, because when I'm talking to him, yeah, I do get turned on sometimes."

"So what does it? What he says, the way he says it, the tone of his voice, what?"

"It's partly his voice—it's low and rich and slow—and he has this laugh that seems to come rippling up from deep inside him. And he treats the whole thing like a game; he sees the humor. But it's also just him. He's honest about being lonely; his wife died four years ago and he misses sex."

"You ever thought of actually meeting him?"

"Lordie, no." Edna studied her knitting, but Polly noticed that color stole up her neck. "I'm just his fantasy. He calls every week or so." She laid down her needles and patted her ample hips. "He'd be shocked out of his mind if he realized what Lilith actually looks like."

"Don't put yourself down." Polly privately thought a beauty makeover would do Edna a world of good. "Maybe he's exactly your type. Look at Maxine and Harry."

Edna shook her head. "I'd be too embarrassed to meet him. He thinks I'm twenty-four

179

and I measure thirty-six, twenty-six, thirty-eight." Her smile was wry. "He's a senior—his heart might not stand the shock of the real me."

"You think you'll ever get into another relationship, Edna?" Having a broken leg left way too much time for thinking.

"After John left, I swore I wouldn't. But now I get lonely. I liked being married. I was good at it, and I don't think all men are like John." She looked pensive. "But I have no idea where I'd ever meet someone. I go to the library, the cinema, and here." She shrugged. "Not exactly a singles beat, huh?"

"What about a personal ad?" Polly, bored out of her skull the last few weeks, had perused the personals on the Internet, amazed at the variety.

Edna looked doubtful. "I'd have to lose weight before I could meet anyone."

"No, you wouldn't; you're sexy the way you are. All you really need to do is maybe get Terry to style your hair, buy some new clothes. We could do that on the Internet, too. There's all sorts of shopping sites."

"Really? You'd help me get a new look? I wanted to ask you that time you did Maxine for her first date with Harry, but I figured it was maybe kinda hopeless. And I don't have a lot of money to splurge with, either."

"That's gonna change now that I have that court order for copies of Gimbel's telephone and credit card records. We'll confirm what he spends and see if there are calls to banks in foreign jurisdictions at the start or end of each month. He's hidden money away somewhere, and by God I'll find it. We're makin' headway, my friend."

"I hate going through this," Edna confessed. "It's demeaning to fight for money from the man who fathered your kids and promised to love you forever."

"Yeah, well, we expect too much of men. Most of them are permanently damaged by testosterone."

Edna giggled. "But Harry seems like a nice man, doesn't he?"

"Yeah, he's one of the rare few who doesn't make me want to hit him with something heavy."

Edna nodded slowly. "How about Dr. Turner? Does he turn *you* on, Polly?"

Polly shook her head vigorously. "He pisses me off. He makes me crazy. He frustrates me to death." Polly thought about Bruce and scowled. "Besides all that, he's obviously not very bright. I insult him and refuse to go out with him and he just keeps right on phoning. Wouldn't you think he'd get the picture?"

"But does he turn you on?"

Edna could be single-minded and downright maddening at times. Polly opened her mouth to deny it, and then heard herself say what she'd been afraid to admit.

"Well, yeah. Maybe a teensy, tiny bit." Her voice was plaintive, and that surprised her too. "That's what makes me so damned mad." She slammed her hands down on her crutches. "I don't *want* to be turned on by a bloody doctor, not even a little bit."

Edna's knitting needles were flying, but she didn't have to look at what she was doing, which always amazed Polly. She was watching Polly's face instead.

"He's a baby doctor, and you know how much you like babies. And all doctors aren't alike. Don't judge Bruce by your father, Polly. Don't judge the future by the past. I did that for years when I was married to John. I thought just because we'd been together so long, we always would be." Edna switched needles without looking.

How did she *do* that?

"It took me a long, hard time to realize that life is change, that nothing stays the same forever, that nothing even needs to be the way it was in the past in order to survive."

Polly wanted more than survival, but she didn't say so. "There you go," she teased instead. "That's what I've been telling you. You need a new hairdo and some new clothes. Change."

Edna thought it over and then gave a decisive

nod. "Let's do it. I'll put it all on my charge card."

The business phone rang. Edna propped it against her shoulder and without batting an eye reverted to Lilith.

Polly listened for a minute. God, she got turned on herself by what Edna was saying. It had been way too long since she'd taken anybody to bed. And maybe that was the way to get Turner out of her system once and for all.

She moved into the kitchen and called Terry on her cell, got Edna in for a styling that afternoon, and then began her own day's work. When Bruce called that afternoon and asked if she'd like to go out for dinner on Friday, she shocked him almost speechless by accepting.

"Maxine, would you have dinner with me on Friday?"

Harry wasn't looking at her, and his tone revealed that he wasn't at all sure how she'd respond.

"Please? I thought we'd go back to the restaurant where we first met and maybe start over."

Harry was smearing peanut butter on bread as Maxine spooned vegetable soup into Graham. On the way home from the park, Harry had asked if she'd like to see where he lived, which was how they'd ended up in his kitchen.

Graham was slumped in the high chair that Harry had brought up from the basement. The baby was rubbing his ears and yawning so often it was almost impossible to feed him. Maxine knew she shouldn't have let Harry talk her into giving the kids lunch here, but she hadn't been able to resist spending just a little more time with him. And she'd been curious about what his house was like.

It was a lot like hers: older, full of toys, Salvation Army modern decor. She loved it.

"What do ya think, Maxine? Should we start over?"

"Yeah. I'd like that. Starting over, I mean."

She glanced over at him and caught the gratified look he shot her. She grinned. "Darn, I blew that, didn't I? I should have pretended to think it over longer, played hard to get. I'll have to practice being mysterious." She gave him a suggestive glance. "I'll start Friday."

"Could we put off the hard to get?" He handed Sadie a carefully quartered sandwich and gave Graham a portion. The baby squished it in his hand, dropped it to the floor, and yawned again.

Harry got up. "Sadie, keep an eye on the baby for a minute, okay? I want to show Maxine something."

Sadie nodded, fixing her eyes on Graham and trying not to blink.

Maxine gave Harry a quizzical look as he gripped her hand in his and pulled her to her feet, leading her down the hall and into the living room.

"What . . ." She gasped as his arms came around her and drew her into a fierce embrace.

"Shhhh," he murmured. "I need to kiss you."

His lips were on hers, warm and firm and certain.

Something melted inside her, and she put her arms around his neck, touching the thick, springy hair on the back of his head, letting her fingers outline his ears and the strong line of his jaw.

He made a sound in his throat and dragged her closer to him, one large palm between her shoulder blades, the other in the small of her back, sliding slowly, enticingly down until he was cupping her bottom. He slid his hand inside her shorts, inside her underwear, and her skin burned.

Her breath caught as she felt the hard ridge of his erection. He was pressing it urgently against her, and she pressed back because it all felt so good, his hand on her bare skin, urging her forward.

"I want you, beautiful woman," he whispered against her mouth, his voice low and thick and dangerous. "I've wanted you since the first time I ever heard your voice." He kissed her chin, her nose, her eyes. "It's nearly killing me. I watched you today in the park, bending over to pick up Graham, that round ass of yours just teasing me. When you ran after the Frisbee, your breasts bounced, and I could hardly walk, I wanted you so much. It's a wonder I didn't get arrested for having a hard-on."

She had to giggle, even though her heart was hammering and her body throbbed. She rocked against him, teasing, unable to subdue her own cravings.

"I'm renting a room at the hotel on Friday," he murmured against her lips. "Say that you'll spend the night with me."

"Daddy? Daddy, come here; this baby's sleeping *sitting up*." Sadie's tone was scandalized. "Daddy?"

They could hear her pushing back her chair and, a moment later, trotting down the hallway.

Harry groaned and withdrew his hand from Maxine's bottom, but his arm stayed around her.

She shook her head at him and gently pulled away just before Sadie burst into the room.

"Daddy?" The little girl sounded anxious. "That baby needs to go for a nap," she insisted. "He can sleep in my bed, okay, Daddy? I don't need a nap today, right, Daddy?"

Harry sighed and turned his attention to his daughter. "Sorry, sport, but you do need a nap."

Sadie's bottom lip shot out and her face began to crumple. "I do not. I'm a big girl; I'm not a baby."

Maxine hastily intervened. "Sadie, you are a big girl, but Graham needs to sleep in his own crib," she explained, aware of the Technicolor

Join the Love Spell Romance Book Club
and **GET 2 FREE* BOOKS NOW—
An $11.98 value!**
Mail the Free* Book Certificate
Today!

Yes! I want to subscribe to the Love Spell Romance Book Club.

Please send me my **2 FREE* BOOKS**. I have enclosed $2.00 for shipping/handling. Every other month I'll receive the four newest Love Spell Romance selections to preview for 10 days. If I decide to keep them, I will pay the Special Members Only discounted price of just $4.49 each, a total of $17.96, plus $2.00 shipping/handling ($23.55 US in Canada). This is a **SAVINGS OF $6.00** off the bookstore price. There is no minimum number of books I must buy and I may cancel the program at any time. In any case, the **2 FREE* BOOKS** are mine to keep.

*In Canada, add $5.00 shipping and handling per order
for the first shipment. For all future shipments to Canada,
the cost of membership is $23.55 US, which
includes shipping and handling.
(All payments must be made in US dollars.)

NAME: _____

ADDRESS: _____

CITY: _____ STATE: _____

COUNTRY: _____ ZIP: _____

TELEPHONE: _____

E-MAIL: _____

SIGNATURE: _____

If under 18, Parent or Guardian must sign. Terms, prices, and conditions subject to change. Subscription subject
to acceptance. Dorchester Publishing reserves the right to reject any order or cancel any subscription.

The Best in Love Spell Romance!
Get Two Books Totally FREE*!

An
$11.98
Value!
FREE!

PLEASE RUSH MY TWO FREE BOOKS TO ME RIGHT AWAY!

Enclose this card with $2.00 in an envelope and send to:

Love Spell Romance Book Club
20 Academy Street
Norwalk, CT 06850-4032

vibes that went right on zipping back and forth between her and Harry. "Maybe you and your daddy would give us a ride home now?"

Instead of agreeing, Harry leered at her and twirled an invisible mustache. "Only if you answer yes to the question I asked, my pretty one. Otherwise we'll have to hold you and Graham for ransom, right, Sadie?"

"Right, Daddy." Sadie giggled and clapped her hands.

"I'll think it over," Maxine purred. "Threats never work on us girls, right, Sadie? Maybe I should call a cab."

"Rats, foiled again." Harry swung Sadie into his arms, and then leaned forward to plant an unexpected kiss on Maxine's lips, which made Sadie giggle and demand a kiss too. He gave her a huge smack, and then said to Maxine with a groan, "The suspense is gonna kill me, to say nothing of the cold showers."

"I suspect you'll survive until Friday," she said in a heartless tone. But as they collected children and keys and diaper bag, Maxine wondered if *she* would.

Polly was in a foul mood by the time Bruce Turner rang the doorbell Friday evening. Deciding what to wear, normally an exciting process, had become a major pain in the ass with her leg in a cast.

"I'm not gonna sacrifice expensive silk trousers by slitting one leg open to accommodate this flaming thing," she fumed. "And I'm not gonna wear one of those stupid jogging suits, either. I'm sick to death of jogging suits."

"So wear a dress." Maxine was getting ready for her own date.

"They're all short, and I'd need to wear panty hose because my legs are white as a fish belly," Polly whined. "But panty hose'll look ridiculous stretched over this cast, and with stockings the garters dangle on the left side."

"So start a new trend and wear just one stocking." Maxine was losing patience; it showed in her voice. Before Polly could protest, she took scissors and neatly snipped off the garters that dangled uselessly down Polly's thigh.

"This is economical—the stockings will last twice as long wearing only one," she said brightly, handing over a lace-topped cream stocking.

Underneath her narrow little blue sundress, Polly's garter belt kept hitching up. Between that and the sight of her one ridiculously pale bare thigh peeking out from under the short skirt, she felt thoroughly pissed off instead of sexy by the time she was ready.

She was also nervous, and that made her even crankier. She hadn't been nervous about a date since she was fourteen and on her way to the junior prom with the captain of the debate team. Since then she'd dated captains of industry, brilliant lawyers, and minor sports heroes without the slightest tremor in her gut, so why should a lowly baby doctor make it necessary to apply extra deodorant?

Edna was taking a call in the kitchen and Maxine was putting Graham to bed when the doorbell rang shortly after seven. Harry wouldn't arrive for another half hour, Polly knew, so it had to be Turner.

She was ready, but she wasn't eager. She wiped her damp palms on a tissue and cursed Edna, the crutches, and the stupid custom of dating as she made her way to the door and yanked it open.

Chapter Sixteen

"Hello, there, Hopalong." Bruce was smiling, and he handed her a bouquet of violets tied with a yellow satin ribbon. She had a weakness for violets. She didn't let him see how much she liked them.

Or how much she liked the way he looked.

He had a mouth that could only be described as indecent, and the golden beard accentuated his lips. He was always smiling. That, combined with the undeniable fact that his shoulders were massive, his waist narrow, and his hips lean, meant that he qualified as a boy toy, she assured herself. And after tonight, she'd have him out of her system.

"Come on in," she said. "Thanks for the flowers." She left him standing in the living room and stumped into the kitchen, violets clutched in one hand. She found a water glass and carefully arranged them. They smelled sweet and innocent, and for a moment she wished she were.

"Where's Maxine and Edna?" He was peering around, obviously curious.

"Turning tricks in the back bedroom," Polly snapped. "That's where they keep the S-and-M stuff."

"Oh, of course, how stupid of me." One eyebrow lifted sardonically and he nodded. "Well, I hope they're practicing safe sex." He reached politely for her purse and her jacket, but Polly snatched them away, forgetting momentarily about her precarious balancing act on the crutches.

"Whoops, careful there, Counselor." He grabbed her by both forearms to keep her from falling, and his hands on her bare flesh sent tingles shooting through her. She felt her nipples stand at attention against the flimsy cotton of her dress, and she knew by the way his eyes flickered down and then quickly up again that he'd noticed. He didn't release her immediately, and the intensely interested look on his face made her decide not to smack him with one of the crutches.

Damn, she fumed silently, allowing the moment to go on and on. *Damn, damn, damn.* She wanted him.

What she'd admitted to Edna was an understatement. Bruce Turner didn't turn her on a little bit. This was big-time, ten on the Richter scale. For the first time she understood what romance novels meant when they described a touch as electrifying. And on her *arms*, for heaven's sake. What the hell would happen when he touched a *real* erogenous zone?

The man was a walking sex bomb, and at the moment she felt like a match on the verge of spontaneous combustion. But she really ought to get through dinner before she seduced him. It was not classy to jump his bones in the first hour.

It was comforting to see that he wasn't unaffected. The perpetual twinkle had faded from his dark brown eyes, replaced by what could only be outright lust. His breath sighed out and his big hands drew her closer instead of releasing her, sliding around to her back to draw her to his chest, bringing her weight fully against him. Feeling safe, feeling supported, feeling horny as hell, she let the crutches drop to the carpet and enjoyed the moment.

He lowered his head slowly, giving her ample time to pull away, but she didn't want to.

She wanted him to kiss her, and when his lips finally came down on hers, she wanted more. Much, much more. And quickly. She tightened her hold on his neck and deliberately pressed her hips into his, rocking gently, teasing herself every bit as much as him.

Damn, the man knew how to kiss. His mouth was firm and confident on hers, applying just the right amount of pressure, using his tongue a little. She didn't even mind the beard; it was surprisingly soft and exceedingly sensual against her skin. He tasted musky, erotic.

She opened her lips a little more and used her own tongue, touching the arch of his upper lip, pushing inside just the slightest bit, exploring his teeth and delving deeper, totally engrossed in the process. He tasted rich and smoky and sexy, and yes, she was definitely going to take this man to bed tonight.

They'd go to her apartment—she'd say she had to pick something up there. She probably did, at that; she didn't think she had any condoms in her purse.

She was really starting to get carried away when he drew back. After a moment spent getting her libido tamed enough to think, she decided he was deliberately insulting her by stopping first.

"Shouldn't it be the *woman* who stops?" Her voice was annoyed, but it was also huskier than she'd expected it to be, and she cleared her throat and scowled up at him, still having to rely on his arms to support her.

"I thought we settled all that with equal-opportunity legislation," he said with an easy grin, somehow managing to hold her steady but not too close while reaching down and retrieving her crutches. "Besides, I didn't want to get my face slapped for making a serious move on you before we've been out together three times."

Three times? "What rule book did you read? Because it must have been ancient history," she snapped as she got balanced on her crutches again. She knew her face was flushed. Her whole damned *body* was flushed.

Never mind. If she knew anything about men, it was the fact that their crotches and their brains never worked at the same time. It would be simplicity itself to seduce him later this evening. "Okay, Turner, go ahead and play hard to get," she muttered, adding in a more audible tone, "So if we're going, Doc, let's get gone."

He gave her a mock bow and swung the door wide. She stomped out, head high, crutches swinging, but she had to proceed with caution on the steps. Much as she hated to admit it, his presence at her side was comforting.

"You rented a *van*?" She'd sweated over how she'd manage gracefully getting in and out of the sports car he'd surely have insisted upon from the insurance company.

"I have two vehicles," he explained. "My grandma is in a wheelchair. I like to be able to take her out for dinner on my days off. She's in a care home and she enjoys getting out once in a while. With the van, I can just wheel her in, wheel her out. Makes life less complicated for both of us."

Kind, she ticked off reluctantly on his report card.

So he had a heart beneath that hairy, manly chest. So what? She'd soon find out where his weaknesses lay. She always had before. By the time she was through with him at the end of the night, he'd qualify for one of the general unflattering headings in her own history book:

Self-absorbed. Cheap. Angry. Boring. Predictable. Unimaginative. Premature ejaculator. One-shot Charlie.

But what he'd just said lingered in her mind, and with the usual stab of guilt and sorrow and pity, Polly thought of her own mother. It would be so wonderful to take her mother out to dinner when she visited in Winnipeg. Her mom was in a care facility, too, but Janet Kelville's mind was far too confused to chance taking her anywhere. She was as likely as not to think she was being kidnapped and scream the place down.

He opened the door of the cherry-red van, and before she could object, he'd removed her crutches, picked her up, and smoothly settled her on the soft leather seat.

So he was strong; so the playboy physique wasn't just to show off at the beach. So what? He was probably insufferably vain about it.

"I'm taking you to my favorite restaurant," he said as he started the van.

Confident, damn his eyes.

"I didn't think they served food in the delivery room."

He laughed and shook his head. "That place tops my list of favorites, all right, but not for dinner. I'm hoping we can avoid the delivery room tonight." He frowned. "None of my moms are actually due today, but in this business that's no guarantee."

"So where are we going?" She'd never admit it, but just being dressed in something besides a track suit and getting out of the house for a couple of hours was a turn-on, regardless of the fact that her one bare leg looked ridiculous above the cast. She felt that the other one went a long way toward making up for it, with the delicate stocking and that tantalizing bit of garter she was making sure showed under the hem of her dress.

But he was concentrating on driving.

Oblivious, she noted, feeling piqued.

God, she badly needed to get her life back if it mattered so much to her that a *doctor* noticed how sexy she was. Maybe it was simply her own abstinence that made Turner seem so attractive.

"Where are we going?" she asked again.

"It's a surprise," was all he'd say. He turned

on music, softly classical, gave her a smile, and drove in silence.

Tasteful. Doesn't need to fill the air with empty words, she added reluctantly.

The surprise was obviously located downtown, but he seemed to know every side street and alleyway that would avoid the heavy traffic, which made the drive interesting.

As they turned onto Robson, Polly began to get anxious. In this location, he was probably taking her to one of the city's nicer restaurants. She worked not far from here, she'd eaten in almost every one, and she was certain to know somebody. She didn't want to see anyone she knew tonight; being on crutches was a humbling experience. She didn't feel like answering questions and putting on a sassy front. She didn't want everyone staring at her one bare thigh.

But he pulled off Robson onto a side street, then nosed the van into an alleyway and somehow slid it into a parking spot that seemed far too small.

"It says, 'Private parking'—you'll get towed," she pointed out, but he just came around and helped her out, making sure she had a firm hold on the crutches before he released his grip on her arm.

Stubborn. Probably hopelessly bullheaded.

"Right in here." He led the way down the dark alley to an unmarked door in a brick wall, opened it, and stood aside as she hesitantly stepped inside.

At first glance it was bedlam. She was in the kitchen of an Oriental restaurant. Steam billowed up from cauldrons, and the tangy smell of fresh seafood filled Polly's nostrils. Her ears rang with what seemed a loud and violent argument being waged at full voice among the dozen or more cooks. They were deftly stir-frying greens in gigantic woks, tipping baskets of live lobster into cauldrons of boiling water, scooping steaming rice into bowls, slipping carefully bundled wontons into fragrant pots of broth, all the while hollering aggressively.

Bruce called out a friendly hello, and the hubbub quieted a little. His appearance was greeted with broad smiles, head bobbings, and a new barrage of noise. A small busboy went scurrying out, and a moment later a tall, distinguished Asian man in a nicely tailored gray silk suit came through the swinging doors, smiling broadly at Bruce. He hurried over and took Bruce's hand in both of his, shaking it heartily, his sculpted face creased in smiles.

"Dr. Bruce, Dr. Bruce, I have been waiting for you. Welcome, welcome, I am so glad you've come."

"Good to see you, Tommy. This is my friend, Polly Kelville. Polly, Tommy Wong."

Tommy bowed formally over her hand, and then indicated that they should follow him.

"This way, this way," he urged, clearing a path through the cooks so that Polly could maneuver her crutches through the swinging doors and along a short corridor into a dimly lit restaurant filled to overflowing with customers.

Tommy seated them at a table that had obviously been prepared and reserved just for them; it was very private, in a curtained alcove at the back, and a special padded armchair and footstool had been prepared for Polly and her cast. She sank down, gratefully propping her leg up.

The moment they were seated wineglasses appeared, along with a bottle of fine champagne. A pretty young woman in a snug fitting red silk dress came through the curtains carrying a fat and beautiful baby whom Polly judged to be about six months old. She handed the baby to Bruce, and he hefted him and let Polly hold him.

She nuzzled his sweet neck and made admiring comments about his weight and beauty and obvious good nature and good health.

"My wife, Way Lin. My son, Rupert," Tommy said to Polly, his gaze on the baby, his voice and eyes brimming with pride. Way Lin bowed and took the baby away.

"You like seafood?" Tommy demanded of Polly, filling her glass with more of the delicious wine.

"Very much." She felt dazed. It was obvious

that Bruce was an honored guest here, part of the family.

Tommy left, and Polly turned to Bruce.

"What's the deal? Why are we being treated like royalty?"

"Way Lin had some problems carrying a baby to term; she'd lost several before I met her. I was her doctor with Rupert, and fortunately everything went well. Tommy and I became friends."

Modest.

Polly knew there had to be more to the story than that, but before she could delve any further, a basket of deep-fried prawns arrived with a tangy dipping sauce.

"I'm starving," Polly admitted, spreading her napkin across her lap. Propping her injured leg up had made her skirt ride high, and she knew that Bruce had to have noticed the garters that held up her single stocking. He'd have to be blind not to, but he still wasn't reacting in any visible way. She was more than a little disappointed.

Low libido? She scratched that out. Not possible.

Maybe she just didn't turn him on?

Nope, that wasn't so either. She had that one kiss to go by, and there'd been no mistaking the lump in his trousers.

Polly was too hungry to worry about it at the moment. She attacked the succulent shrimp with a groan of pleasure.

Gentleman Caller

A perfectly cooked carp on a bed of greens came next, and after that one delicious course followed another in leisurely fashion.

They talked about food, other restaurants, movies, books.

He was smart and amusing and quick-witted, and someone had worked hard on his manners. He was as polite and attentive as a well-brought-up Southern gentleman, not that she'd met any. As the evening progressed, she had to grudgingly admit he was fun to be with.

He asked about her work and listened when she talked. They argued over a recent scandal that involved a female juror who'd fallen in love with the accused and dated him after he'd been released from custody. Bruce felt the woman suffered from low self-esteem; Polly figured she was seriously lacking gray matter, and that what little she had was functional only when she was standing up.

He laughed so hard he had to gulp water.

Intelligent. It was nice to have someone smart enough to appreciate her humor.

She asked how he'd come to be a doctor. He'd wanted to be an architect, he said, but he couldn't draw. So he switched to medicine, and passed out cold watching a baby being born. But then he got hooked. Delivering babies was much better than designing buildings. Better than almost anything. The heat in his glance filled in the blanks on that one.

Innuendo.

Yes. This was going to work.

A final dish of fresh litchee nuts in syrup and a plate of fragile almond cookies marked the end of the meal.

Polly struggled up to visit the bathroom and was surprised to find the restaurant almost empty. A glance at her watch startled her; they'd been there five hours.

"Time to go?" Bruce was waiting with her jacket when she got back. Polly noticed that no bill had arrived. Bruce left a sizable roll of money on the table.

Generous, she ticked off with a sigh.

Tommy appeared as they made their way back through the kitchen. Polly thanked him for the dinner, and Bruce shook his hand firmly as they went out the door.

Back in the van, Polly began plotting. First she'd suggest they take a ride through the park, she decided, and she'd see to it he stopped at one of the secluded spots overlooking the ocean. After a heated, dedicated half hour of driving him out of his mind, she'd let him talk her into going home with him.

Hell, seduction was easier than taking a deposition, she thought with a satisfied grin. And once she'd fulfilled this physical urge to bed him, she'd be able to put him in perspective and move on with her life.

Except that when she suggested the ride in

the park, Bruce shook his head. "I'm taking you home," he announced in a no-nonsense tone. "Otherwise I'll end up making love to you." His big hand reached across and slipped under her skirt, caressing the bare flesh between stocking and garter, sending hot and powerful vibrations up her thigh and higher.

"You're a sexy witch, Polly. I can't look at you without wanting to strip off your clothes."

"My apartment isn't far from here. We could go to my place," she murmured.

"We'll do that, but not tonight," he said firmly.

What was this idiot's problem? She glanced out the window, certain he had to be saying one thing and meaning another. But the van was heading across town, in the general direction of Maxine's house.

"What the *hell* have you got against making love?" she burst out.

He blew out a long breath. "Absolutely nothing. I'm a *really* big fan, believe me. But not on our first date."

He was religious. He was insane. He was impotent? He was a doctor—he'd know about Viagra, for God's sake.

"I tell you, this isn't easy for me, Polly." There wasn't a trace of his teasing grin, and his tone indicated that he was deadly serious. "I want you so much I can hardly think. But I'm determined that we'll get to know each other before we jump into bed together."

"Well, silly me," she said in a snarl. "I had the idea that's exactly how two people got acquainted."

He grinned at her and shook his head. "Nope. Not in my book, not with you. See, it's easy to be physically naked. I want us to do the emotional nakedness first, so that we know we're suited before we take the next step."

She gaped across at his handsome profile, lit intermittently by streetlights, hardly able to believe her ears. She considered hitting him across the head with her handbag, but he was driving. And she already had that damned "reckless driving" charge pending from broadsiding his car.

She seethed for the rest of the time it took to reach Maxine's, planning the perfect insult for the moment when he made the mistake of asking her out again. And if he thought he was going to get a kiss good night, he was wrong, wrong, wrong. Man, was he in for a surprise.

He pulled into the driveway and was out of the car and around to her door before she could locate her damned crutches. He lifted her out and walked protectively close all the way to the door, where he rang the bell before Polly could fumble out the key in her handbag.

Edna answered, phone pressed to her ear, pacifier plugged in her mouth. She winked and waggled her fingers, gave a protracted moan as she sucked hard on the pacifier, and then went back into the living room to finish her assignment.

Bruce stared after her and then gave his head a wondering shake. "What's that all about?"

"Sucking," Polly snapped. "It sounds like she's . . ."

"I get it." He closed his eyes briefly and then opened them and said in a not-too-steady voice, "Thanks for a fantastic evening. I'll be in touch soon." He brushed her cheekbone gently with his thumb, and she waited for him to take her in his arms, rehearsing the blistering lecture she planned to lay on him.

But he drew his hand away and gave her a smart little salute.

"Sleep well, Hopalong," he had the nerve to say as he opened the door. He was whistling cheerfully by the time he hit the steps. Even though she knew full well the penalty for murder, Polly was plotting ways and means as the door closed behind him.

Chapter Seventeen

Harry shut the hotel room door, and Maxine stared around, her heart hammering so hard she was sure he could hear it. All through their elegant dinner she'd barely tasted the food. She'd been thinking about this, about coming up to this room, about taking her clothes off and making love to Harry.

She wanted to, she *really* wanted to, but now that the time had come she was quaking in her high-heeled sandals.

She knew so much about men and how to please them when it came to phone sex, but in actual fact she'd been with only three men in her entire life. She was beyond nervous. She was scared out of her mind.

Harry would be disappointed; she was sure of it. He'd expect her to be a lot more practiced than she was. All the way up in the elevator, she'd been afraid that the sumptuous meal she'd just eaten was going to come back up again. *Nothing like vomit to turn a guy on, Maxine.*

The hotel room was large, and there were soft lamps lit, creating a sense of coziness and luxury. It wasn't just a bedroom, either; there was a small, cozy sitting area with a sofa, a coffee table, and even a fireplace. Beyond, wide double doors showed a slice of king-size bed reflected in a huge wall-size mirror. There was a balcony, and through the sliding glass doors Vancouver's downtown sparkled like a rhinestone necklace.

"This is so luxurious. It must have cost you a fortune, Harry," she finally managed to stammer. "Oh, and look at the lilacs." On legs that felt like sponges she walked over to the vase set on a narrow side table and bent, drawing in the heady, rich scent of the blossoms.

"You ordered these?"

He nodded.

"Thank you for thinking of flowers, Harry."

"Actually, I stole them from Mrs. Campanato's garden."

She gave him a horrified look and then realized by the twinkle in his eye that he was teasing. He was trying to help her relax; he sensed

207

that she was nervous. It was sweet of him, and she gave him a shaky smile.

"How about some wine?" He took a bottle from an ice bucket on the wet bar, and when she nodded, he opened it and poured them each a glass.

"Don't tell me," she said when he handed it to her. "You stole it from Mr. Campanato's wine shed, right?"

He grinned as he reached out and touched her glass with his. "I can see I've told you far too much about myself. You know all my nasty little habits."

"And I love you in spite of them." The words were out before she realized what she'd said. Her face burned, and she tipped the glass up and downed half the wine in one gulp, not looking at him. She could feel tears prickling behind her eyelids. Of all the things she'd been determined not to say tonight, the L-word was at the top of the list. She'd blown it, and they hadn't been in the hotel room for even fifteen minutes.

"Just fooling." But her voice wobbled.

"Maxine." His voice was quiet, and she knew he was standing very close behind her, but she didn't turn to face him. She was too embarrassed. His arms came around her, drawing her stiff form close against his chest, and she could feel his breath, cool on her burning neck and cheek.

"Sweetheart, I know you're joking, but if I

thought you meant that, I'd be the luckiest man on earth." He turned her into his arms and used a finger to tip her chin up so he could kiss her, a reassuring kiss, soft and very tender.

Her lips were trembling.

"Let's make a bargain, dearest."

The endearment made her feel better.

"We'll be totally honest with each other tonight, and anything we do or say stays within this room. We're free to be as shy or outrageous or wild or reserved as we like, as long as it's genuinely how we feel at the moment."

It sounded good. She gave a tiny, tentative nod.

"This is our time; we're totally off the clock until tomorrow comes," he reminded her, his voice husky. "No kids, no phones, no responsibilities. We don't even have to have sex if you don't feel like it."

She managed to look disappointed.

"Although if we don't, you're liable to see a grown man bang his head on the wall and cry," he added sardonically. "What I'm trying to say is, we don't have to do a damn thing unless we both really want to. Okay? What do ya think?"

"Okay." She didn't sound too certain, but she didn't feel too certain about anything just at the moment. At least this way she wouldn't have to worry about what was going to come out of her mouth next.

"Done deal. What do you feel like first?"

Bobby Hutchinson

She considered it. "Let's have another glass of wine and just look around."

Wineglasses in hand, they wandered through the suite, and Maxine began to feel like a child exploring a playground. She opened the mini-bar and examined the contents. "Ohh, chocolate."

"Here we go." Harry removed the huge bar and peeled away the wrapping, breaking off bits and slipping them into her mouth. The sweetness soothed her, melting seductively on her tongue. She liked his fingers touching her lips.

She wandered, admiring the sunken tub and the stacks of navy and plum towels in the bathroom, the scented candles by the tub. Harry took two into the bedroom, setting them on the bedside table.

Without exchanging a word, they flopped down side by side and bounced as hard as they could on the king-size bed. After that they stepped out onto the small balcony.

"It's like being on vacation." Maxine sighed blissfully, staring up at the sky with its canopy of stars, and then down to the millions of twinkling city lights. As soon as he felt her shiver in the damp night air, he took her hand and drew her back into the bedroom.

She sat on the edge of the bed as he lit the candles and turned off the lights. She was relaxed, and now she felt anticipation instead of fear.

He went to get the bottle of wine. When he came back he said, "When was the last time you had a vacation, Maxine?"

She remembered it vividly. "Graham's father, Ricky, took me to Mexico for ten days." It was there that she'd become pregnant. "How about you? When was the last time you went on vacation?"

He thought it over. "My honeymoon, I guess. We went to Bermuda. It was a good time. We went scuba diving and horseback riding." He emptied the last of the wine into their glasses and set the bottle on the floor. "You've never told me much about Graham's father, apart from the fact that he was an asshole who walked out on you when you were four months pregnant." He took off his sports jacket and slung it over a chair, then turned the clock radio to a station that played soft instrumentals. "I'd like you to tell me about him, Maxine. If it doesn't bother you."

She looked up at him. He was dark, dangerous, and killer handsome in his white shirt and loosened tie.

"I didn't think he was somebody you'd want to talk about, Harry."

"But I do," he insisted. "I want to know everything about you, and he was obviously a big part of your life." He knelt at her feet and slipped off her high-heeled sandals, giving each foot a small massage in the process, rubbing her arches, giving each toe a gentle squeeze.

"Mmmm, that feels good." It did. It also felt sensual. She plumped the pillows up behind her and shimmied back on the bed. "You said that to me before," she reminded him. "When we first talked on the phone, you said you wanted to know everything about me." But of course she'd had no intention of being honest then. She did now. "It was the first time in my life that a man had ever said that to me."

"Men are generally idiots when it comes to women," he said with a regretful sigh. "We don't know what to ask, or how to ask it." Harry took off his own shoes and made himself comfortable close beside her.

Her heart had settled down in the last few minutes, but it accelerated all over again when he slid an arm under her shoulders and drew her against his side. She could smell his freshly laundered shirt, the faintly spicy deodorant he wore, and, most arousing of all, the undertones of musky male that were personally his.

"I'm trying to graduate out of the idiot category where women are concerned, sweetheart, so I want to know what attracted you to the guy who was Graham's father," he insisted. "I want to know what he was like, what made you fall in love with him, what his good points were. He must have had some."

"Good points?" She raised her eyebrows and shook her head. It was resting on his shoulder.

She wondered if his heart was thrumming the way hers was.

"I tend to concentrate more on why I was such a fool where Ricky was concerned," she confessed, conscious of his fingers lightly tracing a pattern on the bare skin of her arm. His touch made the tiny hairs stand on end.

"But you're right; of course there were things about Ricky I liked. He was smart, exciting to be with, the kind of guy who has an idea a minute." She shook her head. "And never carries through on any of them. He had this great imagination. He had lots of energy. He was tall and blond. And he made me laugh." She settled more comfortably into his arm. "I'm a sucker for a guy with a sense of humor."

"That's the death knell for me, then," he said in a hopeless tone. "Humor, no less. And here I was already stinging over the physically attractive, tall, blond bit."

She laughed and he hugged her close.

"Okay," he said with an immense sigh. "I think that's all I can stand of his good points. Now tell me his faults so I don't get a total complex."

"Well, for one thing, he wasn't good at paying back loans."

His fingers stopped stroking for a moment. "You loaned him money?" The teasing was gone from his voice.

Maxine nodded. "Only my life savings, which

213

included what I'd inherited when my aunt died." She explained about the airline, and how Ricky had convinced her that the money was an investment in their future. "I have a promissory note; Polly's been trying for months to find him and collect on it." She told him that Ricky had said he was going to Costa Rica. "He's not there, though. He seems to have vanished into thin air."

Harry was silent for several long moments, and then his arm tightened around her.

"Rats. I was gonna ask for a loan, but I guess that's out now."

"Smart thinking." She matched his playful tone. "My bank account's a lot thinner than I am."

"And here I'd hoped you were rich as well as beautiful." He sighed deeply and turned toward her, forcibly pulling the length of her body close against him, sending her breath rushing out. "Rats, I'll just have to be satisfied with kisses instead of money," he said in a growl, bringing his mouth to hers.

She loved the way he kissed, sure of himself, lazy at first, nipping at her bottom lip with his teeth, giving her all the time in the world to get used to being this close to him, to get used to the fact that nothing would interrupt them—if she didn't want it to. Their other kisses had been stolen, hurried, fitted in between the demands of the kids. Now it was only the two of them, and a long, long night ahead.

He was stroking her arms and back through the thin fabric of the simple amber-colored sheath she'd bought especially for tonight. It had been worth every extravagant cent she'd spent, because he'd looked her up and down when he first saw it and whistled low and long.

"You're a knockout, Maxine," he'd said with a funny little catch in his voice that thrilled her.

"You smell like pumpkin pie," he murmured now, trailing kisses down her throat.

"Pumpkin pie?" She giggled. Wait until Polly heard that her expensive pheromone concoction smelled like pumpkin pie.

"It's my favorite smell," he assured her, using his tongue to stroke the exact spot on her throat where her pulse beat hard and fast. "Ummm, you taste good, too. Sweet and creamy. And hot." His mouth and teeth did enticing things to her neck.

Her arms were around him, and she slid them down his back, aware of hard muscles, a narrow waist. She wanted desperately to touch his skin, and she tugged his shirt out and slid her hands underneath.

The contact with heated, smooth flesh made her catch her breath and sent an answering shudder down his body.

"I love you touching me," he whispered, undoing the shirt and tossing it aside. "Do it more. And I need to touch you, too."

Her dress had slithered up, and now his hands stroked downward. They encountered garters and stopped abruptly. He raised his head and looked at her legs, and the groan that erupted was one of pure delight.

"I thought so when you got in the car, and when I was rubbing your feet, but I couldn't be certain it wasn't just wishful thinking. How did you know that garter belts are my weakness?"

Because a year and a half of doing phone sex had at least taught her a few things about male fantasies, Maxine thought with a smug grin.

"I have a psychic streak," she murmured into his ear, taking the opportunity to run her tongue along its rim. She grew bolder and nibbled his earlobe, and he moved his hips against her.

Adept at arousing men sexually on the telephone, she was unprepared for the intensity of her own arousal. Need grew in her, and she rocked against him, aware of the erection that strained against his gray trousers.

Her breath was coming in short gasps, and she suddenly couldn't wait any longer. She wanted him now; she needed him now. She needed to be naked with him.

Chapter Eighteen

"Unzip my dress?"

Maxine's voice was unsteady. She rolled over just a little, so Harry could reach the back zipper. When his fingers tugged it down to her hips, she got to her knees and shimmied a little, letting the silky garment slide slowly down over her low-cut chocolate-colored bra, down past the matching garter belt and the tiny scrap of lace below.

Polly and her belief in the power of thong panties were justified by the expression on his face.

Her lace-topped stockings were the same burnt-amber shade as her dress, and she knew the flesh between was creamy white . . . and plentiful.

Earlier tonight, she'd studied herself in the mirror in her bedroom before she'd slipped into the dress, pleased with the lush cleavage the bra enhanced, but worried about her tummy, conscious of the extra flesh around her waist and hips.

Now, watching Harry's eyes grow heavy-lidded, hearing his sudden in-drawn breath and the low, lusty sound he made in his throat, she felt voluptuous instead of plump.

He got up for a moment, undid the belt at his waist, and stripped off his trousers, snug black briefs, and gray socks. And then he knelt beside her on the bed, putting his hands gently on her arms.

"Let me look at you."

Over his shoulder, she caught a glimpse of the two of them reflected in the large mirror on the wall. Her heart rose in her throat. They looked beautiful, his hard, muscular body with its dusting of dark hair contrasting with her paleness, his erection strong and urgent, her body rounded and glowing, utterly female in the candlelight.

"Maxine, Maxine," he crooned softly, as slowly he reached out and stroked his palms over breasts and hips, using his fingertips to lightly caress the bare skin between panty and stocking.

"Should I touch you like this?" His fingers brushed the damp, throbbing place between her legs and then slid away, teasing, enticing.

"Like that, oh, yes," she whispered, leaning toward him, but he kissed her mouth instead, urgent and deep, and then his head dipped as his lips followed the path his hands had taken, tongue circling, mouth closing over each aching nipple in turn, suckling them strongly through the flimsy lace of her bra.

"Let's get rid of this." He reached behind her and undid the clasp, letting her breasts spill into his palms.

"Ahhh, Maxine, lovely woman. I've imagined what you'd be like, naked in my arms. You're more beautiful than I dreamed."

His words went deep into timid places, a soothing balm that began to heal the insecurities that made her hesitant. Bolder now, she put her hands on his back, learning the hard lines of his neck and shoulder, tracing the straight, strong march of vertebrae past his waist, down to his muscular buttocks. She cupped them and drew him toward her, letting herself fall back. He straddled her, skin to skin, and deftly slid a condom into place.

"I want you, Harry." Her voice was soft, but her hips were urgent, undulating against him, telegraphing her need.

"Good." He kissed her, and now his mouth was savage, drawing the passion that burned in her belly up until her entire body was burning, consumed with craving.

He brushed against her, hot and hard.

She was wet and impatient, almost sobbing with need as she opened her legs wide, mutely inviting him. With a muffled groan he moved against her, and then, at last, she felt him filling her, slowly at first, rocking gently as he adjusted, as he found her rhythm and moved into it.

And then he was losing control, plunging deep and hard once, then again. It was too soon, and she made a frantic sound. He stopped.

"Don't move. God, sweetheart, don't move." His face above her was contorted with the effort he was making to hold on, to wait until she was ready.

But now she was beyond thought, beyond restraint. She writhed beneath him, and then cried out helplessly as the spasms began deep within her, so acute she forgot who and where she was, remembering only his name and her desperate need.

"Harry, Harry . . ."

His head reared back, and with a final long, convulsive thrust he joined her, his cry echoing hers.

His body trembled above her, and slowly he lowered himself, covering her, shuddering with her as aftershocks rippled through them.

She felt his weight and tasted his sweat. His

forehead touched hers, and for long, peaceful moments they lay still, sharing euphoria.

"That was . . ." It was difficult to find words. "That was spectacular," she finally whispered. Her lips were close to his ear. She pressed her nose against his neck, drinking in the musky male scent of him, using her tongue to taste him.

"Spectacular," he repeated. "I think that's an understatement." His voice was thick and deep. "I was so afraid I wouldn't be able to make it good for you. I worried about it all through dinner," he murmured. "You drove me out of my mind with wanting, you witch."

"*You* were afraid?" Consumed by her own fears, she'd never given a thought to his, or even suspected he might have any.

He made a sound against her shoulder and nodded. "Scared shitless," he admitted in a rueful tone. "As your lawyer friend would say, the burden of proof is on the man in these situations."

Maxine giggled. "Polly doesn't think that. She says that women are responsible for their own orgasms."

He chuckled. "You could have given me that news flash before we started. It would have saved me a lot of stress." He rolled to the side, sliding one of her legs between his, holding her close. "But if that's the final word on the subject, then from now I'll just throw caution aside and proceed with wham, bam, thank you, ma'am."

"Polly and I don't agree on everything, you know."

She felt him smile. He was stroking a hand lightly down her side, leisurely tracing the generous curves of breast and bottom. "Your skin is like a newborn's," he said, scattering kisses on her shoulder and neck. "And this . . . ahhh, Maxine, this is perfection." He cupped her breast and ran his forefinger across the nipple, sending a shuddery response through her. He replaced forefinger with tongue, moving his hand down between her legs, and at his touch she felt her body begin to glow and throb.

"We've got all night. We'll take our time," he promised. "We'll have to. I'm not exactly a teenager anymore." She felt his smile as he claimed her mouth with his. "Still randy, but older."

With lazy ease, he used his lips and hands in clever ways that made her breath catch in her throat and her body pulse. Against her leg she could feel him growing hard again, and after a long, pleasure-filled interval filled with kisses that traveled from one heated spot to the next, she gave herself up totally to the pleasure of loving him and being loved.

He knew the exact moment when she fell asleep, and it made him smile. Her breathing changed, and a small snore erupted close to his ear, followed by another. They were endearing, and he felt his chest constrict with an emotion he couldn't quite identify. Tenderness? Affection?

Both, and something more, something that both thrilled and terrified him. He was falling in love with Maxine.

He probably had been from the time he'd first laid eyes on her, in the restaurant downstairs, but it was only now, holding her sleeping body close to his, hearing her soft snores, that the full realization ripped through him with a force that would have knocked him flat were he not already lying down.

Some things in life came slowly, logically, piece by gentle piece, until they fit together like a jigsaw. His knowledge that he was a writer had come to him that way, gradually, over a period of years.

Other things arrived out of the blue, with the force of a tsunami. He'd experienced this overwhelming sense of recognition only once before, when the nurse in the delivery room had handed him the naked, bloody little scrap that was his Sadie, and aweful love had overwhelmed him, bringing tears to his eyes and constriction to his chest.

He felt those things again now and knew them for what they were. He loved this woman. He wanted her beside him, not just now, but always, for whatever time they had left in their lives. She was the woman he wanted to marry, the woman he wanted as wife and companion and lover and mother for Sadie. He wanted babies with her, brothers and sisters for Graham and Sadie.

Maxine was cradled close in his arms, oblivious to the earthshaking revelations he was experiencing. Their lovemaking had exhausted her, and no wonder. He should be exhausted too; it was after three. The candles on the bedside table had guttered out long ago, and he'd turned the music off. Morning wasn't far away.

He, too, should be asleep, just as she was, but instead his mind was alert, leaping from one thought to the next. He felt as if he'd never sleep again.

How could he have made love four times in as many hours and still not be satiated? His body was—he felt weary in every cell—but his mind just didn't get it. In his head he wanted her more than ever, with a desire that went far beyond the physical.

And mixed in with the rest of the conflicting emotions was a sickening sense of guilt. She'd reminded him tonight of what he'd said, early on, when he'd first phoned her: that he wanted to know everything about her.

She didn't know that he'd taken notes on the things she'd confided and sold them to Sullivan. The article was due the following week, and his stomach felt sick when he thought of it. For days now he'd tried to figure out how to get out of writing it. His brain went over the entire mess again, the pathway all too familiar, with no detour in sight.

He'd considered giving back the advance money, difficult as that would be, seeing that he'd already spent it. But the money wasn't really the issue here, he reminded himself. He could always borrow the money; he knew that.

It was his reputation as a freelancer that he couldn't afford to compromise; his income was dependent on assignments from editors, and they were a tight-knit group. Failing to deliver on a major assignment was a serious matter. He'd have trouble getting work if he reneged. Sullivan had gone out of his way to give him the advance he'd asked for, and he'd let Harry control the tone of the article.

His arm tightened around the lush woman sleeping so trustingly at his side, and panic rose in him. He'd betrayed her; there was no other word for it. He'd sent Sullivan that detailed outline for the proposed exposé. In it, he'd used pseudonyms—Aurora instead of India—but it contained many of the things she'd confided in him.

On the basis of that outline, Sullivan had paid him the advance, and now he had to write the story.

Harry knew he should have told Maxine the truth. He'd had opportunities during the past weeks, and especially tonight. He should have told her tonight; he'd promised himself he would. But he knew that if he had, it was highly probable she wouldn't be sleeping in his arms right now.

Hell. He should have told her regardless. She was going to find out anyway, and when she did, he hated to think how she'd react. He was a craven coward.

He shifted a little, and Maxine stirred, turning toward him trustingly, sliding her arm across his chest, sighing with contentment, and he closed his eyes tight, knowing he was caught in a trap of his own making.

The article would run whether he wrote it or not. Sullivan was hot on the concept, and if Harry backed off, the editor would simply find someone else to follow up on the information Harry had supplied in the outline.

Writing the article gave him control as to how Maxine was depicted, how the telephone sex business was portrayed. He wanted it to be honest, to show exactly how and why women did phone sex, how circumstances could force someone into a situation she might otherwise never consider.

He thought over what Maxine had revealed tonight about loaning Ricky Shwartz money. For a moment Harry indulged himself, fantasizing about beating the other man to a bloody pulp.

The pen is mightier than the fist, he reminded

himself grimly. If he was going to tell Maxine's story—and he didn't see he had much choice in the matter at this stage—he'd at least make damned good and certain to use Shwartz's name and description in the article. What could the jerk do, sue? He'd have to come out of hiding to do it, and then Polly would nab him.

And maybe Maxine wouldn't even see the piece, he consoled himself as the numbers on the bedside clock moved from three-fifty-nine to four A.M. Maybe nobody would. How many articles had he poured his heart and soul and blood into, only to have them buried on page twenty-three of section C? For the first time in his writing career, he prayed fervently that his work would go unnoticed.

But just in case it didn't, he knew he'd have to tell her at breakfast, and the knowledge was agonizing.

He'd ordered from room service, and judging by the display on the serving table, Maxine might assume he'd simply told them to bring everything on the menu.

She lifted the silver top from one of the numerous serving dishes. "Mmmmm, eggs Benedict. And potato pancakes, and ooh, look at these shrimp, Harry."

"I'm looking, I'm looking."

"Lecher." She grinned at him and pretended to adjust the white terry cloth of the hotel robe so that her breasts didn't show quite as much, but it was a token gesture. Harry's eyes weren't on the food, and she liked that.

Hers were, however; she was starving. It was after nine. She'd come slowly awake, already aroused, aware that in the sensual dream she'd been having, he was making love to her. She'd opened her eyes to find out that it was really happening. That slow, early morning sex had been explosive. When it was over, he'd looked down into her eyes and whispered, "I'm falling in love with you, Maxine."

The words repeated and repeated in her heart. They were a precious gift that she held clasped close to her soul.

She hadn't said she loved him, too; it seemed to her that it would sound as if she were just being polite. She wanted to wait for exactly the right moment. She'd know it when it arrived.

It wasn't now; now, she needed food.

"Let's start with fruit salad, okay?" She spooned it into two bowls and placed one in front of him. He, too, was wearing one of the lush white robes. His dark hair was still wet from the shower, and his long legs poked out from under the hem, deliciously hairy and masculine. He was cute. He was irresistible. He was falling in love with her. Life was perfect, and after they ate, she planned to lure him back into the bedroom.

She'd eaten her way through several lavish

servings of everything before she realized he wasn't keeping up.

"Aren't you hungry?" She spread a toast triangle with blackberry jam and popped it into her mouth.

"I'm enjoying the scenery," he said, his eyes caressing her. "The sun sets your hair on fire."

The table was set in front of the open French doors. They were being bathed in morning sunlight, deliciously tempered by a cool breeze off the ocean.

"Thank you." She could feel her cheeks grow warm at the compliment, and she smiled across at him. "Harry, I'm so grateful to you for planning this. I can't remember the last time I felt so happy, or so pampered."

"You deserve everything, and more." There was a note of tension in his voice, and she glanced over at him. He was frowning, and the food on his plate was still untouched.

"Harry, what's wrong?" She put her coffee cup down and leaned across to touch his arm.

"I have something to explain to you, Maxine."

"Okay." She nodded and smiled at him, but her stomach gave a little lurch at the solemn tone of his voice. "So go ahead and explain."

"I'm a writer."

"Yes, I know that." She frowned at him, confused.

"I freelance, I work for magazines and news-

229

papers. Sometimes I propose articles, sometimes editors request them."

"You told me that before." She was staring at him, puzzled. "What's this about, Harry?" The tension in his voice was affecting her, making her nervous.

"That first time I called you? It was because an editor had asked me to do an article on phone sex."

"Did you do it?" She'd wondered about his call many times. "Because it doesn't matter, I've had reporters call me before. And you didn't really know me then anyway; you just knew India." But it stung, the fact that he'd never told her the truth about that first call.

The line of strain between his eyebrows was distinct and deep. "I did an outline, using some of the personal stuff you confided to me."

Her heart was starting to race. She kept her voice even. "What sort of personal stuff?"

He was looking increasingly miserable. "Oh, what you told me about growing up, about finding yourself pregnant with no chance of employment, the way you started your business and why you did. The thing is, I used *you* in the story, Maxine. Not your name, but certainly you. I used the things you confided in me."

She stared at him. She had to clear her throat before she could speak. "What magazine was it for?"

"The *Star*. It isn't published yet. It's coming out next weekend."

"Oh." She swallowed. Her throat was dry. "So you've already written it."

"Not completely. Partially. I wrote an outline, but I haven't finished the story yet."

"Then you can stop it."

"No." He shook his head. "I can't." He started to explain about outlines and advances and integrity and his reputation, but she wasn't listening. Deep inside her, something new and fragile was disintegrating, and before the pain of destruction became unbearable, she had to get away from him.

She drew the robe around her tightly and got to her feet. She was shaking in earnest now, and she didn't want him to see. She'd already shown him too many of her weaknesses.

"Maxine, please sit down. Talk to me."

She shook her head and went into the bedroom. She gathered up her clothing and took it into the bathroom.

He was waiting when she came out. He didn't try to touch her. "I never intended to hurt you," he said. "Everything I wrote about you was written with admiration. I'm in awe of your courage, Maxine."

"But it was a betrayal." She was amazed at how reasonable she sounded. "I told you those things because I trusted you, Harry. You should have told me you were just interviewing me.

Bobby Hutchinson

You shouldn't have pretended you cared."

"I do care. I told you I cared. I said I'm falling in love with you—how much clearer can I get?" He sounded angry.

She swallowed hard against the lump in her throat. "That's exactly what Ricky said when he borrowed my money, you know. He said he loved me." She stuffed her things into the classy overnight bag she'd borrowed from Polly. "Don't worry about driving me home, Harry. I'll take a cab." Her handbag was on the dresser and she looped it over her shoulder.

"The hell you will. Just hold on a minute till I get my stuff together. Don't you dare just take off. . . ."

She heard the fear and the hurt in his voice as the door closed behind her. She ran down the hall, and fortunately there was an elevator waiting, and a yellow cab just outside the hotel door. She wanted to go home, lock herself in her bedroom, and stay there the rest of her natural life.

Chapter Nineteen

"Maxine, it's in this morning's edition." Edna came bursting through the kitchen door, holding out a folded newspaper. "I saw it on the newsstand when I stopped for milk, and I figured your paper wouldn't be delivered yet, so I brought it back."

It was barely seven-thirty. Polly was spooning Cream of Wheat into Graham while Maxine made toast and a fresh pot of coffee.

"Thanks, Edna." Maxine suddenly felt sick and cold. "You shouldn't have bothered to come all the way back with it. I'd have seen it soon enough anyhow."

Better to get it over with sooner than later, though.

Maxine took the paper and flipped it open on the table, so that Polly and Edna could see too, and she could feel her body start to tremble and gorge rise in her throat.

TALK TO ME, BABY; PHONE SEX FOR PLEASURE AND PROFIT, the front page trumpeted. Harry's name was on the byline.

"Do you have the gift of gab and a feminine voice? You, too, could be earning big money without the danger of sexually transmitted disease."

This ad or one like it appears weekly in the Help Wanted section of newspapers across North America. The telephone sex trade is flourishing, some of it from offices set up exclusively for that purpose. But phone sex is also a thriving home-based vocation. There are an increasing number of entrepreneurs, like Aurora, who operates her business from a modest bungalow in a quiet Vancouver suburb.

"Aurora, huh? Well, Aurora's not bad. At least he picked an imaginative pseudonym for you, Maxine." Polly put a sympathetic arm around her shoulders and together they all bent over the table.

Upon request, the telephone company installed a 900 number, and Aurora signed a

*contract, agreeing to pay them 40 percent of
her profits. On a good night, Aurora and her
employee might take in an estimated fourteen to sixteen hundred dollars. There's
nothing illegal about it; Aurora keeps careful
records and religiously pays her income tax.*

"At least he got his facts straight so far,
right?" Polly asked.

"It's not at all degrading," Edna commented.

Maxine couldn't say anything. Her skin prick-
led with dread as she skimmed down the page,
and bile burned in her throat.

*Although her customers can't see her, Aurora
is young, beautiful, titian-haired, green-eyed,
curvaceous. She's also excellent at her job;
her unusually deep, throaty voice and creative imagination often keep customers en-
thralled for upward of forty minutes. What
she does is tough and time consuming but
financially lucrative. It has to be; Aurora is
a single parent, raising her year-old son
alone. The daughter of a small-town minister whose rigid and judgmental standards
drove her away from home at an early age,
Aurora had no one to turn to and nowhere
to go when she found herself pregnant and
jobless. . . .*

Graham, feeling abandoned in his high chair, began to squirm and whine. Fingers clumsy, Maxine fumbled with the straps and lifted him out, heedless of the sticky cereal that covered his hands and cheeks. She hugged him close, aware of the blood pounding in her temples.

"Hey, listen to this." Polly read the next portion aloud: Ricky Shwartz, an airline pilot, disappeared long before his son was born, taking with him Aurora's life savings and leaving her pregnant and destitute.' "

Maxine gasped. "That traitor. I told him about Ricky and the money only last weekend. He must have waited until I was asleep and then scribbled down notes."

"Hold on, it's continued on page two." Polly flipped to it eagerly, but Maxine had had enough. She felt as if she'd been punched in the stomach.

"How could he? How could he do this to me?" she raged.

Polly glanced at her and shrugged. "It's not a bad article, Maxine. It's obvious the guy cares about you. And this stuff about Shwartz is the best news I've heard since Judge Crandall retired. If there's anybody out there who knows where Shwartzie is, this might just be the way we'll locate him." She sounded exuberant, and Maxine felt suddenly outraged.

"You think there's nothing wrong with this?" She was hollering, and Graham gave her a shocked look. His mouth puckered and he started to sob. Maxine lowered her voice and patted him, but she had to tell her friends how she felt. "You think it's okay that he got me to spill my guts, and then copied it all down and sold it?" Her voice trembled and went up an octave. "I can't believe you'd be so callous, Polly."

"Shall I take him?" Edna held her arms out and Graham went to her gladly. Edna smiled at him and headed to the bathroom to wash him off while Polly and Maxine glared at each other.

"No, I don't think this is all right. That's not what I meant at all," Polly said forcefully. "I think he was a rat and an idiot not to tell you sooner what he was doing. But I also think it could have been worse. Here, read the rest of this, he's presented you exactly as you are, a smart and hardworking businesswoman with a kid to support. He's sarcastic about the guys who use the service and sympathetic to you. Hell, he actually makes you sound like a heroine—is that so bad?"

"Victim is more like it." Maxine snorted. "Some idiot female who didn't have enough sense to use birth control."

"Maxine, that's not true. Look here; he says that you're highly intelligent and inventive, that—"

"Obviously you don't get it," Maxine snapped. "And I don't need to read about my life. I lived it, remember?"

She couldn't be around Polly or that miserable paper one moment longer, or she'd start screaming. "I'm going to change, and then I'm going grocery shopping. I don't want to hear another *word* about this. I just want to forget it ever happened."

"Okay." Polly held her hands up, palms out. "Okay, you got it; we'll never mention it again. And I'll baby-sit while you're at the store, give you time to cool off."

Maxine shook her head. "I'm cool. I'm taking Graham with me. He likes the supermarket." She knew she was being snippy and she didn't give a damn.

"Fine." Polly did her best to sound soothing. "What about the business phone? If it rings, I could give it a try. . . ."

Maxine had heard Polly talking to her secretary often enough to know that only a caller wanting a demented dominatrix would stay on the line with her longer than two seconds.

"Thanks, but I'll program the business phone for call forwarding and take any calls on my cell."

"Whatever," Polly sighed. "Well, then, if you don't need me to baby-sit or answer the phone, maybe I'll go to the beach. I could use some fresh air, and it's actually hot out there today. And I do have that new silver bikini." A calculating look stole over her face. "Maybe I'll give

Doc a call and see if he wants to be my chauffeur."

"You know seeing him is gonna put you in a foul mood," Maxine reminded her. "The last three times he took you out, you weren't fit to live with for days afterward."

"So I've got short-term memory loss where he's concerned. He's a challenge—sooner or later he'll give in. The bikini might do it. It's got a thong bottom."

Maxine didn't want to hear about thongs, either. They reminded her of the night with Harry.

She tried to put him and the article out of her mind as she went to retrieve Graham. Edna was kneeling beside the tub, giving him a bath.

"You okay?" She gave Maxine a worried look.

"Yeah, I'll get over it. Thanks for bathing Graham. I'm sorry I was so short-tempered."

"You had a right." Edna got to her feet and hugged Maxine. "I'm sorry Harry hurt you. I'm going home now to get some sleep. I'll see you tonight."

"Thanks, Edna. You're a good friend." Edna's kindness touched her, and Maxine had to struggle to keep the tears back. She searched for a subject that would take her mind off the newspaper. "You look really pretty with that new hairdo."

Terry had cut Edna's thick club of hair into a stylish wedge that brought out the beauty of her classic features and emphasized her eyes.

Edna blushed with pleasure. "I've already had two responses to the ad Polly helped me put on the Internet," she confided in a shy tone. "One of them sounds really nice. He wants me to meet him for lunch next week."

"Go for it. You deserve somebody who appreciates you."

"Don't we all." Edna sighed. "Trouble is, what we deserve and what we get are often very different things."

She left, and Maxine dried her son and dressed him, determined not to let the article devastate her.

"C'mon, dumplin', let's go in the car."

"Car?" Graham's face lit up. He was learning new words every day. He pressed his lips together and made the car sound that Sadie had taught him, and Maxine's heart hurt. She'd fallen in love with Sadie as well as with Harry, and now she wouldn't see the little girl again.

Fighting tears, she changed into jeans and a shirt and hurried out to the garage.

The supermarket was busy when they arrived. The first thing Maxine noticed was an overflowing rack of *Star* newspapers, Harry's headline blaring. There seemed no getting away from the article.

She fastened Graham into the buggy and slunk off down the aisles, reminding herself that no one could possibly know she was the Aurora in the article.

Graham babbled cheerfully as she tossed in cereal, crackers, tomato sauce, toilet tissue, garbage bags, juice. The cart was nearly full by the time she reached the produce section, and she glanced around, praying that it was Leonard's day off. She just wasn't up to fending off his slavering advances this morning.

She shoved a head of lettuce into the cart and was filling a bag with apples when she heard her cell phone ringing. Her heart sank. The last thing she felt like doing was taking a business call, and on top of it all, Graham was beginning to get restless. She thought of just letting it ring, but business was business. No matter how terrible she felt, there were still bills to pay and groceries to buy.

She snatched up a box of crackers from the cart and hastily fumbled it open, handing one to her son as she clicked the receive button on the phone and frantically looked around for a quiet corner where she could take the call, but there were shoppers everywhere.

"India? Hey, babe, long time no talk. How ya doin'?"

"I'm fine, darlin'." It was a superhuman effort to sound languid and sensual. "I wondered when you'd call. I've missed you." It was one of her regulars, but for the life of her she couldn't place him. Charlie? Chip? Chuck? She racked her brain for a name, but Harry was the only name she could think of. And where was she going to go that was reasonably private?

There was a short corridor leading to the back storage area, with a sign saying *Employees Only* on the swinging door. Maxine maneuvered the laden cart in and stood with her back to the store, hunched over the phone.

Chad, that was it. Forcing lightness and sensuality into her tone, she cooed, "Gosh, Chad, I just got out of the tub. Give me a minute to dry off and put on some panties."

Graham shrieked and reached for another chunk of banana.

"Who's there with you?" Chad sounded suspicious.

"It's just Candy, my little poodle—you remember her?" Maxine improvised, propping the phone between her shoulder and ear and frantically thrusting another cracker at Graham. "There, now, I've put on a black negligee and these teensy thong panties. You do like thongs, Chad?"

"Describe them. Tell me how they feel." His voice was thick, and Maxine went into a breathless and detailed description involving a narrow strip of lace hiding amidst lavish buttocks.

Graham had had enough banana. He wanted a drink, and she was fumbling in her handbag for his bottle and encouraging Chad with suitable murmurs and gasps and moans when she heard a squeak behind her.

She whirled around. Leonard was standing a bare foot from her and he seemed to be choking. He was holding a large head of emerald green broccoli against his chest, but his face was beet colored. Obviously he'd overheard her conversation.

It was far too late to deter Chad. Maxine waved Graham's bottle at Leonard in a half-hearted salute and plugged it in her son's mouth. She panted as Chad gasped and moaned his way past the point of no return, and when he was coherent again Maxine stared Leonard in the eye and gave Chad the line about how wonderful it had been for her.

Leonard, whose open mouth and round eyes made him resemble a fish, gulped and wheezed as she disconnected the phone and stuck it into her jacket pocket.

"Hi, Leonard." She pulled the loaded cart backward, forcing him to move out of the way. "Sorry about that. Business call."

"Hi, Ms. Bleckner." Leonard's voice was little more than a whimper. He stood to the side and let her edge past. She had the creepy feeling his eyes were going to pop out of their sockets and roll straight down the neck of her blouse.

"Did . . . did . . . did you . . . ahhh, did you happen to notice the zucchini, Ms. Bleckner? Fresh in this morning."

"I'm in no mood for zucchini, Leonard, thanks anyway."

Maxine headed for the checkout, praying that she wouldn't get another call until she was safely out of the store.

She made it to the car, unloaded the groceries and Graham, and slid behind the wheel. Her hands were trembling, and she didn't know whether to laugh or burst into tears.

"I've got to get another job," she said with a moan.

"Dog," Graham pronounced, pointing a fat finger into the middle distance.

"You got it, sweetie. This job *is* a dog."

She thought of the two night-school classes she'd attended at broadcasting school. They'd done breathing exercises and enunciation. They'd be learning elocution, how to work with a microphone, timing, and diction. The instructor was an ex-announcer named Dave Boxman, and he'd been enthusiastic about her voice.

"Hardest thing is breathing," he'd told her. "You've gotta be able to read three or four pages at a time without gasping; you have a tendency to gasp."

She hadn't told him that it had taken her a long time to learn to gasp properly, and now she'd have to unlearn it. Gasping aside, could she even manage to finish the course? There were ten more sessions. Polly had baby-sat Graham, and Edna had come early twice last week to take the business calls. How much longer could she impose on her friends?

Even if she finished, there were a limited number of jobs available. The B.C. Institute of Technology had a daytime credit course, eight weeks long, in communication arts, and Maxine had heard that its graduates got priority when it came to jobs.

She was a long way from being able to support herself doing what she wanted. And in the meantime she'd simply have to go on yakking into the phone, regardless of how much she was beginning to hate doing it.

She turned the key and held her breath until her ancient Toyota coughed and came reluctantly to life.

This was all Harry's fault.

She backed up and then steered her way out of the parking lot, wishing she could press her foot on his neck instead of the gas pedal.

She'd fallen in love with him, damn his sneaky soul, and as if that weren't enough of a disaster, being with him had also made her dissatisfied with her job. Before she'd found out he was a liar and a cheat, she'd experienced what it was like to have all the separate parts of her come together as a single whole. It had felt powerful and right and good.

And because of it, she no longer wanted to be India, pretending to make love to faceless men on the telephone.

Chapter Twenty

It was two A.M., and Edna knew the caller on the line was young. By the sound of the half-stifled laughter in the background, he wasn't alone, either.

Edna also knew by the telltale echo that he had her on a speakerphone. *Group sex*. She shook her head. It happened occasionally, usually when young men got drunk and rowdy.

"So, Lilith, tell me what you're wearing."

She could hear the smothered giggles in the background. Edna shook her head and smiled. "You sound like a nice young man, but I'm not comfortable doing something this intimate when we've got an audience," she explained.

246

"Maybe you could call back sometime when you're alone, honey?"

The trick was to let them know what the rules were without insulting them.

There was silence on the other end of the line, and Edna was about to hang up when there was the muted sound of a scuffle; then another male voice, obviously close to the receiver, said in a strangled tone, "Mrs. Gimbel? That's you, isn't it, Mrs. Gimbel?"

Edna froze. Horror overwhelmed her. For an instant, as bright spots swam in front of her eyes, she thought she might even faint.

"Mrs. Gimbel, I know it's you," the young man was shouting now in an accusing, angry tone. "I'd know your voice anywhere. It's you, isn't—"

Edna's numb fingers finally managed to push the button that disconnected the call.

Kenny Henderson. God help her, it was Kenny. She'd know *his* voice anywhere, too. He'd grown up next door; he'd been like a brother to her own sons, Gary and Marshall. She'd made him countless peanut-butter sandwiches; she'd put Band-Aids on his knees; she'd cared for him one entire summer, while his parents went on a second honeymoon to Tahiti. He'd wet the bed every night, and she'd kept it a secret from her boys so as not to embarrass him.

Kenny. He was in college now, with Gary and Marshall.

The next thought made her heart pound even harder, and bile rise in her throat. Her sons. Were they there, too, with Kenny, with the others? Had they heard her pretending to be Lilith?

The idea was so horrible she let out a long, keening howl of absolute anguish, and then another, louder one. She was going to be sick. She needed to get to the bathroom, but for several moments she couldn't move. When she finally managed to struggle to her feet, her rubbery legs wouldn't support her and she had to flop down again hard. She gagged and tipped her head forward between her knees, gulping in air that wouldn't reach her lungs.

"Edna? Edna, honey, are you okay? God, I thought at first it was Graham howling like that." Maxine put an arm around her shoulders. Maxine's hair was wild, her face swollen from sleep, her flannel nightshirt creased.

"What's going on?" Polly came out of her bedroom, half glasses perched on her nose, crutches thumping. "I was reading and I heard somebody making a terrible noise. Was that you, Edna?"

Her friends' concerned voices barely penetrated the terror and despair that were rolling through Edna like bowling balls, intent on knocking her to her knees. She moaned and crossed her arms on her chest, rocking back and forth in agony.

"What happened, Edna? Is someone hurt?" Maxine knelt at her side, but Edna could only shake her head.

Polly panicked. "Edna, either you talk to us this minute or I'm calling an ambulance," she ordered. "And believe me, you don't want to go to Emergency unless it's life and death."

Edna managed to sit up. Polly took one look at her face and dropped her crutches to the floor. She collapsed on the arm of the chair, got her balance, cursed, and reached for the phone. "I'm calling a bloody doctor anyway. You're having a heart attack."

"No." Edna's voice was faint, but the sickness was starting to fade a little. "No. I . . . I just had a bad shock, that's all," she managed to whisper.

"That's *all*?" Polly scowled and shook her head. "It must have been pretty major to make you look this green. What the hell happened? Oh, my God, it's not your kids, is it? A car accident?"

Edna clasped her hands over her heart. It was hammering against her chest wall. "I . . . I . . . took a call. It was . . . there were young men, more than one. But one of them was . . . was . . . and, and he said . . ." Her voice failed her. Sobs rose in her throat and choked her. Tears gushed from her eyes.

"Okay, now, let's calm down here. Just take it easy. What did this asshole say, exactly?" Polly patted her back and smoothed her hair, and Maxine held her hand until Edna was able to talk again.

"Oh, God, it was ter-terrible. It was . . . it was a close friend of my sons. His name is Kenny. He . . . he recognized my voice. He knew me; I . . . I took care of him when he was younger."

Maxine made a shocked sound in her throat.

"Holy shit." Polly, too, realized what the situation might mean. "Were your sons . . . D'you think your boys were there with him?"

Edna shrugged hopelessly and a fresh flood of tears poured down her cheeks. "I . . . I don't know." Renewed panic made her shiver. "But the others heard him; he called me"—her voice broke—"he called me *Mrs. Gimbel*. They all heard him. Someone's bound to tell Gary and Marshall, whether they were there or not."

"Take deep breaths, Edna." Maxine found a box of tissues and shoved a handful at her.

"Blow your nose and let's think this thing through," Polly ordered. She groped for her crutches just as the business phone rang. She was closest to it, and she snatched it up before Maxine could move.

"Yeah?" She listened for a moment. "Yeah, well, snookums, you do sound horny as hell, but I'm afraid we're not doing phone sex just now. Try masturbation on your own." She hung up.

Maxine rolled her eyes and blew out a breath. She switched the phone over to the recorded message and got to her feet. "I'm gonna make some tea. C'mon in the kitchen, you two. I've got some brandy in the cupboard—I'll put some in your cup, Edna."

Edna shook her head. She was shaking, both inside and out, and she didn't think brandy would help. "What am I going to do? I'll never be able to face my sons again." She started to cry harder. "And they'll . . . they'll tell Jooooohn," she wailed. The thought of her ex-husband finding out that she did phone sex made her hysterical.

"Damn crutches. Ouch." Polly was struggling with a chair as Maxine set teapot, cups, and a bottle of brandy on the table.

"I could use a shot of that." With a sigh of relief, Polly flopped down, adding a good amount of brandy to the mug Maxine set in front of her. She took a swallow and slumped back in her chair. "Okay, let's look at this head-on, Edna. Let's say the worst has happened and the truth is out."

Edna could feel panic building again. Her hands were shaking so much that her tea splashed on her Mickey Mouse sweatshirt. The tea was hot, but she barely felt it. Shame and fear made it hard to breathe.

Polly reached over and patted her shoulder. "I know this is tough for you to hear right now,

Bobby Hutchinson

Edna, but from my point of view this is the best thing that could have happened. If your sons don't tell Gimbel, I'd strongly suggest you let me tell him."

"*You'd* tell him?" Anger, shock, and betrayal mingled with the other emotions Edna felt, and she swiped at her nose and glared at Polly through her tear-streaked glasses. She could feel her chin trembling. "How . . . how c-can you say such a heartless thing?"

"Easy." Polly added more brandy and took another swig of tea. "Look, here's the deal." She leaned forward and took Edna's stiff fingers in hers. "Now you've got nothing to lose, Edna. That's a very powerful position to be in. I'll apply a little pressure to dear old John, letting him know that unless he coughs up every cent of the money he legally owes you, I'll see to it . . ." She thought for a moment; then her face took on an expression of unholy glee.

"I'll see to it that Watson writes a follow-up to his exposé, naming names and explaining how a wonderful lady of fifty-three got forced to do phone sex in order to pay the rent because of her lawyer husband's lies." There was jubilation in her voice. "Hallelujah, this is the break we've been waiting for, girls. Let's attack, okay, Edna? *Pleeeease*, Edna?"

Edna couldn't think straight, but Polly *was* her lawyer. Edna had spent endless hours listening to John and his colleagues lament the

252

fact that clients hired them and then didn't follow their advice.

"I . . . I don't know," she said, her voice quavering. "What would *you* do, Maxine?"

But Maxine was glaring at Polly. "You'd actually ask *him* to write a follow-up to that article?"

No one had to ask whom Maxine meant by *him*. Edna and Polly had watched helplessly for the last week as Maxine refused phone calls, insisted that no one answer the door when Harry came by, and, worst of all, tossed a dozen beautiful long-stemmed red roses in the garbage can.

"Yeah, of course I'd ask him," Polly said. "Edna and I've both told you countless times that the article wasn't that bad. So the guy made a mistake—you could cut him a little slack. At least he didn't withhold sexual favors, did he?"

"Is that what *you're* doing with Bruce Turner, cutting him a little slack?" Maxine's tone was downright nasty.

Polly's face grew crimson. "There's no similarity at all between Watson and that . . . that sheep in wolf's clothing," she snapped. "Watson didn't lead you on, rub suntan lotion on practically every inch of your body, kiss you brainless, and then refuse, for the fourteenth time, to go the distance with you. I've told you before, the good doctor obviously has some major sexual issues."

Edna and Maxine had already heard Polly's views on the doctor's hangups, numerous times and in scathing detail. The last—and worst—episode had occurred—or not—the day he and Polly had gone to the beach and then to Polly's apartment, ostensibly to pick up clothing she needed. It seemed she'd done her inspired best at getting Turner into bed, only to have him tell her quietly but firmly that the consummation of their relationship would be on his terms.

"He actually said," Polly had fumed, "can you believe this, that he's a trifle old-fashioned about sex. Old-fashioned?" Her voice had dripped venom. "He's antediluvian, for God's sake."

Both Edna and Maxine had noticed that Polly never once said the doctor was impotent. And in spite of being furious with him, Polly still never hung up when he called.

"And anyway, we're not discussing Bruce Turner here; we're talking business. Edna's business. Let me do this, Edna. I know it'll work. Your ex wouldn't like the kind of publicity I'll spell out for him."

Edna still hesitated. "What do you think, Maxine?" she asked again. "What should I do?"

Maxine thought it over. "I'd go for it," she finally said with a resigned sigh. "This telephone sex thing isn't the kind of business anyone wants to be in long-term, and if you got a decent settlement out of John, you wouldn't have to do it anymore."

"But then you'd have to hire someone else," Edna said. Although the work itself wasn't what she'd spent her life dreaming of doing, Maxine had become her closest friend.

"Yeah." Maxine gave her a weary smile. "But that's my problem, and it hasn't happened yet. Let's take one disaster at a time here." She yawned and got to her feet.

"Anyhow, I'm going back to bed; Graham'll be up in another couple hours. Night, you two."

"So what do ya say, Edna? Yes or no?" Polly drained the last of her tea and, after a moment's hesitation, she poured another generous inch of brandy into her cup.

"I guess yes," Edna said tremulously. Polly was right. She had nothing left to lose. She got to her feet and found that she wasn't shaky in the least anymore. Making the decision had calmed her. It was probably the same calm victims of earthquakes described.

"I'll get back to work before we lose all our customers," she said in a rational tone. "Thank you, Polly."

"Atta girl." Polly held up the cup in a toast and downed it in one swallow. "I'll get on it first thing in the morning. I'll bet we have some action by dinnertime. Yahoo and alla kazaam."

*　　*　　*

It was only four the following afternoon when Polly turned off her cell phone and gave a shrill, prolonged shriek of triumph.

"Johnny boy caved," she warbled to Maxine, who was making a pot of soup in the kitchen. "He's agreed to spill the beans about all those foreign accounts. It'll take a few days to draw up the papers and get them signed, and then Edna's gonna get a check that'll make her very happy. I'll call her right now with the good news. She oughta be up by now. And if she's not, this is worth waking up for."

"Tell her I'm thrilled for her." She was, too, Maxine told herself as she sampled the soup.

It was tasteless, and she couldn't think what to add to give it flavor. Soy sauce, maybe? She stepped over Graham, who was happily unloading the pots-and-pans drawer. The clatter he was making was giving her a headache, but at least he was happy.

She hadn't taken him to Motoring Munchkins since the breakup with Harry, and she felt guilty about it; he needed the contact with other children, but she couldn't face the possibility of meeting Harry there. *Not yet*, she told herself, pouring a liberal dose of the sauce into the soup and tasting it again. Maybe later, but not yet. She was still too mad. Too sad. Too resentful.

Now the damned soup was too salty; Graham wasn't going to like it. She felt the ready tears building behind her eyes and grimly attacked the dishes in the sink, determined not to cry. Again. She'd been doing far too much crying the last week, and far too little work.

Her mind went from Harry to her job, and the dark depression that she couldn't seem to fight off overwhelmed her.

She knew that she wasn't doing a good job with the calls that came in. For the first time it was almost impossible to be India. She found herself wanting to tell the sad, silly men that she was actually a mother, that she usually wore jeans, that she had a few too many pounds around her hips, that she wore practical cotton underwear and the only orgasms she'd had recently were in the arms of a man who'd lied to her and used her trust for his own purposes.

She hadn't really done that to a caller, at least not yet. But her clients definitely sensed that she wasn't putting her imagination into her work. The number of incoming calls from regular customers had dropped sharply in the past few days, and all Maxine could feel was relief.

The truth was terrifying, but it was impossible to avoid. She didn't want to be India anymore. She *couldn't* be India anymore. The article Harry had written had done more than ruin their relationship; it had also made it impossible for her to go on doing the work that earned her a living.

If she didn't snap out of it soon, she warned herself, she'd be in serious financial trouble.

She'd already paid the fees for her night-school courses, which had depleted her meager savings.

Get a grip, Maxine. You vowed never to let a man ruin your life again, remember? So put Harry out of your mind and get on with your life.

Harry felt as if he were living at Motoring Munchkins. For the fourth time in a single week, he walked with Sadie into the huge room. His head ached, and his stomach churned. The place smelled like a dog kennel. The high-decibel sound level felt as if he were inside a kettledrum. But he kept coming because he kept hoping Maxine would be here.

So far he'd struck out, just as he'd struck out trying to locate Ricky Shwartz. In the past two weeks he'd called in favors with policemen, asked for tips from detectives, and used every search engine on the Internet with no results. Finding Shwartz was fast becoming an obsession; it was the single thing he could think of to do that might help Maxine.

"I'm gonna go make pictures, Daddy," declared Sadie, heading off to the easels under the window.

"Okay." Harry's eyes were scanning the room like radar detectors, desperately searching for Maxine.

"Harry, thank goodness you're here. I need a big, strong man to help me move the gym equipment when this session is over. They're putting in new mats for us."

Rosalie's lilting voice and heaving breasts finally registered, and he gave her a lackluster glance.

"You will help me out, won't you, Harry?"

He wanted to refuse, but she *was* the Campanatos' daughter, and he owed them for being good neighbors and helping out with Sadie.

"Sure. Do you know if Graham and his mom are coming today, Rosalie?"

"Gosh, I doubt it." Rosalie looked anything but sorry. She did manage not to smile, but it was a close thing. "They've missed . . . what, about six or eight sessions now. I guess I should call and see if Graham's sick or something." She didn't seem at all eager.

"Yeah, could you do that for me?" He pulled his cell phone from his pocket, punched in Maxine's private number, and handed it to Rosalie. He'd gone way beyond caring what anyone might think. He needed to know if there was the slightest possibility Maxine might be coming here, and when.

Rosalie's round spaniel eyes looked as if he'd just kicked her, but she waited obediently while the phone rang.

"Hi, this is Rosalie from Motoring Munchkins; can I speak to Ms. Bleckner, please? Oh, hi, Ms. Bleckner . . ."

It was agony knowing Maxine was on the

other end of the line. Harry longed to snatch the phone and beg her to talk to him, but he'd done that numerous times and she'd hung up. He waited, anxiety gnawing at his stomach.

"Okay, sorry about that. I see. Okay, we'll miss Graham. 'Bye."

"What? What'd she say?" It was all he could do not to reach out and shake the answer out of Rosalie.

"She says she's lost her job, and until she finds another one, Graham won't be coming back." Rosalie gave him an injured look and flounced off.

Shocked and worried sick, Harry cursed at length and received a reproving look from a tiny, birdlike mother whose son resembled a miniature Arnold Schwarzenegger.

Polly. He'd talk to Polly; she'd know what was going on. Trouble was, he didn't have the number at her office. Making certain Sadie was still occupied with the poster paints, he hurried outside to a booth that actually had a telephone book hanging from a chain.

Polly propped her foot on a stool and rested the phone against her shoulder. "Maxine, Harry's a gentleman. And you're being a stubborn idiot. I know because it takes one to know one."

She listened and rolled her eyes heavenward, praying for patience. "He's been trying to find Shwartz, and when he heard you weren't working, he called me and suggested, get this, that I pretend I'd located flyboy, and he—*Harry*, no less—would cough up the amount Shwartz owes you. Talk about putting your money where your mouth is."

She listened again and blew out an exasperated breath. "So it's not entirely honest; it *is* chivalrous, for God's sweet sake. And sweet and touching and rare as an honest politician. Anyway, I told him I wouldn't lie to you, which is the only reason I'm telling you all this right now. But I think you oughta stop being such a bonehead and at least talk to the guy."

She listened again and scowled. Maxine was using diversionary tactics, and Polly didn't want to talk about Turner; she didn't want to think about him; she certainly didn't want to dream about him the way she did most nights. And she *really* didn't want to explain to her friends that she still hadn't made one iota of headway with the seduction thing. It was humiliating.

"No," she snapped in answer to Maxine's question. "I haven't heard more than two sentences from him for three days. He's busy delivering babies—people must have been screwing like rabbits last November. Anyway, to hell with him. I'm not wasting any more time waiting; I'm not getting any younger. There's a new attorney over at Morgan and Jones. He asked me for a drink after work, and I'm gonna go."

Polly listened again and fumbled among the

scraps of paper on her desk. "I don't know what his name is; I must have it written down here somewhere. I'll just call him 'sweetie' if I can't remember."

Shirley poked her head in and made significant faces, and Polly nodded at her and said to Maxine, "Gotta go—my three-o'clock appointment's here. And take the advice of your attorney, okay? Call Harry."

Slowly Maxine hung up. As she'd just told Polly, Harry Watson was not an honest man. But it was impossible to stop the warm and tender feelings that had come over her when Polly told her this latest evidence of his generosity and concern.

It was also impossible not to remember that he was a fantastic and imaginative lover, a wonderful, caring father.

Kind, her rebellious brain added to the list; *don't forget kind. Attractive*, she admitted reluctantly. Even handsome, when he remembered to shave.

Devious, she reminded herself.

Fluent at lying.

And impossible to forget, she confessed sadly. The bond between her and Harry had gone deeper than just sexual pleasure. He'd wormed his way into her heart and soul, and try as she might, she couldn't displace him.

She'd had a lot of time to think lately, too

much, in fact. Polly had moved back to her apartment, and Edna had received her settlement. Maxine was deeply touched when the older woman offered to go on working until Maxine could find and train someone new.

Maxine refused, of course. There was no point; the simple truth was that the business had died a natural death.

After a week with no calls, she'd canceled the 900 number. Soon, very soon, she was going to have to find day care for Graham and search for a job. She kept putting it off, unable to summon the energy necessary to make the effort.

Edna offered both money and free day care, but again, Maxine gently and gratefully refused, except for the two nights a week she attended night school.

She had enough money in her savings account to last two months, and she was going to take a little break, a sort of holiday, she lied to Edna.

The truth was, she couldn't dredge up enough energy to even think about what to do next. She spent the days caring for Graham, taking him for long walks, planting a late garden in the backyard, and trying not to think about either Harry or her aimless life.

Trouble was, there wasn't a whole lot else to do these days but think. Maxine kept the house tidy, worried over bills, made a lot of soup, weeded the sad excuse for a garden, and cared for Graham, who was napping at the moment. Caring for a year-old baby, although physically challenging at times, wasn't exactly brain surgery. It left a great deal of time for contemplation.

Thinking about Harry had forced her to consider a lot of other things, such as how she'd come to fall in love with Ricky Shwartz in the first place, and what demon kept her from accepting the profuse apologies Harry had gone to such lengths to make.

Once she'd gone beyond blaming Ricky, and Harry, and everyone else she could think of for her misfortunes, there was no one left to consider except herself and her own deep lack of self-esteem.

Why had she made such a mess of her relationships with men? The question invariably led her back to the first man in her life: Zacharias Bleckner, her father.

She thought of the little girl she'd been, and her heart hurt at the painful memory of how hard she'd tried to please Zacharias, all to no avail.

She'd watched Harry with Sadie. He'd given her a picture of how a father could be with his daughter. It wasn't at all the way her father had been with her.

She couldn't remember Zacharias ever complimenting her. She didn't remember a single spontaneous embrace, or a time when she'd wanted to run toward him in greeting.

She'd heard Harry tell Sadie countless times how pretty she looked.

Zacharias had only criticized.

She'd heard Harry tell Sadie how much he loved her.

Zacharias had never once let Maxine know he cared.

The specter of her father was a roadblock to every relationship she would ever have with a man, Maxine concluded. And now she had a son to consider. Would her own insecurities rub off on him unless she did something radical about them?

There wasn't any detour around the problem. She was going to have to meet it head-on, and try to dismantle it.

She swallowed hard as the truth she'd done her best to avoid smacked her between the eyes.

She was going to have to see her father again, and try to make peace with him. There was no other way, and the very thought terrified her so much, she kept shying away from it.

Zacharias had no idea he had a grandson. She could predict what he'd say when he found out she was a single parent. God, it was so much easier just to let things stay the way they were, with no contact.

But easier wasn't always better. It was going to have to be done, and there was no time like right now to do it.

She reached for the phone three times before she could make herself dial the number that had always been there in the hidden recesses of her mind.

She heard the ringing begin and she prayed passionately that he wouldn't be home.

"Hello?" The familiar gruff voice made Maxine jump, and she almost dropped the phone. Her throat closed and she couldn't speak.

"Hello, who is this?" There was a note of impatience in Zacharias's voice that she was all too familiar with.

She closed her eyes and cleared her throat, gulped twice, and then said the hardest words she'd ever had to say.

"Hello, Papa. It's me. It's Maxine."

Chapter Twenty-one

Two days later, when he came walking toward her at the airport, Maxine's first thought was how old he'd become.

She remembered him as a tall, muscular man. He was still tall, but now his wide shoulders were stooped, and under the worn black suit and stiffly starched white shirt, his body was stringy.

"Hello, daughter." His deep, distinctive voice, as always, was portentous and stern, but Zacharias's faded blue gaze wasn't on her. Graham, heavy in her trembling arms, had been squirming to get down. Now he was still. He was staring, eyes round and curious, straight back at his grandfather.

Bobby Hutchinson

"Hello, Papa. This is my son, Graham."

Zacharias's hand rose slowly, seemingly of its own accord, and one finger gently touched Graham's cheek.

"Hello there, boy." The words were choked. Could there be a trace of moisture in her father's eyes?

She had to be mistaken. "How was the flight, Papa?" She was finding it hard to talk. Her throat felt constricted, and her entire body was shaking. She hoped he wouldn't notice. She didn't want him to know how terrified she felt. She'd vowed to be totally honest with him, radically honest, but she'd also promised herself she wouldn't be apologetic for a single thing. Her life was her life, and it was up to him to accept it.

But it was easier to make vows alone in the middle of the night than to live up to them in the light of day, she admitted now.

"Takes longer for me to drive to the airport than to get here on the plane," he grumbled in answer to her question. "Now where's the suitcase I gave them?"

Maxine indicated which way to go to the luggage carousel, wondering if she'd made a terrible mistake by inviting him to visit. But she hadn't felt there was a choice; there were too many important things to be said for a telephone call. And she'd wanted him to see Graham. She was proud of her baby. There was a

268

part of her that desperately wanted her father
to acknowledge how beautiful her child was.

"Can't that boy walk?" Zacharias was striding
along, and Maxine was having a hard time keeping up. Graham was heavy.

"Yes, he can walk." Instantly defensive, Maxine hugged Graham closer to her and glared at
her father. "But not in a place like this, he
learned how only a little while ago, and he's still
a bit unsteady."

"Give him to me, then."

It was the last thing Maxine wanted to do. It
felt like handing her baby over to the enemy.
"He'll make a fuss," she protested.

"No, he won't." Zacharias made a dismissive
noise in his throat that she remembered very
well. It had always made her feel as if her opinions were trivial. "I'm his grandfather. Give him
here, Maxine."

Short of making a scene, there was nothing
she could do. Reluctantly she handed Graham
over, hoping he'd scream bloody murder.

He stiffened, and for a long, considering moment, he studied Zacharias's face. Then he
looked for Maxine and gave her a tentative
smile and waved his fist at her before sticking a
curious finger into Zacharias's ear.

Maxine felt totally betrayed.

They reached the parking garage and the Toyota.

"Don't you lock the car doors?" Zacharias

gave the battered vehicle a frowning once-over and gingerly climbed in.

"The lock on the driver's side is broken. I figure nobody will steal it if there's something better around."

"Hmmmph." The sound indicated exactly what Zacharias thought of the car, and of her reasoning.

At home she fed Graham and put him down for his nap, and then served the lunch she'd sweated over earlier that morning.

"Can't eat green onions," Zacharias immediately declared, picking them out of the egg salad. "Soup could use a dash of salt." He emptied most of the shaker into it.

Maxine held her tongue.

"You own this house, daughter?"

"No, Papa. I rent it."

"How much?"

She told him, muscles tensed for the inevitable critical reply.

"Blessed heaven." He swiveled his head around, taking stock. "That much, for *this* tumbledown place?" That throat sound again, making her cringe. "And what are the utilities?"

She told him, adding, "You want some tea, Papa? I usually drink herbal, but I've got regular." She thought longingly of the brandy. She could use a shot.

"Never drink tea. Coffee either. Bothers my stomach. Only Postum. You got any Postum?"

She didn't.

"Piece of apple pie, Papa?" She'd slaved over the damned pie most of last evening.

He accepted, and after the first bite announced that it was too tart for his liking. He liked his pie sweet.

She sweetly wondered which blunt object might be best to use on his head. At least now she was beyond nervous and well into outraged. She gulped chamomile tea and tried not to think about the four endless days and one eternity of an afternoon that remained of his visit.

"And who's the boy's father?"

She'd known it was coming. She took a deep breath and explained, without apology, about Ricky. She'd made a vow about honesty, so she went into detail about the money she'd loaned him, and about Polly's efforts to get it back, and when she was finished she felt proud of herself.

"Hmmmph."

That noise again, but for some reason it didn't bother her as much as it always had. And to her amazement, he didn't lecture or even comment on what she'd revealed.

"I think I'll go for a walk," he announced instead. "Always walk after lunch, and then have a little liedown. Not as young as I once was."

With profound gratitude for the respite, Maxine saw him out the door and told him where the nearby park was. He disappeared down the street and she took two aspirin for the headache pounding at her temples and decided she needed a little liedown herself. She hadn't slept more than an hour last night, contemplating this visit.

She glanced in Graham's room, thankful that he was sound asleep, padded bottom in the air and thumb firmly plugged in his rosy mouth.

She went into her bedroom and collapsed on the bed.

Zacharias could get lost wandering around Burnaby alone, she thought drowsily. Her last thought before she fell deeply asleep was that she should be so lucky.

The house was silent when she swam up to drowsy consciousness. Graham and her father must still be asleep.

She rolled over and looked at the clock, and then sprang up so fast the room tilted and whirled.

Twenty to six. She'd been asleep almost four hours. Graham never slept this long. She raced along the hall, into his bedroom.

The crib was empty.

So was the rest of the house. Zacharias's bed was mussed, as if he'd lain there, but he was gone.

In the kitchen, two empty jars of baby food, spilled milk, and clumps of bread on the floor by the high chair told her that, incredibly, her father must have fed Graham. A sodden diaper in the bathtub showed that he'd also changed him.

The stroller was missing from the front porch.

Unbelievable as it seemed, Zacharias had taken Graham for a walk. Dazed, Maxine sloshed water on her face and brushed her hair. She put on a fresh tee and a pair of clean shorts and cut up the chicken and prepared the vegetables for dinner, pausing every few minutes to peer anxiously through the window.

The chicken was baked and the vegetables ready by the time she heard them coming up the front walk.

She flew to the door.

Graham's face, hands, and clothes were covered with a gooey mixture of chocolate and ice cream and something red. One shoe was off, and he was banging on the front of the stroller with both chubby hands, making his car noises.

Zacharias still wore his three-piece black suit, but he'd added a straw hat. His face was magenta, and sweat trickled down his temples. He had a huge carrier bag balanced on the stroller's handles, and a large plastic grocery sack in one hand.

"Papa, where on earth did you go with him? I've been worried sick," Maxine blurted.

"Went to find a store to buy Postum. Don't just stand there, girl; come and take this sack. It's hot as Hades out here. Thought Vancouver

273

was supposed to have a marine climate."

Defiantly, Maxine knelt by the stroller and started unbuckling Graham, but Zacharias shoved the bag at her before she could lift the baby out.

"Leave him alone; do those straps up again. We're gonna go in the backyard and blow up this wading pool and fill it with water. Boy needs a place to splash around in this heat."

Maxine felt instantly guilty. She hadn't even thought of getting Graham a wading pool. She'd been watching her money too closely to consider buying anything except diapers and food and Kleenex.

"Dinner's ready."

Zacharias shook his head. "Not hungry—we had hot dogs and fries. Likes fries with ketchup, this fellow."

Maxine opened her mouth to say that she didn't believe in feeding Graham junk food, but she closed it again.

Once wouldn't hurt, and anyway, what good would it do to object? Her father wouldn't pay one iota of attention to anything she said. He never had.

"Well, I'm going to eat." She realized she was starving. She flounced into the house. The grocery sack contained milk, bread and butter, pork chops and a roast, toilet tissue, and a jar of Postum.

Maxine put the groceries away and filled a

plate, then sat alone at the kitchen table, aware of water running in the backyard and then squeals of excitement from Graham.

Damn. She wasn't as hungry as she'd thought. She set the plate aside and went out to see what was happening.

The wading pool had several inches of water in it, and Graham, stripped to his diaper, was standing inside it, squealing and frenziedly splashing.

Zacharias had dragged a chunk of wood over and was perched on it, his long, bony bare feet in the pool. He looked ridiculous, still wearing the straw hat and the black suit, shirt buttoned tight up to his Adam's apple. But he'd rolled the trousers up almost to his knees.

Maxine went inside and filled two glasses with instant lemonade. She added ice and took them outside, handing one to her father and holding the second so her son could take huge, choking gulps. She sat down on the grass and pulled her knees to her chin.

"You need lawn chairs out here," Zacharias complained. "Garden isn't looking too good, either. Needs water and some fertilizer, ask me."

Maxine had had about enough of his criticism. She took a swallow of the lemonade to fortify herself.

"I suppose there's lots of things I need, Papa. But I don't have money to buy them."

"On welfare, are you?" The very way he said

it made it sound as if it was all he expected of her.

Instead of feeling hurt, Maxine exploded. "No, damn it, I'm not on welfare. Don't you think I have enough gumption to support myself and my son?"

Gumption? My God. She was even using his vocabulary.

His bushy eyebrows shot up. "No need to blaspheme, Maxine."

"I'll damn well swear if I feel like it, I'm a grown woman, Papa. You can't tell me how to act or talk, or . . . or what I should be thinking. Not anymore." It felt good to holler at him, but Graham was staring at her, eyes startled and chocolate-covered chin quivering. She gave him a strained smile and lowered her voice.

"Until a few weeks ago, I had my own business. I ran it out of this house so I could take care of Graham. I even had a woman working for me. I managed to save a bit of money. But then I couldn't do it anymore, so I gave it up. I only have enough money saved to pay the bills for another two months, so I'm going to have to look for good day care for Graham and find a job. I'm going to night school. I want to eventually work in radio as an announcer, but it'll take a while to earn a living at that."

"Hmmph. What kind of business were you running?"

Here it was. She hadn't planned to tell him

just yet, but why not? The moment he heard the truth, he'd leave, and good riddance. Despite his surprising acceptance of Graham, she couldn't take any more of his jibes.

Hearing that she'd done phone sex might even give him a heart attack, a cautionary voice inside her warned, and she hesitated for a moment before blurting it out.

Well, there was another way to tell him. She got to her feet and hurried into the house, coming out a moment later with the article Harry had written. She'd kept it as a bitter reminder to herself that men weren't to be trusted.

She thrust the paper at Zacharias. "I'm the woman in this story, Papa."

He frowned at her, confused. Then he fumbled in his jacket and pulled out a pair of reading glasses, taped together at the bridge. It seemed to take forever for him to position them on his nose. At last he tipped his head back and peered down at the paper.

Maxine felt giddy and sick at the same time. She went over to her son, lifting him up and letting him splash his feet in the water. His solid little body was comforting. Graham giggled and Maxine cooed to him, but her heart was hammering against her ribs, and she was horribly aware of her father's impassive face as he slowly read, turning methodically to the inside section.

God, how long could it take him? How long before he stood up and waved a fist in the air, the way she'd seen him do so often when she was a child, sitting in the front pew cowering at his hellfire-and-damnation sermons?

She could hear her neighbors on one side, laughing and talking as they barbecued. Across the alley children hollered as they bounced on a trampoline. All of them were going to hear Zacharias loud and clear when he blew, she thought dismally. Her father had a good voice for preaching and ranting, deep and resonant and carrying. She'd never thought about it, but it was probably where she'd inherited her own distinctive vocal cords.

She pretended to be totally absorbed with Graham, but every nerve ending was alert and waiting.

Silence. She stole a sidelong glance at Zacharias.

The newspaper had fallen on the grass. He was absolutely still. His chin was lowered, the hat pulled down over his eyes.

It dawned on her that he was probably praying for her immortal soul. This was only the calm before the storm.

She remembered how he used to make her wait this way when she'd done something he disapproved of. She remembered shaking so hard she couldn't stand, even wetting her pants when she was really little.

It was emotional blackmail, and she wasn't going to let him get away with it, not anymore.

Chapter Twenty-two

"Well, Papa?" She was proud of sounding both defiant and confrontational. If he was going to holler, she'd holler too.

He lifted his head and looked at her, and she couldn't believe her own eyes. Tears were rolling slowly down his face, getting caught in the deep wrinkles around his nose and mouth. He sniffed, then sniffed again.

"I failed you, Maxine." His voice was thick, and he fumbled in the pocket of his vest and pulled out an old-fashioned snowy handkerchief, the same kind she'd ironed for him countless times when she was a little girl aching for his approval. He mopped his face and blew his nose, a harsh, prolonged honk that made Graham jump and then giggle.

"Why didn't you come home, daughter? You got yourself in trouble; you should've come home"—he gestured at the newspaper—"instead of doing *that*."

Speechless, Maxine stared at him. She'd never once even considered going home. She'd known all too well what her reception would have been.

Zacharias obviously read in her face what she was thinking, because his face flushed and he nodded and dropped his gaze.

"It's a small town," he said rhetorically. "People talk; I'm the minister; there have to be standards."

You've made your bed; now lie in it. He'd left out that part. She remembered all the words vividly, because they were what she'd heard all her life, the very reason she'd left when she did, the same reason she'd never returned. But the way he said them this time was different, as if he might suspect they had flaws.

"The prodigal son came home, and was met with rejoicing," he said softly. "You might have given me a chance, at least, Maxine."

"Oh, Papa." Feeling frustrated and confused, she realized that once again he'd found a way to blame her, even if it wasn't for what she'd expected. She didn't know what to say to him. If she had gone home, she knew her reception would have been the nightmare she imagined.

But then, how could she be certain? It was obvious that Zacharias needed to think otherwise, and what was the point of arguing? It was a hypothetical situation. This was here and now.

"I'm taking this little guy inside—he needs his diaper changed." She scooped Graham more firmly into her arms. "Do you want any dinner, Papa, or should I just put it away?"

"No, no. I'm coming in now." He got up, scuffing his feet on the grass to dry them. He picked up his shoes and socks, Graham's clothing, and the newspaper. He folded the paper carefully, and then followed her inside in silence.

Maxine bathed Graham and fed him dinner. Zacharias was quiet. He made a pretense of eating, but Maxine noticed the food on his plate was untouched. He watched the television news and was seemingly deep into *Law and Order* while she was putting Graham to bed.

Zacharias looked away from the television when she came tiptoeing out of the baby's room. "You always rock the boy to sleep?"

"Always." She sighed, waiting for the lecture on child rearing she was sure would follow.

"Your mother did that with you." The words were terse, but there was no criticism in them.

"I remember." Tears sprang to her eyes. There was also much about her mother she didn't know, things she longed to ask.

Bobby Hutchinson

Zacharias surprised her again. "I brought some old picture albums for you," he said. "The boy should know where he comes from. I'll get them."

It was hard to look at the yellowed photos, images of her parents, her grandparents, herself as a baby and a young girl. The last photo of Maxine had been taken on her sixteenth birthday. She traced her finger over the smiling young girl with the unruly hair.

"Your mother was always the picture taker," Zacharias said almost defensively. "I never held much with that sort of thing."

Maxine's throat was thick with tears. "Thank you so much for bringing me these, Papa." It was hard to believe he'd been so thoughtful. "I'll treasure them; it means so much to me to have them."

"Hmmmph. They were in that drawer in the sideboard. I never bother with them."

Judging by the well-worn pages, Maxine didn't think that was strictly true, but she didn't say anything.

"I want to talk to you, daughter." He sat up straighter in the armchair, and she waited silently, heart sinking. Maybe the showdown had only been postponed.

"I want to pay for this night school you're taking, and send you an allowance each month to live on," he began, holding up a hand in the imperious way he'd always used to stop her from saying anything.

Not that she was about to; she could feel her jaw hanging open and she closed her mouth abruptly.

"I have a fair bit of money from investments over the years. It'll go to you and the boy anyway, when I'm gone. Might as well make use of it now when you need it." He scowled ferociously at her. "And don't argue, Maxine. My mind is made up."

She opened her mouth to refuse and saw the vulnerable look in his eyes. He needed to help her, she suddenly realized. He cared about her. It wasn't the way she wanted him to care, but maybe it was the only way he knew how.

And she had no doubts at all about his feelings for Graham. She'd brought the baby, bathed and in fresh blue pajamas, to say good night. Zacharias had smiled, taken him in his arms, and kissed him soundly, once on each cheek, and then he'd actually closed his eyes and cuddled him against his chest for the moment Graham allowed it.

She had to accept. "Thank you, Papa. I appreciate it very much. It's really generous of you."

The surprise on his craggy face was almost funny. He'd fully expected an argument.

"Well, then," he said gruffly. "We won't speak of it again." He turned back to the television, and Maxine watched him instead of the screen. Maybe the rest of the visit wouldn't be as bad as she'd feared.

A commercial came on, and he turned to her. "The locks on your doors are a disgrace, Maxine. Same as the car. It's careless of you and dangerous not to protect the boy better than that. I'm calling a locksmith first thing in the morning. And when was the last time that car had an oil change? Motor sounds like a washing machine. An ounce of prevention is worth a pound of cure, I always say."

He always had said that. He had a million such sayings, all of which seemed designed to drive her wacky. She knew she was going to hear every single one in the endless days ahead.

She gritted her teeth and used her fingers to count the number of days remaining in his visit, and she wished with all her heart that there were someone else around, someone who'd know how to buffer the sharp edges between her and her difficult father.

"The man who wrote that article in the paper. You knew him well?"

Maxine jumped. It was as if Zacharias had read her mind and then gone one step farther.

"Yes, I did."

"Was he, one of your . . . your, ummm, your callers . . . ?"

"Yes. No." She took a shaky breath and wondered how best to describe Harry to her father.

284

"He did call, but he wasn't at all like the others. I thought at first he was a gentleman. But then he . . . he . . ."

"Lied to you, did he?" Her father's expression was thunderous. "Can't abide liars; it's the worst sin."

Maxine thought it over. She was seeing things in a strange new way tonight. "Actually, Papa, Harry told me the truth."

And maybe that was why she couldn't seem to forget him.

Chapter Twenty-three

"But I wanna see *Graym*, Daddy." Sadie's bottom lip stuck out, and she gave Harry an accusing look. "Why can't I see *Graym*? You know how to *drive* to his house, so lets go. Now."

Harry sighed and searched for an explanation that would stop her incessant nagging. "Graham's mommy is mad at me, punkin. She doesn't want me to come to her house."

"Well, '*pologize*, Daddy. Say you're sorry and you won't do it again."

"I tried that, Sadie. It didn't work."

"Try *again*. You always say to me, try *again*."

He had tried, numerous times. He'd finally admitted that the next move had to be Maxine's. He stared down into his stubborn daughter's

286

eyes and, coward that he was, felt immeasurably relieved when the phone rang.

"How about drawing a picture, sweetheart?" He shoved a pad of paper and ink markers at Sadie. "We can send it to Graham, okay?"

Grudgingly she nodded, and with a sigh of relief he picked up the phone. "Hello?"

The woman on the other end said she was calling from Seattle. "I read your article on phone sex?" she began.

He felt like vomiting. The feature had been picked up and reprinted by newspapers and magazines on both sides of the border. Harry had already made more money on it than he ever had on a single piece, and not an hour passed in which he wished to God he'd never written it.

"I'd rather not tell you my name," she said in answer to his question. "But I do happen to know the guy you mentioned in the article, Ricky Shwartz?"

Harry's hand tightened on the receiver and he started to sweat. The bitterness in her voice and the way she said the name told him that it was no longer the love match of the century; obviously she was royally pissed off with Shwartz.

His toes curled inside his shoes. It took effort to keep his voice calm. "You don't happen to know where he is now, do you?"

"Yeah, matter of fact, I do." There was vindictiveness and triumph in her tone. "That's why I called you, actually. Until a couple weeks ago, I was with that louse, until the night I found out he was double-dipping. He's not in Costa Rica like you said in the article, either, the lying SOB. We never went there at all. He's at a ski resort in the B.C. Rockies, a town called Fernie. He bought a Cessna. He flies in skiers in the winter and fishermen in the summer, but I don't know how long he'll stay there. He's got a new pal and she's married. I think he's planning on moving before her husband catches on." She made a sad noise that should have been a laugh. "Which might be real soon, because I just called the poor sucker."

"D'you know where Shwartz is staying?"

"He's got a basement suite; here's the address and phone number." She read them off and Harry copied them down. He thanked her profusely, heart thumping with excitement. The cursed article might do some good for Maxine after all. He hung up and frantically searched his address book for Polly's cell number.

"I made this for Graym, Daddy." Sadie held up a vivid red and purple abstract.

"That's beautiful, honey. He'll love it." He had a sense of urgency now. "Daddy has to make one more phone call, so you do another picture for Mrs. Campanato, okay?"

Sadie gave him a look and shook her head. "I did her lots already. I'm gonna make one for

Maxine. To tell her you're sorry, Daddy. Then she'll like you again, right?"

He swallowed hard and gave his optimistic angel a wry smile. "Hope springs eternal, kiddo. You never know your luck." He found the number, picked up the phone, and dialed.

Polly's cell was ringing, and it felt like a reprieve. Bruce was sitting next to her, on her sofa in her apartment. He was asking her to have sex with him, but now *she* was the one having second thoughts. He was really scaring her, damn his unpredictable hide.

She'd been about to head off to work an hour ago when he appeared at her door, blond hair rumpled, brown eyes bloodshot, jaw sprouting stubble. He'd been up all night delivering a baby girl, he explained, and he'd stopped off on the chance that maybe she had some strong coffee brewed. But if she was just about to go to work, he added, he'd head home and get some sleep.

There was something about him, an elusive expression in his eyes, a certain tone to his voice, that kept her from snapping out that that yes, she *was* going to work, and maybe he ought to have accepted her invitation to *coffee,* and what that stood for, the last time they'd been out together.

Instead she invited him in and poured him a cup from the pot she'd made earlier that morning. She called the office and had her secretary cancel her ten-o'clock appointment. Eleven as well, she added on impulse. Maybe, just maybe, the guy had come to his senses at last. She wasn't averse to morning sex—not at all.

Bruce didn't say anything at first. He gulped the coffee and walked around her living room, but she didn't think he was really noticing anything, which was probably a blessing, because she hadn't picked up the slacks, bra, and underpants she'd discarded on the rug when she got home from work yesterday. Not that they really stood out amongst the rest of the litter. Even without her leg in a cast, she wasn't the tidiest person in the world, but then, he wasn't exactly moving in, so what did it matter?

"You're probably wondering what I'm doing here," he said a bare second before she was about to ask. "See, we nearly lost the baby's mother."

For an instant Polly didn't get it. She was thinking *lost* as in *misplaced* and thinking, *Isn't that typical of a bloody hospital?* But the expression in his eyes brought sudden, shocking understanding, and without another thought, she made her clumsy way over to him and put her arms around him, letting the crutches fall where they would.

"That must have been so scary." She could smell hospital on him, but for some reason it didn't even bother her.

"It was." The words began slowly and then

accelerated. "The pregnancy was very high-risk—she has a heart condition. I advised against her getting pregnant in the first place, but she wanted this baby so much."

She felt the shudder go through him.

"It was close, too close." His strong arms were supporting her, although she had the strangest feeling it was she holding him up. "It was a brave and foolhardy thing for her to do, having this little girl. Beautiful baby, but what a price."

Polly thought about the woman. "I think I'd do the same."

There was a pause, and then he said in a different tone, "*You* want babies that much?"

"Yup." The yearning in her voice surprised her. "More than almost anything."

His mouth was close to her ear. "Enough to take a chance on commitment, Polly?"

She stiffened and moved away from him, hopping on one leg over to the nearby sofa and plunking down, scowling up at him. She was having trouble getting her breath. "Just what do you mean by that?"

He rubbed his tired eyes with his fingers and sat down beside her. "Only that as soon as someone gets close or shows signs of caring about you, you dump them."

"How do you know that?" Her temper flared. "*You* should talk about getting close. *You're* the one who avoids sex as if I had some contagious disease."

"Yeah, and it's almost killing me. See, I don't want to lose you, Polly, and that's exactly what would happen if I took you to bed."

She sputtered out a denial, but it didn't sound very authentic, and he didn't buy it.

"I happen to think we could be good together," he went on as if she hadn't made a sound. "Really good." His voice was firm and a little wistful. "But you'd have to commit to staying around long enough to get to know me. You'd have to trust, and that's a big learning curve." He held her stormy gaze, even though she was shooting killer rays at him with her eyes. "I know, because you and I are alike, Polly. I went along for years doing exactly what you do, love 'em and leave 'em before they had a chance to do it to me."

She wanted to laugh and say that he didn't know the first thing about her, but she couldn't. His words, his assessment of her, went straight to the place inside where the truth lived. On some level, she'd known for a long time what she was doing. She just hadn't been able to look at it and stop.

"How brave are you, Polly? Will you commit to more than sex with me?" There wasn't a trace of teasing or laughter in his voice or in his eyes. "Getting naked physically is easy. It's getting naked emotionally that takes guts and fortitude."

She wanted him more than she'd ever wanted anyone. She wanted to step off the cliff and agree to what he was proposing, but the fear was overwhelming, and before she could face it, she heard the cell phone in her handbag start to ring.

Chapter Twenty-four

Bruce got up and got Polly's bag for her. He sat down and waited patiently as she spoke at length to Harry.

"I have to go to the office," she said when she hung up. "A man I've been searching for has surfaced, and I have to have him served quickly, before I lose him again."

He nodded. He looked disappointed, but resigned.

She took a deep, shaky breath. "I'll be a couple hours at least." It took all her courage to add, "I don't suppose you could stay here and wait for me? The bed isn't made, but the sheets are clean."

The look in his eyes sent a shudder through her.

"Unless one of my patients decides to go into labor, I'll be waiting in your bed when you get back. No matter how long it takes."

And then he kissed her, and one tiny strand of the huge ball of fear inside her began to slowly unravel.

Edna dropped by two days after Zacharias finally left. She rang the doorbell just after Graham went down for his afternoon nap, and Maxine was pathetically glad to see her. Having her father stay for ten days had taken its toll.

"You look absolutely fantastic." Maxine studied the older woman. "You've lost weight. That dress looks great on you—where'd you get it?"

It was a robin's egg–blue silk shirtdress, with a daring slit that showed off shapely legs Edna had been hiding.

"Polly saw it in a window downtown and practically ordered me to buy it." Edna's clear skin glowed, and her gray eyes sparkled. "She told me the wonderful news about locating Ricky Shwartz and getting your money back, and I wanted to say congratulations and tell you how thrilled I am for you." She handed Maxine a huge bouquet of deep blue irises, already arranged in a tall copper container.

"Oh, Edna, thank you. They're so beautiful."

Maxine set the flowers on top of the bookcase. "I'm lucky to have a friend like you." She led the way into the kitchen. As she made tea and set out chocolate biscuits, she gave Edna the highlights of her father's visit.

"He was going to stay only five days, but somehow it got extended to ten." She explained how generous Zacharias had been financially, related his surprising reaction to the news that his daughter had supported herself by doing phone sex, and confessed how difficult it had been to keep from losing her temper and thumping him.

"He criticized, complained about everything, repaired things that weren't broken, sharpened every knife in the house so that now I keep cutting myself, and spoiled Graham so badly I can hardly stand him. He's taken to throwing himself on the floor and kicking and screaming if he doesn't get his own way, and if he wakes up at night he has a fit if I don't appear instantly."

Edna laughed. "Sounds like his grandpa did a good job on him." She bit into her cookie. "I'm so glad things turned out the way they did with your dad, Maxine."

"Me too. I still have issues with him, but we also have something in common. He thinks the sun shines out of Graham's eyes, and when the kid's not being a tyrant, I think so too."

Zacharias's visit had healed sore places inside her. The ones that were still bleeding had nothing to do with her father. "And how about you, Edna? How're things with your sons?"

Coached by their father, Edna's boys had both confronted her, angry and accusing, after finding out about the phone sex.

"Gary's still pretty mad at me, but Marshall comes by and visits. He's beginning to realize his father isn't always right. Marshall's got a girlfriend John doesn't approve of." She smiled and shook her head. "And some of his friends have told him they figure it's cool to have a mother who actually did phone sex, so that's helping things along as well."

They laughed and Maxine asked, "What's happening with the personal ads?"

"I've met three nice men," Edna said nonchalantly. "I've dated all of them, but there's one, Stephen, whom I particularly like. He's a retired doctor. He's invited me to go on a cruise with him to Portugal." She blushed. "Sex with him is fantastic, and conversation isn't so bad either."

Maxine laughed, but Edna's words evoked painful memories of Harry. They'd also shared good conversation and great sex. Something wistful must have shown on her face, because Edna said softly, "Have you heard from him?"

Maxine shook her head. "Graham's gotten several pictures in the mail from Sadie, but that's it."

"Call him." Edna reached out and put a hand

on Maxine's arm. "It's only because of Harry's article that Polly found Shwartz. At least you owe him a thank-you."

Maxine nodded. She'd been dithering about it for days. "I'm scared," she admitted now. "I'm afraid that he'll hang up on me the way I did with him." And if he did, her heart would truly break. She took a breath and blurted out the other half of it. "With him, I'm Maxine, but I'm India as well. That wild, out-of-control part of me is right there when I'm with Harry, and it scares me." She gave Edna a beseeching look. "You understand, don't you?" Edna was probably the only one who *could* understand. She was Lilith as well as Edna.

Edna nodded. "The hardest thing I've ever done was let Stephen see who I really am. I thought it would drive him away, being radically honest, telling him about the phone sex, telling him I *enjoyed* being Lilith. But I had to do it, to be true to myself." Her smile was radiant. "He loved it. And I think I'm starting to love *him*, and I'm so happy I go around singing all the time." She patted Maxine's hand. "You were happy like that when you were with Harry. Call him, Maxine. You'll always regret it if you don't."

Edna left, and Graham woke from his nap. For the remainder of the afternoon Maxine busied herself with laundry, ironing, weeding the garden, making a summer stew. She made certain she was too busy to make a phone call.

But inevitably evening arrived, Graham went to bed, and things were quiet. Maxine, palms sweaty and heart hammering, knew the time had come. It was a warm summer night, but she was shivering as she lifted the receiver and dialed.

He answered almost instantly.

"Hello?"

His voice set off explosive reactions in her, a rush of warmth, a sense of dread, terrible longing, and fear that gave way to certainty. She hadn't planned it, but now she knew what she had to do. Courage came, and with it, a tiny measure of confidence.

"This is India McBride, Harry."

He made a startled sound and began to say something, but she interrupted, her voice low and smooth and sexy. "I want you just to listen to me, please. There are things I need you to hear."

His silence told her he was paying close attention.

She closed her eyes and let herself recognize her truths. "When Maxine first created me, we both thought it was because she needed the money. She did, but that wasn't all of it, Harry. See, she was always ashamed of me. I was this lush, sensual, outrageous part of her, and she was scared that if she let me out, no man would really love her the way she longed to be loved.

299

Because I'm bad, I want to do all the nasty, delicious things Maxine was taught were sinful."

This was hard. It was like exposing her plump naked belly to a photographer. "But I'm part of her, Harry, an important part. And by doing phone sex, we got to know each other and she realized I wasn't so bad after all. We weren't exactly soul mates, but we got to be friends. And then you came along, Harry. And Maxine and I both fell crazily in love with you, and for the first time the two parts came together. But loving and trusting are two different things. When the stuff came up about the article, it was easier not to trust you, just in case . . ." Her sexy India voice wavered and she became Maxine, insecure, shy. "Just in case you didn't love me back."

Tears were close, and the tissues were in the kitchen. She sniffled and swallowed and blurted out the rest. "I've made peace with my father. I'm changing my job. I think I know myself now, for the first time. But life's empty and awful without you and Sadie. See, I love you with all my heart, Harry." Her belly was in knots as she waited for him to say something. It took a couple of long, agonizing seconds for her to realize the line was dead.

She stared at the silent phone in disbelief. He'd hung up on her. She'd gambled and lost, and she hadn't even gotten around to saying thank you to him for locating Shwartz.

Damn. Waves of desolation rolled over her,

too intense even for tears. The future stretched ahead, long and straight and dusty, devoid of Harry, and she tried to tell herself that it would get easier than this—it had to, but she couldn't begin to believe it.

After a while she got to her feet and stumbled into the kitchen, but tea didn't hold any appeal. She opened the cupboard and searched for the brandy bottle. There were a few pathetic drops in the very bottom. She couldn't even get dramatically and tragically drunk.

The only thing left was a hot bath; her knees were grubby from gardening and her nails had dirt underneath them. She headed down the hall and turned the water on, but before she could get her shorts off, the front doorbell rang.

To hell with them, whoever they are. She couldn't imagine talking to anyone right now.

It pealed again, and yet again, and at last she turned the taps off and stomped back down the hallway.

She jerked the door open and her mouth dropped as her heart rose.

"Harry? Oh, God, Harry, come in."

He had a blanket-swathed Sadie asleep on his shoulder, and he walked over and gently put her down on the sofa. Then, less gently, he pulled Maxine into his arms and kissed her hard before he dropped on one knee to the carpet.

"Before another single thing happens to interrupt us, will you marry me, Maxine? Because

I love everything about you, the stubborn part, the shy part, the part of you that's insecure. I love Graham. And India. God, Maxine, I *love* the part of you that's India. So what do ya say? Will you marry me?"

His chin was covered with stubble, and his jeans were stained with what might have been spaghetti. He'd been running his fingers through his hair, and it stood up in a rooster's comb on the back of his head.

He was the most desirable man she'd ever seen in her entire life, and she wanted him so badly her thighs quivered. The kids were asleep, her bedroom was just down the hall, and they had the whole long night ahead of them.

"I will, Harry. I want you. Yes, I'll marry you."

Sadie stirred and sat up, rubbed her eyes, and peered around. "Daddy, you *'pologized*. Hi, Maxine. Where's Graym?"

Down the hall, a whimper began and escalated rapidly into a roar of outrage.

Maxine looked at Harry, and together they started to laugh. With two little kids around, making it to the bedroom was going to present a challenge. But they were equal to it, and they had time on their side.

They had a whole long lifetime ahead of them.

Don't miss this uproariously funny
novel from bestselling author

KATIE MacALISTER

Move over, Bridget Jones. Alexandra Freemar has
taken over London, where she has two months to write
the perfect romance novel. But even though she may
know every imaginable euphemism for the male
member, she has a lot to learn about love.

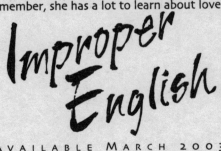

AVAILABLE MARCH 2003!

Chapter One

Lady Rowena gasped in horror at the sight of Lord Raoul's majestic purple-helmeted warrior of love.

"Lawks a-mercy," she swooned, her eyes widening as the warlord strode forward, his massive rod waving before her. "However will you fit that mighty sword into my tiny, and as yet untrammeled, silken sheath?"

"Thusly," Raoul growled, and throwing himself upon her, he plunged deep, deep, oh so deep into her depths, rending from her that most precious jewel of womanhood, making her scream with pleasure as he drove his lance of love home.

"So, what do you think?"

A pronounced silence met my ears.

Katie MacAlister

"C'mon, Isabella, you said you'd help me with this. What do you think of it so far? You can be honest, it won't hurt my feelings."

"Well . . ."

"It's vivid, isn't it?"

"Well . . ."

"Do you like the imagery? I tried to make it colorful." I reached for the teapot and felt its round little brown belly. It was cold. Rats. I hoisted myself off the floor pillow and padded barefoot over to the cubbyhole that passed for a kitchen.

"Yes, it's colorful . . ."

"And you'll notice I have them in bed in the first chapter. Sex sells, you know, and I've started things off with a bang. Ha! A bang! Get it?" I snorted to myself as I checked the water in the kettle and plugged it in.

"Erm . . ."

"Heh. So what do you think? Do you think it's good?" I marched back and stood in front of the vision lounging on the wicker chaise. Isabella bit her bottom lip and looked vaguely uncomfortable, despite being in possession of the most comfortable piece of furniture in the flat. "Alix . . ."

"Yes?"

"It's dreadful."

I frowned at my critic. Dreadful? *My story?* "Surely it's not that bad?"

Isabella grimaced and waved a rose-tipped, slender hand at me in a vague fashion as if she was swatting an unimportant gnat. "I'm sorry, darling, it is. It's perfectly dreadful. Terrible. Trite, in fact, and almost sickeningly brutal."

"Brutal? It's not brutal, it's erotic! There's a difference."

She shook her head at my protest, her hair a shimmering curtain of silver-blond that aroused the fiercest envy in my brunette-headed heart, and eased herself into a sitting position. She tapped at the stack of manuscript pages sitting on the small wicker end table at her elbow. "This isn't erotic, it's tantamount to rape. There are no emotions involved in either character, no foreplay, no affection, just a man bent on taking what he can."

"Oh." I felt my face fall with my spirits, but immediately began the buoying process. After all, Isabella herself admitted that she didn't read romances and probably wouldn't recognize a good one if it came up and bit her on the backside. Still, it was important I get this right on the first try—I didn't have long to prove myself with it. "You didn't like Lady Rowena? Or the dashing Lord Raoul? What's not to like about Raoul?"

"Neither. No, I tell a lie, I liked Rowena. And I suppose Raoul shows promise." She waved her hand again and gave a little shrug as I hooked my foot around a three-legged stool and pulled it over, carefully lowering myself to it. I'd had experience with that stool during the ten days I'd been living in the flat, and now approached it with the respect it was due. More than once I had been unwary, only to have it buck me off, resulting in gruesome rug burns from the horribly scratchy polyester burnt-orange carpet.

"Honestly, Alix, it's not the characters, it's the writing."

I sat up straighter and snatched the plate of lemon biscuits from where she was about to snag one. Now this was hitting a little too close to home! "What's wrong with the writing?"

"Well . . . it's a bit purple."

"Purple!"

"Yes, purple. Exaggerated. No one calls a cock a purple helmeted warrior of love."

I blushed a little. "Well I don't call it . . . it . . . *you know*, either."

"What?"

"You know. What you called it. The c-word."

"Cock?"

"Yeah."

"What do you call it?"

"I use creative euphemisms instead," I said with great dignity and allowed her to have just one lemon biscuit. They were my favorites and very expensive, but she was my landlady and she had volunteered to give me her opinion on my work in progress. Sacrifices were sometimes inevitable. "I am, after all, striving to be a writer. I am expected to be a bit on the exuberant side, verbally speaking."

Isabella pursed her lips and tapped an elegant finger to their rosy fullness. Seeing her perfect mouth in her perfect face, topping her perfect body made me suck in my bottom lip and gnaw off the few tendrils of chapped skin that graced it, all the while making a mental note to check out whether or not the National Health insurance plan for visiting Americans covered plastic surgery.

"Euphemisms like *lance of love* and anything with a helmet are passé, Alix. I suggest you try something a little less flowery."

"Flowery, huh?" She nodded. I thought about it. "How about if I change that first line to read *Lady Rowena gasped in horror at the sight of Lord Raoul's throbbing manhood . . .*"

"No," Isabella said firmly, shaking her head at me, her pageboy swinging emphatically. "No throbbing. Nothing should throb, it sounds like it's infected. Find another phrase."

"Mmm . . . gear and tackle?"

She raised a perfectly shaped pale eyebrow. "I should think not."

"Um . . . donkey rig."

"No."

"Nature's scythe?"

"Really, Alix, you're not being serious."

"How about tarse? Tarse is good. I like tarse.

Tarse sounds manly and firm, and not in the least bit infected."

"Nooo," she drawled after considering for a moment. "It's too blunt. If you'd take my advice—"

"Pintle?"

"What?"

"Too archaic?"

"Definitely."

"How about poll-axe?"

She shuddered delicately. "Too violent. Why must you beat around the bush—if you won't call it a cock, simply use the word *member*."

"Member," I scoffed. "Member! How prosaic. Member."

She glanced at the thin gold watch on her delicate wrist. I abandoned my protests and hurried on, deciding it was better to fight the big battles. If it's one thing I've learned, it's not to sweat the little stuff. "Well, all right, for the sake of moving on, I'll go with member. Now, about the next scene—"

"You know, darling, honestly, I think you're just a bit over your head with this project. You said yourself that you've never written anything, and to plunge in with a romance seems a bit . . ."

"Daring?"

She sighed. "Ambitious. Alix, I think you should reconsider your plan; surely your mother would understand if you decided it was too much for you to do in two months? Why don't you just enjoy your holiday rather than trying to write the entire time? You could travel about, visit Europe, see the rest of England—" She stopped when I made a rude face.

"I don't imagine you learned too much about my mother from the draft she sent for this flat, but I can tell you that our agreement is iron-clad, with no changes allowed: She pays for this very expensive flat for two months, and I write a book. It's as simple as that. If I don't succeed . . ." My mouth went dry at the thought of the alternative. "Well, I'd rather not think of that. Assuming I do finish the book, I'll be sitting in clover. Mom's agreed I can spend a year rent-free in the apartment over her garage, allowing me to establish myself as a writer. After that, my future is negotiable."

A languid hand reached for the red lacquer fan sitting next to the tea tray. I avoided the questions in her eyes, and went to check on the water.

"In case you're wondering, I threw away those tea bags and I'm making tea the way you like, although I have to admit—it never fails to amaze me how you English drink hot tea in the middle of summer." I swished out the teapot with hot water and added fresh tea. "You'd think everyone would drink iced tea when it gets this hot out."

Isabella examined her perfectly painted rose-colored toenails. "Tea should be hot, not iced," she said pedantically, then allowed a smile to curl her lips as I carried the tea to the small table next to her. "And coffee should be white, not black."

I shuddered as I kicked the floor pillow next to the table. "You're not going to get me into that argument again. You forget I'm from Seattle—if it's not strong enough to strip paint, it's not real coffee."

"You say that with pride."

A smart-ass retort rose immediately to my lips, but it withered when I met the look of concern in her eyes. I hadn't told her much about my life, but Isabella seemed to have an uncanny knack of seeing through the usual screens. I gave her a rueful smile instead, and plopped down on the pillow. "Seattleites take their coffee very seriously."

"What will you do if you don't finish your book?"

I considered what to tell her while I played mother and poured tea, adding milk to hers and lemon to mine. I'd only known Isabella for a little more than a week, having met her the day I took over the sublet on the flat. She was polite but rather distant then, warming a little each day until the previous day when I admitted my purpose for being in London. Although our contact was limited to a few hours each afternoon, our friendship had grown into something very comfortable. I trusted her where I trusted very few people.

"If I can't cut it as a writer, I will . . ." I paused, staring into the tea, hoping for inspiration, hoping for a life-altering event, hoping for hope. ". . . I will be an indentured servant with no future. None. Ever."

Her eyelids dropped over her brilliant blue eyes. Outside, a siren dopplered against the building and in through the three open windows as a panda car swerved in and out of the busy afternoon traffic, around two corners of Beale Square, finally heading off for God-knows-where. We sipped our tea in companionable silence, the fragrant smell of Earl Grey mingling with the tang of fresh lemon and the faintly acid bite from the bouquet of flowers I'd bought at the corner shop. I stopped avoiding the inevitable and glanced at Isabella.

"I must be going," she said with what sounded like genuine regret, and set her cup down next to the few pages of my book. A slight line appeared between her eyebrows for a moment as she eyed the papers, then her brow smoothed as she rose gracefully from the chaise and ran her hand down the tunic of her hand-dyed primrose silk hostess pajamas that I had coveted almost as much as I had coveted everything else she had worn. "There is such a thing as trying too hard, darling. Perhaps if you were to forget everything you've read about writing a book, your prose might be less . . ."

I stared at the hostess pajamas for a moment, calculating how much they must have cost, finally determining that they were probably more expensive than my entire stay in England. "What?" I scrambled up from the pillow and walked the ten feet over to the door. "Purple?" I tried on a little pout for size.

She smiled suddenly, tiny laugh lines appearing around her cerulean eyes. She patted my hand reassuringly as I smiled back. "Ghastly."

My smile slipped a little, but I managed to murmur my appreciation for her advice.

"Do you know what you need?" she asked, her head tipping to one side as she ran her gaze over me. I straightened up from my habitual slouch, and wished I had on something more elegant than the plain Indian sundress I'd picked up at a tiny shop in the tube station. I also toyed with the idea of wishing I wasn't quite so Amazonian and more in the line of Isabella's sylph-like figure, but shrugged that thought away. Wishing wouldn't make me shorter, skinnier, or more graceful.

"What do I need?" I asked as soon as she completed her survey of my rumpled dress, bare legs, and unpainted toenails.

Her smile deepened, a dimple peeking out from one side of her mouth. "A man."

"Ha!" Surprised, I hooted with laughter.

"Sure, you got one in your pocket? I'll take him!"

One perfect blond eyebrow rose quizzically.

"You thought I was going to say I don't want one, didn't you? You can think again, sister. I've been looking for a man my whole life."

"I see."

"I've had some, too—I don't want you thinking I haven't, because I have."

"I never imagined you hadn't."

"It's just that they've all been creeps. I'm a bit of a creep magnet, you see. If there's a flaky guy around who thinks it's sexy to rub Cheetos all over your erogenous zones, I fall for him."

"That sounds rather uncomfortable."

"The Cheeto-rubbing or the creeps? Doesn't matter, they are both uncomfortable, so if you have some guy just hanging around looking for a babe, I'm your girl."

"I'm not sure he is hanging around looking for a babe . . ."

"Course, he's got to be fun. I don't like those stodgy types, like lawyers and what-have-you. And I don't have time for a real romance, you understand, just a quickie or two."

Isabella frowned. "I'm sure my friend would want more from a relationship than just casual sex."

"Oh. Damn. Well then, you'd probably better not fix me up with him. I don't have the time or strength to go through the whole serious relationship thing with a guy. Do you know of anyone who does want casual sex?"

She smiled a distant, rather cold smile. "I'm sure you could find any number of such men at Drake's Bum."

I made a face. I'd been to Drake's Bum—it was a local pub that had been modernized within an inch of its life. Now it was a trendy hangout, populated with people there to see and be seen; not my type of crowd at all. "I was kind of hoping for a guy who had been creep-vetted already."

"I'm afraid I can't help you there. I seldom count creeps amongst the men of my acquaintance." She tried to sidle past me.

I turned to block her progress and took a moment to wax philosophical. "You know, Isabella, I've always said that men are like a bag of potato chips. They may look scrumptious and tasty, but once you've had them, all you're left with is an empty bag."

She paused, frowning slightly. "I don't quite see the analogy."

I waved a dismissive hand. "It doesn't matter, the point is that unless you know of a non-creep who wants a fling, I'm not interested in this guy of yours."

She eased past me. "If you change your mind, let me know. The man I have in mind is a perfect match for you. I thought so the day you arrived, but I wanted to know you a little longer before I suggested him."

A matchmaking landlady—just what I needed to complete my happiness. "Thanks, but no thanks."

She nodded and stepped out the door. I watched her start up the stairs to the floor above, which was divided between her and another tenant, and leaned back against the doorjamb to scratch an itch between my shoulder blades. A perfect man. Ha! In the whole of my twenty-nine years I'd yet to see such a thing. Perfect for someone else, no doubt, but not me. I wasn't going down that slippery slide into hell again. No sir, not me. Once burned, twice shy. Fool me once, shame on you; fool me twice, shame on me. A bird in the hand is worth two in the . . . oh, dear.

"Um . . . Isabella?"

"Yes?" she called down without pausing her ascent.

"You said this guy is a *perfect* match?"

"Perfect for you, yes."

She rounded the landing and disappeared up the last flight of stairs.

"How perfect?" I yelled after her, good manners flying out the window even as I told myself I wasn't in the slightest bit interested.

"Perfect." Even her voice was elegant, all rounded vowels and languid English richness.

I walked to the banister and peered up the

stairwell. "Is this *perfect* man a friend of yours?"

"In a manner of speaking," her voice drifted downward, growing fainter. I heard the chimes that brush her door tinkle softly as she went into her flat. "He's my lover."

Chapter Two

"Oh, that my sainted Lord Raoul would find me here in this evil place!" The Lady Rowena's *creamy, bounteous bosom heaved as she wailed to the silent cell she had been imprisoned in, wringing her hands and rending her clothing without regard to modesty or economy. "Oh but that I could at this dark moment kiss his firmly chiseled lips! Oh that I could hold him in my arms, stroking the tousled curls back from his broad and manly brow! Oh that I could seat myself upon his manly pillar of alabaster and ride him as he's never been ridden before! Oh! Oh!"*

"Be honest now, is that something you'd like to read more of?"

"Well . . . it's very explicit, isn't it? I mean, what with his pillars and her bosom and all."

I leaned forward onto my knees, and wriggled my right ankle to bring the feeling back into my foot. I'd been squatting next to the library cart so long my feet were going numb. "All romances have sex in them in the U.S. You did say you read romances, right?"

The librarian ducked her head in a shy gesture and pushed the cart down the stack. I followed on my knees.

"Other than his pillar and her boobs, what did you think? Is this a book you would buy?"

The woman looked around nervously, then leaned her head close to mine and whispered, "I think you should take the smut out of it. Romance isn't about sex, you know. It's about two people committing themselves to each other."

She smiled a tense little smile and nodded as she wheeled the book cart away. I looked at the manuscript in my hand. *No sex?*

I considered the no sex angle while I marched home to my lovely little flat, the same lovely little flat in which I had laughed long and hard the day before, chortling merrily over Isabella's offer of her latest boy toy. Oh yes, I laughed when Isabella called down to me that this perfect man—the man she thought was meant for me—was her lover. I laughed and rolled my eyes as I wandered back into my tiny little flat to ask the room, "Yeah, right, like I just fell off the stupid wagon?" The sad reality is that after I got through laughing, I started seriously considering what Isabella had said.

I suppose a few words are needed to explain just exactly why an offer of Isabella's *homme de l'heure* would strike a chord of interest in someone who spent the last ten years of her life bouncing from creep to creep, with a few intermittent losers tossed in just to break up the monotony.

My mother's best friend from school married a rich Brit, and they had a daughter, Stephanie. Steph was off to Australia for the summer, leaving her flat in an old house on a relatively quiet square in need of a subletter. After six long weeks of negotiation, Mom and I came to an agreement, with her agreeing to pay for the flat while I tried my wings as a writer.

There was much more riding on the situation than just an agreement between Mom and me, though, there was a little matter of my entire life, my future, my hopes and dreams and . . . well, I'll be honest, I've never been much of a success at life, something my mother brings to my attention frequently. I'd been married once, to a workaholic Microsoft yuppie who divorced me after telling me I was bad luck. I've had eighteen jobs in the last ten years, doing everything from scraping up gum at a movie theater, to staring blindly at microfilmed checks at a bank, to walking dogs for people who were too busy to walk their own dogs. I've had a slightly fewer number of boyfriends in those same ten years, hooking up with some guys who could easily out-creep Charles Manson.

Although it may seem that my one and only goal is being successful at writing a book—and the motivation for success is strong, since failure means I'll have to give up my life to stay in a hick town in a desert in Eastern Washington taking care of my paternal grandmother's bodily needs—more important than *that* is my need to prove to my mother once and for all that I can succeed at something. Anything. Just once, I'd like to come out on top and have her witness my triumph.

The need for parental approval—it's a massive, unwieldy weight to bear.

When I first arrived at the house in London, Isabella greeted me politely, gave me the keys to the doors, showed me my new home for the next two months, and briefly explained who the other tenants were.

"The ground floor has two families and their children," she said in a plummy English accent that sent little goose bumps of delight up and down my spine. England! I was really in England!

She frowned for a moment at an oversized gold floor pillow, and adjusted it infinitesimally to the left. "The families are related—sisters— and both spend their summers in Provence.

Their flats are let to visiting scholars. This should be fixed."

I looked where she was pointing at one of the side windows which didn't quite close all the way. "It's not a problem, I doubt anyone would scale three floors to crawl into the flat."

"Mmm." She moved on to straighten an ugly Van Gogh print. "The first floor is shared by Dr. Bollocks—he teaches at London University—and the Muttsnuts." She pursed her lips and shook her head briefly at the mention of the last name. "They're newlyweds. We hardly ever see them."

Dr. Bollocks? Muttsnuts? Quaint English names—you gotta love 'em!

"The second floor has two women, Miss Bent and Miss Fingers, and Mr. Aspertame. Philippe is from the Bahamas."

I watched as she fussed briefly with a hideous yellow-cracked vase full of wilting daisies, and wondered when she was going to leave so I could quietly collapse on the small daybed that lurked in the corner. "Fingers. Aspertame. Bahamas. Fascinating."

Isabella pushed back the beads that hid the entrance to the cubbyhole of a kitchen while I sent a brief glance of pronounced longing toward the bed, but as she showed no signs of leaving, I stiffened my knees against the jet lag that was threatening to make them buckle, and tried to pay attention to what she was saying.

"You'll be careful with this gas ring?"

I nodded my agreement. Honestly, I was willing to forgo ever using the bloody thing if she'd just leave me alone.

"The third floor consists of this flat, and across from you are two university students, Mr. Skive and Miss Goolies. They're very quiet, so you need have no worry about late night parties, loud music, or any other violations of the house rules. You did say you were looking for a quiet flat?"

I maneuvered all the muscles necessary into a smile, but I was sure the result was less than pretty. Isabella's startlingly blue eyes quickly slipped away as I confirmed that I was indeed seeking quiet to work on a personal project.

"Mr. Block and I share the upper floor," she said smoothly as she opened a battered wardrobe and wrinkled her nose at the musty smell. "You should air this out before you hang your clothes in it."

"Thank you," I said firmly as I sidled toward the door. "I'm sure everything will be perfect, and I'll fit right in."

"Mmm." She looked rather disbelieving as she glided past me and out the opened door. I kept the tepid smile on my face for the count of ten, then closed the door softly, took a proprietorial look around the small flat, and headed straight for the bed.

By the time ten days had elapsed I had met

most of my neighbors, and felt happy in my new digs, happy enough to smile at Isabella's ridiculous offer before trotting out to do a little research for my book. It was a Regency romance, and I wanted to be sure to have all of the twiddly bits right—descriptions of Rotten Row, Kensington Park, White's, and other such landmarks. I spent an agreeable hour getting a reader's card at the British Museum's new library, returning home in a most satisfied state of mind. Satisfied, that is, until I came face to face with my nemesis.

Isabella's house wasn't really what we west coast Americans think of as a house—it was part of a long line of connected buildings that ran the length of one side of the square. Made of white stone, each house had nearly identical black metal railings, white stone steps, and white net curtains at all of the front windows. Our house had a rich mahogany colored door that I swore came straight from the depths of hell. That door hated me—or rather, the lock did. I'd seen it work for other tenants so I knew it wasn't defective, but let me approach it with my arms full of shopping, and it would turn its face away as if it couldn't bear to allow me across the threshold.

"So, you're in *that* sort of a mood today," I muttered as I jiggled the key in the lock, twisting it back and forth in an attempt to engage the mechanism. "Well, my steely friend, I have news for you—I have a little something here guaranteed to make you see the error of your ways!"

I set down a stack of paperbacks I'd picked up at a mystery bookshop, my bag of groceries, and a small spiky plant I bought off a street vendor. "Aha!" I cried, flourishing the small metal awl I had found in a jar with a bunch of Stephanie's ceramics tools, and subsequently had placed in my purse for just such a moment. "Vengeance is mine, you little bastard!"

I set to work poking the awl into the lock and muttering imprecations under my breath. "We'll just see how you like to be gutted," I said with a particularly vicious jab at its inner workings. "Won't open up to me, will you? Ha! No lock can keep me out, I'm . . ." I struggled with the tool and leaned my weight into it. The metal in the lock squealed against my prodding. "I'm . . ." A slight metallic snap sounded. Sensing victory, I gnawed on my lower lip and jabbed the awl in at a different angle. "I'm . . ."

"Breaking and entering is, I believe, the term you're looking for."

"Bugger and blast," I swore, and whirled around with the awl still clenched in my hand. The man standing on the steps leading up to the house wasn't familiar, so I assumed he was there to visit one of the residents. I stared for a minute into the loveliest pair of green eyes I've ever seen on a man, and let my gaze trail upwards, over a forehead with a few faint frown lines etched in it, up higher to gorgeous chestnut hair that hung over his forehead with just a hint of curl, then back down over his nice cheekbones, long nose, lips that were thinned with annoyance, and a gently blunted chin. I made a concerted effort to pull myself together and tried not think about what his lips would look like if they weren't mashed together in a thin line.

"Um . . . the lock doesn't work."

He looked again at the awl in my hand, and one dark chestnut colored eyebrow rose in question. I felt a little blush moving upwards from my neck. "I have a key, it doesn't work, so I thought I'd try this and see if I couldn't—"

"—persuade the lock to open, yes, I heard you." He looked me up and down in an arrogant manner and shifted a leather satchel from his right hand to his left. From his pants pocket he pulled out a key ring and without so much as a by-your-leave, shouldered me aside and fitted the key. The bloody door opened without a peep.

"It hates me," I muttered as I gave it a good glare, then stooped to pick up my belongings.

"One moment, if you please," said the green-eyed locksmith, holding up a restraining hand. He stood rigidly, clutching his satchel and keys, a faint sheen of perspiration beading on his forehead. It had to be at least eighty, and this joker was decked out in a black and charcoal suit, looking like a hot, mildly pissed lawyer. He reached behind him and pulled the door shut.

"Hey! You can just open that again." I reached into my bag of groceries and pulled out a loaf of French bread, waving it in what I hoped was a suitably threatening manner. His eyes narrowed as I took a step closer, ignoring the whiff of spicy cologne that curled around me in an intoxicating manner. "You open that door up again, or I'll bop you on the head with my bread, and I just bet you wouldn't like a head full of crumbs! They might get on your suit!"

His eyes widened in surprise. "Are you threatening me, madam?" he asked in a low, rich voice that reminded me of Alan Rickman, the dishy English actor.

"You got that right. I live here, buster. See, I have a key!" I showed him the key clenched against my palm, along with the straps of the shopping bag, the awl, and the three paperbacks. I hefted my fresh-baked weapon a bit higher. The man was a good four inches taller than me, but even though he was on the step above me, I figured that if push came to shove, I could beat him about the head and shoulders with my bread until he opened the door.

He didn't look intimidated by the threat of being impaled by a loaf of French bread, but he didn't look happy about it, either. His eyebrows came together in a frown as he gave me the once over. It was apparent from the look of distaste that flickered across his face that he wasn't impressed with what he saw.

"You're no prize, either, you know." He blinked in surprise as I poked him in the chest with my handful of books. That was a lie, but I wasn't going to stand there and be examined like I was a piece of moldy cheese.

"I beg your pardon?"

"That look you gave me—it wasn't very flattering. I just wanted you to know that you can speak in that Alan Rickman voice all you want— it's not going to do a thing for me." I nodded and pulled myself back from where I had leaned in to deliver my warning. Somehow that cologne he wore seemed to pull me in closer. I fought a curl of lust that flared briefly to life, and matched his frown.

"I see. Thank you for telling me that. Now perhaps you would care to show me your identification?"

I goggled at him. The nerve of some people! "My what?"

"Your identification. I assume you're American or Canadian?"

"American, not that it's any of your business. Just open the damn door, Bulldog Drummond, and let me get to my flat before my ice cream melts."

"You must have a passport," he insisted.

I looked around in an exaggerated manner. "Gee, I could have sworn I went through passport control at Heathrow. If you won't open the door, the least you can do is step out of the way so I can kick it down."

He gazed over my head for a moment, sighed, then slipped his hand into his suit jacket and pulled out a leather wallet. He flipped it open. A thumb-sized image of his face, minus frown, stared back at me. I read the words at the top.

"Metropolitan Police."

"That's right."

"Scotland Yard?"

He closed his eyes briefly and nodded. I looked again.

"You're a detective inspector! Cool! Who are you visiting here?"

"No one, I live here, which puts me in the perfect position to know that you, my fair little bread-wielding house-breaker, do not. Now please show me your identification."

"I'm subletting Stephanie Shay's flat," I told him, suddenly noticing that his hands were large, but nicely shaped. I admit to having a thing about men's hands, and the combination of a real live Scotland Yard 'tec, his hormone-stirring cologne, and those hands was making me a bit woozy. "You can ask Isabella. You're not one of the people who lives on the ground floor?"

"No, I live on the fourth floor."

It was my turn to blink in surprise. "You live above me?"

"Evidently." He frowned once more for good measure, then picked up my spiky plant and gave it a curious look. "Are you accustomed to carrying illegal drugs around with you?"

"Huh?"

He held out the plant. My fingers overlapped his as I tried to take it, but he wouldn't let go of it. I tugged harder.

"You're aware that this is a marijuana plant, aren't you?"

I stared at my cute little spiky plant. It looked so innocent! "I . . . no! I bought it off a guy outside the tube station. He had a whole row of them—he said it was . . . oh."

He cocked an eyebrow at me, but released the plant. The sensation of his fingers sliding out from under mind made me babble. "The guy selling it said it was a homeopathic herb used to bring enlightenment and peace, and was harmless." I felt my face flame up as I admitted to my naivety, but said nothing more when he unlocked the door and held it open for me. I gave him a quick, crooked smile, the door a muffled promise of retribution, and swept into the tiny hall.

"I *will* ask Isabella about you," he warned as I started up the stairs.

I shrugged as best I could with my arms loaded, and heard his footsteps follow me up

333

the uncarpeted stairs. "It's no skin off my nose; she'll tell you the same thing I did."

I looked over my shoulder as I turned on the landing and was delighted to see his eyes had been solidly fixed on my derriere. "Well, well, so there is flesh and blood beneath that suit!"

His emerald gaze shot up to mine. I cocked my head at him. "Gee, I can't remember the last time I made a man blush."

He seemed to grow more rigid, if that was possible, his jaw tightening until the muscles there jumped with tension. Obviously Mr. Detective didn't get a whole lot of yucks during his day. Poor guy, here he was sweltering away under a hot suit and I was teasing him.

"Hey, it's all right," I said with reassuring smile, giving the hand clutching the banister a friendly little squeeze. "If it will make you feel any better, you can walk in front of me and I'll ogle your ass."

His eyes bugged out a little at that and he looked like he couldn't decide whether he wanted to yell at me, or laugh. I turned my smile up a notch and poked him in the ribs. "It was a joke, Sherlock. You're supposed to laugh. You know, ha ha ha?"

One corner of his mouth twitched, then the other, and then lo and behold, Mother Mary and all the saints, he smiled. I took a step back and clutched the bread to my chest. "Oh, be still my heart! I shall have to avert my eyes lest such a devastating smile brings me to my knees and strips me of what sensibilities I possess," I said in my best Regency heroine voice, and grinned when he laughed a rusty sounding little laugh.

"Don't use that laugh much, do you? I bet it's all of those dead bodies and master criminals you investigate, right?" I started back up the stairs, adding a little hip action just to see if he was watching. He was.

"You're doing that on purpose," he accused me.

I tossed a flip smile over my shoulder. "You take your pleasures where you can," I said archly, and rounded the next flight, pausing so he could come alongside me. "Hey, can you get me into that Black Museum I heard about? I'd love to see all of that Jack the Ripper stuff, and the death masks, and the Dr. Crippen memorabilia."

Detective Grumpy gave me a weary look and shook his head. "The Crime Museum is not open to the public."

"I know, that's why I want you to get me in."

"Miss . . . Mrs. . . . what *is* your name?"

"Alix."

"Yes, and your name?"

"Alix. What's yours?"

I stopped in mid flight when he grabbed my elbow. "Why are you asking me if you already know it?"

"What? What are you talking about?"

The frown was back. "I asked you what your name was."

"And I told you—it's Alix. Short for Alexandra, if you hadn't guessed."

The frown deepened for a minute, then smoothed out and a smile flirted with the corners of his mouth again.

"You better watch out for that, it'll become a habit soon." I marched up the rest of the stairs and stood fumbling for my keys in front of my door.

"My name is Alex as well," he said in a monotone voice as he plucked the plant and bread from my hands so I could unlock the door. He held the door open for me and watched as I unceremoniously dumped the carrier bag, books, and my purse on the distressed table next to the entrance. I took the proffered bread and added it to the stack.

"You're kidding! You probably thought I was an idiot just then," I grimaced, wondering what was behind that emerald gaze. It was amazing how much heat it suddenly seemed to carry. "Imagine that, we've both got the same name. Well. Bob's your uncle!"

One eyebrow went up infinitesimally.

"What?" I asked.

"Bob's your uncle?"

"I didn't say it right? I heard someone use it on the telly. I thought it meant *there you are.*"

One side of his mouth twitched. "It does."

"Then why did you give me that funny look?"

He reached toward my cheek and tucked a strand of hair that had come out of my ponytail behind my ear. A rush of blood swept up my chest, tightening my nipples and making my breath catch low in my throat.

"It sounds a little ridiculous when Americans say it."

"Oh." It occurred to me I had just been insulted. I ignored my nipples' pleas to throw themselves on him, thinning my lips and frowning at him instead. "Bollocks! That's a stonking great lie! You're trying to cheese me off, aren't you? What a load of cobblers! That's total pants! Why, I can speak—"

He held up his hand in defeat and a real, honest-to-goodness smile danced across his face. "I concede the point! Bob's your uncle it is."

I smiled back at him for a few moments, watching his eyes darken as the smile faded from his lips. I had an almost overwhelming urge to taste him, just run the tip of my tongue on that spot where his jaw met his neck. I ignored the sensible voice in my head when it pointed out that I had just met him and he wouldn't be interested in the likes of me, and humored the other voice, the fun voice, the voice urging a little flirtation just to see where it would get me. I leaned in toward him and breathed in his scent. It was cologne and man and . . . something else I couldn't quite put my finger on. "Have you been there, Alex?"

A muscle jumped in his jaw, but he didn't step back. He didn't grab me and lay his lips on me, either, but we can't have everything. "Have I been where?"

I leaned a little closer and gave him my best sleepy bedroom eyes. "The Black Museum."

I could see the pulse beating strongly in his neck. His Adam's apple bobbed up above the knot in his tie. "Yes, I have."

"Take me?" I whispered.

His pupils flared in those lovely green eyes. "What?"

I tipped my head slightly and blew a little line of breath at his ear. "I lied to you, Alex. That Alan Rickman voice does do something to me. Will you take me to the Black Museum?"

"Do you always seduce someone when you want a favor?"

I grinned when he took a step closer. I could feel his breath fanning around my face, mingling with the spicy cologne I swore was made up of pure pheromones. "Not always. Only when threats of assault with bread don't work."

"I see," he said in that sexy voice, turning his head slightly. I tilted my head and opened my mouth just enough to steam his lips. "So will you?"

"Take you?" His lips brushed mine as he spoke, feather light and very warm. I gave a little gasp and wondered what happened to all of the air in the room. "Yes, Alix, I suspect I will take you."

I let my lips curve a smile against his, enjoying the frisson of heat that contact started in my belly. I hadn't felt anything like this before—not even when I was dating my ex-husband. "Good," I breathed. "When?"

"Soon. I'd like to know you a little better first, but . . . soon."

"Good," I repeated, wishing I had the nerve to just wrap my arms around him and plant my lips on him, but I am nothing if not circumspect. I clutched my hands behind my back instead.

He made a little hum of agreement and slowly stepped backwards until he was outside the doorway.

"Let me know when you want to go," I said with a rueful smile, a little worried about the sense of loss I felt with his withdrawal. I'd just met the man, for heaven's sake, surely even my starved libido couldn't set its cap at the first gorgeous Englishman it clapped eyes on. "My schedule is pretty easy, and all I need is a day or so warning in advance."

His lips weren't smiling, but his eyes were. Veeeeery interesting. He nodded his head and turned to take the stairs up to the top floor.

"My sister is going to be terribly jealous, you know," I called after him.

"Is she?" he stopped and looked over his shoulder with an inscrutable look.

"Yep. She's a really big mystery fan, and she's always wanted to see the Black Museum. She'll be spittin' kittens when I tell her you're going to take me there."

Both chestnut eyebrows rose. "I believe I mentioned the Crime Museum was closed to the public, Alix."

I watched him step onto the landing, then snapped my mouth shut. "Wait a minute, you just said you would take me, and now you're saying you won't?"

He had one foot on the bottom step of the last flight of stairs. The stairwell was too dark to see the expression on his face until he leaned to the side, into the light from a window behind him. He looked just like the Cheshire Cat—my jaw dropped at the sight of his grin. The little frisson of fire that had started with our flirtation burst into a full-fledged roaring volcano, threatening to consume me where I stood. I grasped the doorframe to steady my suddenly weak knees.

"You asked me to take you, Alix, and I fully intend to honor that request. Unfortunately, it's not possible for me to bring you to visit the Crime Museum."

I felt as if every bone in my body had melted to pudding under the influence of that wolfish grin. "But . . . but . . . you said . . . you'd take me. . . ." A light bulb lit up over my head. I stared at him, unable to believe what I was thinking. Surely he hadn't meant . . . he couldn't, he was English, and everyone knew Englishmen were cold and reserved and didn't flirt like that, certainly not suit-wearing detective inspectors. "Uh . . . ."

"Close your mouth, Alix," he said softly, and with a graceful tip of his head, he disappeared up the stairs.

"Well, stone the crows," I said to no one, looking after him at the dark passageway. "I'll be . . . hoooo!"

I closed the door quietly behind me and leaned against it, reviewing what he had said, what I said, wishing I hadn't been such an idiot, then allowing myself to bask for a moment in the warm promise that was heavy in his voice. I had just gotten to the point where I was imagining him stark naked on the chaise when I remembered what I had said to Isabella about her perfect man. Although Fourth Floor Alex was my type, I was sure he wouldn't be interested in the sort of relationship I wanted. He didn't look like the quickie type. Besides, there were other drawbacks.

I mentally ticked off all of his bad points as I picked up the bag of groceries, my books, and the bread. He clearly had little to no sense of humor, was arrogant, prickly, serious-minded, wore a wool suit even in the middle of summer, and probably wouldn't know fun if it came up and dropped its drawers in front of him.

I looked down at the books and groceries, then frowned and added another sin to the list. "That little rat! He took my pot plant!"

Chapter Three

The Lady Rowena was on her knees in supplication before her lord, tears streaming down her ivory cheeks, over her chin, down her neck, up over the neckline of her gown, splattering and streaking the thin muslin of her gown, making that fabric nigh on translucent, baring her breasts and her pert little pink nipples to Raoul's heated gaze. She hiccupped, then dabbed at her running nose with the hem of her gown. "Oh, please, my dearest darlingest beloved! You cannot abandon me and marry the bastard daughter of a duke!"

Lord Raoul turned his back to the sight of the damp woman, and looked out upon the velvety green lawns at Firthstone. He was saddened he had to give up the bit o'fun that was Rowena, but *after all, she didn't have nearly the dowry that Pruenella, the natural daughter of the Duke of Colinwood had, and dammit! One didn't pay for the cow when one had the milk for free!*

"Why should I not marry her?" he asked carelessly.

Rowena looked at him as if he'd lost his senses. "Er . . . well . . . for one, she's a bastard, Raoul. Not legitimate. Her parents weren't wed. You do understand that concept, don't you?"

"So, what do you think? Is it too harsh? Do you think Lady Rowena would speak in such an insolent manner to her beloved Lord Raoul? Is he too unsympathetic?"

Kamil the grocer had that look peculiar to deer caught in the headlights of a speeding truck, but he gamely rallied a smile and smoothed a hand over the stack of evening tabloids next to the cash register. "I'm sorry, I can't help you. You talk to someone else, a woman, maybe, someone who reads books. I can't help you. You want to buy something else, maybe?"

I scooted over so a customer could plop down his packet of shrimp-flavored crisps and a six-pack of shandies in the tiny clear space on the counter. It wasn't much of a space, about a foot across, the rest of the counter being taken up with racks of candy, newspapers, snack foods, postcards, and miscellaneous odds and bobs. Kamil's store was one of a dying breed, a tiny oasis of fascinating British and Pakistani food-stuffs crammed together so tightly on the shelves, it was impossible to extract an item without a positive cascade of tins, packets, and jars falling upon the unwary shopper. I peered through the stacks of items on the counter to wave a friendly goodbye to Kamil, and gathering up my manuscript pages and groceries, headed out the door toward home.

I like walking around London. It has a nice feel to it for one of the world's major cities—neighborhoods have a distinct feel to them, some warm and homey, others hip and exciting, and still others dusty and dry with history. I lived within walking distance of the British Museum in a very pleasant area that had several green squares, aggressive squirrels who panhandled anyone incautious enough to bring food to the square, and lots of dark, mysterious little shops filled with intriguing antiques, books, and artifacts guaranteed to delight even the most sophisticated of hearts.

Heat shimmered up through the thin soles of my sandals as I strolled down the pavement, swinging my bag of groceries and breathing in deeply.

"Ah, the smell of diesel on a warm summer's eve," I said happily to an elderly lady who stood at the zebra crossing with an armload of shopping.

"It's terrible, innit?" she nodded, shuffling

forward at the traffic break. "You'd think with the price of petrol these days, fewer people would drive, but it seems like more and more are." She sniffed and gave me a curt nod, then marched off toward a block of flats.

I turned and started down the street toward Beale Square, content to listen to the sounds of life around me—music drifting out from opened windows and shop doors, the dull roar and whine of traffic as it started and stopped up and down the street, and the wonderful ebb and flow of conversation. It's amazing how many variations there are on an English accent, everything from the guttural and harsh Cockney and its variants, to rounded words of the western counties, the occasional swoop and sway of an Irish accent, the warm burr of the Scots, and the plummy, silky smooth BBC-type accent that sounds just too, too teddibly top drawer. I loved them all, even the ones I couldn't for the life of me understand, and secretly lay in bed at night and worked on perfecting my own English accent.

I hummed a bit of "Moondance" to myself as I strolled along, wondering what Mr. Dishy Detective Inspector Alex would be doing that evening while I was up visiting his neighbor. Isabella had invited me to meet her friend, *the* friend, her perfect lover friend who was even more perfect for me. I had agreed to meet him only after I spent two days thinking non-stop about the man upstairs, telling myself with more than a hint of desperation that maybe Isabella was wrong, and Mr. Perfect would be interested in a little summer fling. Mr. Alex certainly wasn't—I hadn't seen neither hide nor hair of him since he ran off with my cute little spiky (alleged pot) plant.

"This fascination with him is not a good thing, Alix," I had told myself sternly the day before when I caught myself staring out the window and picturing Alex lying starkers in the patch of sun that warmed the chaise. "Keep your mind on business. Work, work, work, that's what you need."

I grimaced at my own words—I had experience with workaholics before, and had no desire to become one of those obsessed perfectionists. Life was too short and too uncertain to do nothing but work, especially when there were green-eyed Englishmen reposing seductively on the chaise, offering up their sleek, muscled bodies to be kissed and caressed and licked and nibbled . . .

"Sweet Fanny Adams, I'm doing it again! Right, that's it, I clearly need help." I scribbled out a brief note, marched upstairs, and wedged the paper between Isabella's door and the frame. I will admit to glaring briefly at the door opposite hers, but went back downstairs feeling much better, convinced that if I met this perfect man of Isabella's, the less than perfect Plant

Thief would be washed from my mind.

It didn't strike me until the next day when I was dressing for Isabella's dinner that the two men might be one in the same. I stood naked, balancing on one foot while the other hovered in the air as I paused in the act of pulling on a pair of underwear, blinking at nothing as the thought swam around in my mind. Alex? My perfect man?

I finished donning the appropriate under-things while I mused over the pertinent facts, but could find no validity to the idea. All Isabella had said was that the guy was perfect for me, and Detective Inspector Starched Shorts was anything but that. Besides, if she had meant him, she would have surely said so, since he was so handy for introductions. As for him being her lover . . . I pushed away a vague sense of unhappiness over that idea and shrugged at my image in the mirror on the wardrobe door.

"So they're doin' the nasty—big fat hairy deal. Means nothing to me, nothing at all, and you can just stop shaking your head at me, because that's my story and I'm sticking to it!"

I gave my reflection a good glare just to let it know it wasn't going to goad me into admitting anything, and sat down to apply rarely-used cosmetics. I couldn't remember the last time I wore make-up. Probably one of the few times Matt dragged me out to a corporate dinner.

"This one's for you," I said, saluting the mental image of my ex-husband with a five-year-old container of mascara. It was a bit stiff and clumpy, and I managed to get mascara damn near everywhere, including the bridge of my nose and my left earlobe, but at long last I had several coats on, enough to turn my brown lashes the same shade of inky black they wore in the 1960s. It was really, really black, and not a little sticky feeling. I peered at the small hand mirror I was using and decided it looked better than it felt. I tried to remember if I was supposed to put blush above, on, or under the cheekbone for maximum effect, and decided a bit everywhere would give me a healthy glow. A small dusting of gold glittery powder turned into an unexpected avalanche when the container spilled down my cleavage, but I got most of it out without too much trouble. A dashing bit of crimson lipstick, a splash of my favorite perfume, and the face staring back at me from the tiny mirror was ready to dazzle the pants off of my prospective perfect man.

It was just too bad that Alex wouldn't be there to view my triumph. I was conscious of a deflated sort of feeling around my mid-section when I thought of how disappointing the evening would be without him.

"Stop it," I told myself sternly as I pulled on the nicest of my dresses. "Stop it right now. This is the perfect man we're talking about here—

let's not screw this up with foolishness over a guy who thinks you're an idiot."

I was about to pull my hair back, but I decided it was sexier hanging down my back, so I fwoofed a little gel in the front to keep it out of my eyes, and blow-dried it into submission. The final step was to debate the panty hose issue—I hate wearing the things, I really do, but there are times when bare legs just look too informal. Since my dress ended a few inches above my knees, there was a lot of leg showing. I eyed them critically. The fact that I had gone European and hadn't shaved them in a while decided me—I dug out a my sole pair of pantyhose and pulled them on, praying I wouldn't run them before the night was over.

Hated pantyhose on, I grabbed the bottle of wine I'd bought from Kamil and prepared to march upstairs, determined to enjoy myself despite the fact that the Wonder of Scotland Yard would not be present. I wouldn't think of him, I told myself as I checked my face one last time. I wouldn't dwell on his fascinating green eyes that changed color so quickly, I wouldn't remember that knee-melting cologne he wore, I wouldn't recall his sexy voice, and I wouldn't allow myself to feel even one atom of desire for him. He was history as far as I was concerned, and the immediate attraction I had felt was nothing more than a sign I really should consider finding someone to scratch that particular itch, someone who wouldn't *mean* anything to me, someone who knew how to have fun, and who wasn't interested in anything serious. I was, after all, prepared for just such an eventuality. When my sister Cait asked if I was bringing any raincoats with me on the trip, I had pointed out that it was July, and unlikely to rain an amount where I'd be needing a raincoat. She had laughed and handed me a box of condoms, saying, "It's time to get over Cheeto Boy. Here's some raincoats. Put them to good use."

Curiosity got the better of me, so I dug around in the bottom of my travel bag until I found a somewhat squashed box of condoms. I chortled to myself at the image of me casually inquiring of a sexual partner if he preferred the strawberry, banana, or "Kiss of Mint" flavored raincoat. I tossed the condoms on the table next to the chaise, and snickered my way up the stairs to Isabella's. I was feeling pretty good, and for once, in complete control. My cute red swishy dress swished sexily when I moved. I felt very seductive. I didn't even look over at Alex's door when I knocked on Isabella's—Alex was totally gone from my mind, finished, finito.

"Nevermore," I said firmly as the door opened.

"Quoth the raven?" Alex asked.

I goggled for a moment. He was even more drool-worthy than I remembered.

"Sorry, I must have the wrong . . ." I looked

across the landing. I wasn't mistaken, I *was* at Isabella's door. "Oh, you've been invited too?"

Stupid, stupid, stupid! He's standing right there in her flat, of course he's invited!

He stepped back so I could enter. I felt my uterus stutter once or twice as the Alex Scent of Manly Man hit me, but I successfully fought the urge to rip off his clothes and wrestle him to the ground by frowning at him. "Don't you wear anything else but suits?"

"Seldom."

"Alexandra! I'm so glad to see you. Do come in."

Isabella stood in a small room by a solid glass dining room table, lighting tall white tapers. She was dressed in a flowing white and silver dress, and looked like a vestal virgin.

It struck me as I walked past Alex that his presence here meant he *was* the man Isabella had intended for me. I was curiously elated and depressed by that thought, but had no time to say anything before Alex grabbed my arm and hauled me up close to his side. Good lord, he was going to kiss me! Right there in front of Isabella! Should I meet him halfway, or should I play it cool and pretend I didn't know he was going to kiss me? My mind ran around in frantic circles like a deranged hamster on a wheel, and just as Alex leaned in close to me I decided that while modesty had its benefits, so did brazenness. I drooped against him and offered up my lips.

"You need to adjust your dress," he hissed, his mouth an inch or so from my ear.

"I—*what?*" I turned slightly so I could frown at him. Our noses brushed. His eyes glittered emerald as I stared at him, unable to think of anything beyond how attractive he was. He seemed to be likewise affected, but managed at last to speak.

"Your dress. You need to adjust it."

I dragged my gaze off him and looked down at myself. Sure, the area between my boobs was awfully gold and glittery from the powder spill, but there was none on the dress.

"What are you talking about?" I asked him in a breathy voice.

He made a sound of annoyance, grabbed my shoulders, turned me around and tugged at the back of my dress.

"It was tucked up in your . . . erm . . ."

Oh good Lord! I spun around, mortified. A smile flirted with his lips. He leaned in to whisper, "I didn't think a face could turn that color of red. It matches your dress," just before Isabella came over to us, holding out both of her hands.

"You look charming. That color suits you, although Alexander must have said something quite risqué to make you blush like that. You have met, have you not? He said he had seen you having trouble with the front door."

"Yes, we've met," I choked, damning the owners and all the shareholders of the pantyhose company all the while I wondered what he had told her about me. I hoped she didn't know I was threatening to do the door bodily harm.

"Good. Now come and let me introduce you to Carol."

I looked at her in surprise. Carol? Who was this Carol? I thought she was just having an intimate dinner for Mr. "I See London, I See France" and me.

"Carol?"

"Carol. The man I told you about." She patted my hand and gave me a brilliant smile. "Alexander must have said something quite unforgivable if he's rattled you this badly. You do remember that you are here to meet the man I think is perfect for you?"

"I—" I looked back to where Alex was stalking behind us, a familiar frown affixed to his face. "Well, yes, but I thought . . . that is, I assumed . . ."

Isabella glanced at me out of the corner of her eye as she steered me toward a candle-lit sitting room. "You thought I meant Alex? Lord, no! He's the last man I'd pair you up with."

Well, hell, it was that obvious?

"This is Carol Coventry, Alix. Carol, this is my summer tenant Alexandra Treebark. Alix is here to do research for a book she's writing."

I stared at Isabella, aghast at her cruel joke. *Treebark?* I was about to correct her when she grabbed Alex's arm and insisted he look at a new print she had framed. I watched them leave the room then turned back to the man who had stood to shake my hand.

"My name is Karl," he said with a wry smile and offered his hand. "Karl Daventry. You have to excuse Isabella, she has a terrible memory for names. I assume you must be an Alicia or Allison if she's calling you Alix."

I shook his hand and smiled. He really was quite pleasant looking—a bit taller than me, dark hair and eyes, long English face, and a cute little skull and crossbones earring. He was nice, but . . . I couldn't help but think he wasn't perfect. Or maybe he *was* perfect, but perfect in that white bread, bland, unexciting sort of way. Even his earring was the perfect balance of hip and different, and yet not silly looking or offensive.

"Actually, my name is Alix, although my last name is Freemar, not Treebark. That's a little odd about Isabella's name hang-up. Does she do that to everyone?" I couldn't help but wonder about Dr. Bollocks and the Muttsnuts newlyweds.

He smiled. It was a nice smile with nice teeth. Perfect teeth, in fact. I waited for a wave of emotion to roll over me at the sight of his perfect smile—love, lust, happiness, excitement, pleasure—any emotion would do. I waited while he speculated as to the cause of Isabella's little memory problem, then I waited some more while he told me about the joys and sorrows of being a dentist (it explained his perfect teeth).

I was still waiting for Karl to generate some sort of emotion within me, something—*anything*—when Alex and Isabella returned. The hair on the back of my neck stood on end when I glanced over at them; Isabella was laughing up at Alex, her arm tucked around his, her head of silver-blond hair contrasting beautifully against the stark black of his suit. He was smiling back at her in a way that made me want to rip his traitorous lips right off his face and do a spot of Riverdancing on them. In clogs.

The evening went downhill after that. My eyelashes underwent a hideous mutation into giant clumps of sticky black tar that clung with a fervor I hadn't expected from eyelashes to the skin just above my eyes. It made blinking a dangerous experience.

"Erm . . . you've got something there," Alex said softly to me, gesturing toward my face. We were all sitting at Isabella's glass dining room table, enjoying her scampi fettuccine, my wine, and fresh basil-garlic rolls that were so good they made me want to weep with joy. Isabella's table was all in white and silver, matching her ensemble perfectly. I couldn't help but wonder if she had chargers, candles, napkins, and accoutrements to match all of her evening wear.

I stopped counting the candles on the table and looked to my right, where Alex was sitting at the foot of the table. "I've got lots, buster, but don't be thinking you're going to be trying it on for size, because you're not. At least, not now. Well, maybe a little later, but I haven't made up my mind yet. Not completely."

His face was a study in puzzlement, with surprise, confusion, and finally a tiny flicker of annoyance all taking a turn in the spotlight. He narrowed his eyes and lowered his voice as he stared pointedly at my left cheek. "You have a black smut on your cheek."

I crossed my eyes trying to look down at my cheek, but couldn't see anything. "Oh. Thank you. Just forget I mentioned trying anything on for size."

I reached up to see if I could feel it and encountered a blob. It was a dung-beetle sized ball of mascara with several eyelashes stabbed through it. "Great," I muttered, the blob of mascara on my fingers, "now my eyes are going to be bald."

"You're very outspoken," Alex said sotto voce in a tone that indicated it was not a compliment. "Are all Americans like you?"

I shrugged and looked covertly around the table but didn't see anywhere I could dispose of the blob. I'd be damned if I ruined one of Isabella's nice linen napkins with it, but I really couldn't sit with it in my hand all night. "It depends. I come from a family of outspoken women. We believe in calling a spade a spade. Why, does that bother you? Don't tell me you are one of those guys who gets into playing head games with people—the kind who is into power trips?" I peered at him suspiciously. "You're not one of those weirdoes who goes in for bondage and domination, are you? Cause if you are, I'll tell you right here and now, there's no way in hell I'll put a dog collar on."

His eyes widened and he started to shake his head.

"And don't expect me to wear stiletto heels and call myself Mistress Cruella, either, because this girl doesn't go in for that."

"I never said—"

I pointed my blobby finger and shook the black ball of mascara at him, half hoping it would go flying off on its own accord. It didn't, of course. They should glue the tiles on the space shuttle with old mascara. "And if you're into being dressed up in diapers and being spanked, well, just don't come running to me to get your jollies! Well, OK, maybe the spanking, but no diapers! I draw the line at diapers!"

A dull color tinted his cheeks a faint pink. I watched, fascinated, feeling a bit wicked and very powerful with this skill at making him blush before I realized that no one else was speaking. I looked over to Isabella and found her and Karl looking at Alex with speculation. I peeked at Alex out of the corner of my eye. He was glaring at me, his fingers twitching like he wanted to get them around my throat.

"Strangling someone is a felony," I murmured at him when Isabella turned back to Karl. "You'd go to jail for the rest of your life."

"It might be worth it," he growled, and looked away.

I was about to poke him when I realized the black blob of mascara and eyelashes was still holding steadfast to my finger. My opportunity to dispose of it came a few moments later. Under the cover of laughter from Isabella and Karl over an amusing anecdote, I wiped it on the side of my plate, hoping it would blend in with the arrugula. It didn't. It clung to the rim of the plate, proudly sporting its growths like a great, hairy black gonad. I stared at it in horror, but I didn't know what else to do with the damned thing. I looked around the table frantically, but there were no tissues or anything else I wanted to ruin with the beastly thing. My palms went all sweaty when I glanced at Isabella—she was speaking with Karl, but I knew the minute she looked over at me, she'd see the horrible malignant growth sitting there on my plate. I swear I could see its feelers waving around in the warm air generated by all of the candles. I watched it carefully, horrified that it might start moving of its own accord.

"Alex?" Karl asked.

"I've never seen it before in my life!" I shrieked, startled. Three pairs of eyes turned to look at me. I laid my fork across the hideous thing, but the eyelashes it held hostage poked through the tines.

Isabella looked a bit taken aback, but Karl looked downright worried. I didn't look at Alex. I had a feeling he had seen me with the thing, and would think the worst of me.

"Sorry. Daydreaming. You wanted to know something, Karl?"

He glanced over to Alex. "Actually, I was asking Alex what he thought of the Wolves and Dons game."

"Oh, hockey." I glanced down at my plate. Had the forked moved a little bit?

"Football, not hockey, Alix," Karl said with a smile.

With the attention off me, I picked up my fork and tried to think of an excuse to take my plate with me to the bathroom so I could dispose of The Entity.

"It's a bit confusing with so many Alexes here," Karl laughed, raising his eyebrows at Alex. I looked at him as well, expecting to see him respond to the comment, but he was staring at the atrocity on my plate with the same look of horrified fascination one wears when passing a particularly bloody accident.

"Is something the matter, Alexander?"

I whipped my head around so fast that I almost knocked a candle over with my hair. Isabella was leaning slightly to the side to peer through the forest of flames to see what it was that had generated such a look of horror on Alex's face.

"It's nothing, Isabella," he replied, pulling out a handkerchief from an inner pocket.

While the talk turned to local sights that I shouldn't miss in my quest to visit all of the tourist attractions within the greater London area, Alex's hand disappeared under the table. I felt it nudge my knee. I groped for it, sent him a look of ardent gratitude that promised him the moon and the sun if he only cared to take me up on it, and with cautious glances all around the table, wrestled the thing off my plate.

I had only to dispose of the handkerchief, since I was fairly certain Alex wouldn't want it back. I noticed a painting across the room, and leaned forward to wave toward it. "Is that a Monet print, Isabella?"

A slight frown wrinkled her brow as she turned to look. "Monet? No, I did that myself. It's a watercolor of wildflowers in Scotland."

I stuffed the handkerchief down the front of my dress while everyone was looking at the picture, then flipped my hair back over my shoulder and would have given a sigh of relief had Alex not chosen that moment to go insane. He threw his napkin over my head and start beating me.

"What the hell do you think you're doing!" I yelled, and struck out with my fists. I connected with someone a couple of times, presumably Alex since the response was a deep, masculine grunt of pain.

As the napkin was pulled off my head, I jumped from my chair and grabbed Alex by his lapels, shaking him while yelling that he was an idiot. He held me off with one hand, cradling his right eye with the other. As soon as I let go of him he sank back into his chair, groping blindly for his napkin. I picked it up off the floor and threw it at his head.

"You rat! How dare you treat me like that? Well, I've got witnesses to your assault, and don't think I won't use them!"

I spun around on my heel and would have made a highly dramatic exit except Mr. Mad as a Hatter ruined it.

"Your hair was on fire," he said in a distracted tone. I looked back. Isabella was standing at his right side, pressing a wet napkin to his eye and making tutting noise at him. Karl was on his other side, offering to see if the couple of blows I had landed had damaged his teeth. I reached to the back of my head to swing my hair around and show him it was just fine, but what my hand pulled forward was an alien thing made up of ragged, charred, *stinking* strands of hair. Most of it wasn't even there to be pulled forward.

"My hair," I whimpered. I may not be vain about many things, but I do have nice waist-length hair. It's not an exciting color, but it's thick and it has a lot of body, or it did, before the raging inferno took most of it.

"You're going to have a black eye," Isabella told Alex, and pressed his hand over his eye to hold the compress in place while she came to examine my hair. She tsked over it. "You'll have to have it cut. There's not much of it left past chin-level."

"I never cut my hair. It hasn't been cut in anything but a trim in over five years," I said, my lower lip definitely quivering. I felt like bawling, I honestly did. There is just so much humiliation a girl can take before she starts wailing.

"I know a very good stylist," she said, patting my arm in encouragement. "I'll ring him up tomorrow and tell him it's an emergency."

I stared at the motley strand of hair that was the sole survivor below my ear on the right side of my head. "Isabella?"

"Yes?"

"Thank you for dinner. I've had a lovely time, if you can forget the embarrassment of walking around with my dress tucked up into the waistband of my pantyhose, the huge black blob of mascara that has probably melted through Alex's hankie and is even now coating my breasts, and of course, setting fire to my head. I would like to go home now."

"Of course you would," she said soothingly. "I'm sure Karl would be happy to walk you downstairs."

"Certainly," he said, standing up from where he was trying unsuccessfully to get Alex to open his mouth.

"It's not necessary," Alex said with a little grunt as he stood and set the wet napkin down next to his plate. "I think I'll go as well. I'll make sure Alix gets to her flat safely." He glared at me out of an eye that was starting to swell. I winced. Isabella was right—he was going to have one hell of a mouse.

"I can walk down a flight of stairs by myself," I said with dignity, and turned toward the door. Alex grabbed my arm, muttering something about Isabella needing to increase her insurance on the house while I was staying.

He said nothing else as we went down the flight of stairs, and stood equally silent while I fumbled to unlock my flat.

"I'm sorry about hitting you," I said as I opened the door. "I thought you had lost your senses or something."

"I'm not accustomed to losing my sense at a dinner party," he said, gingerly feeling first his eye, then the area below his cheekbone. He looked pitiful—wounded, and needful, and sexy as hell. I told myself that since I had caused the problem, it was my responsibility to fix it, so I grabbed his hand and dragged him inside the flat before closing the door.

"Sit," I told him, and nodded toward the chaise as I started for the tiny kitchen. "No, wait, lie down. It'll help take the swelling down."

He stood in the middle of the room for a minute, then gave a little sigh of resignation and sat down on the wicker chaise. It creaked ominously as he lay back on it, careful to keep his shoes off the cushions. I poked around in the tiny freezer compartment of the refrigerator, and ousted a pint of ice cream.

"I'll be there in a sec, I just have to look for something to put this in . . . oh, well, I guess a plastic bag is as good as anything else." I scooped the contents into the bag with a muttered, "waste of perfectly good toffee crunch," sealed the bag, and went over to see how the wounded warrior was doing.

He was lying down with his eyes closed. I plopped the makeshift ice pack onto his injury. He jumped, swore, and tried to sit up.

"Stop being such a baby," I said, holding him down, and replaced the bag of ice cream on his eye. I sat down on the edge of the chaise and pried his hand away from his face and gently felt his cheek. It was a bit swollen, and looked like it was going to bruise.

"You look horrible," I said, shifting the bag of ice cream to see if it was helping to reduce the swelling at all. The flesh beneath his eye had taken on a dark, mottled red color that indicated it was going to be very colorful in a day or so.

"You don't look much better," he replied, cracking his good eye open to examine my head. I reached back for my hair, grimaced at the few strands long enough to be pulled forward, and went to find the scissors. Popeye watched me with a faint frown showing on half of his forehead.

"You're going to cut your own hair?" he eventually asked.

"Nope," I said, returning to the chaise and sitting down on the floor next to him. "You're going to do it for me."

He sat up, lowering the bag of ice cream from his face, a faint shimmer of panic in his eyes. "I don't think so."

I pushed the scissors into his hand and turned my back to him. "Don't look so scared, I just want you to even it up. I can't stand having a few straggly long ends and the rest charred stumps. Just cut it off so it's all one length."

"But—"

"I'd do it for you," I said slowly, watching him over my shoulder. He gave me a long, unreadable look, then nodded for me to turn my head. His hands were tentative at first, fingers almost unwilling to touch me, but he snipped diligently away with only minor murmurs of distress.

"Thanks," I said when he was finished, turning halfway around to take the scissors from him. I ruffled my hand through my hair and encountered his fingers as he pulled a cut strand of hair from where it was dangling from my shoulder. Heat flashed through my fingers as if someone had splashed me with a bucket of hot water, tiny little flames licking their way down from where my hand was touching his, up and over my chest like a flush, pooling lower, deep within me.

"Wow," I breathed, mesmerized as his pupils dilated slightly, his eyes turning almost black. His fingers rubbed against mine, slowly stroking them from knuckle to fingertip. "All that from just fingers."

He didn't say anything, but a shuttered look fell over his eyes. He glanced toward the door. "I should be leaving."

"No, what you should be doing is lying back and letting this ice cream take the swelling down on your eye." *He's not for me, he's not for me*, the little voice chanted in my head. I told the voice to get stuffed, and reached down to push him back onto the cushions. He resisted for a minute, his eyes wary, then he allowed his body to sag backwards.

"Here, put this back on your eye. It won't stay cold for long, but it's all I have." I handed him the ice cream, and gathered up the scissors and my comb.

Neither one of us said anything for a few minutes, other than me asking if he'd like coffee, and him accepting. I pulled out my precious container of pre-ground Starbucks, plugged the kettle in, and assembled a couple of mugs, milk, and my secret stash of chocolate orange truffles on a tray.

"How do you like England?" He finally broke the silence.

"I love it," I answered, wishing I had an exotic pastry or two to compensate for Alex having missed what I'm sure was a fabulous dessert at Isabella's. "I haven't been anywhere but London, but I plan on doing a few touristy day trips in a bit."

"To where?"

I poured water into the French press and added it to the tray. "Oh, here and there. Windsor Castle, Bath, Cambridge, the Lake District—those sorts of places."

"Ah. The Lake District is nice. Isabella said you're writing a book?"

I hauled the tray out and set it on the end table, then dragged both around from behind Alex's head to a position alongside the chaise where he could easily reach them. As I pulled the table into place, a magazine slipped off the edge, exposing the box of condoms Cait had given me. I had a brief moment of sheer panic as a picture rose in my mind of me trying to explain away grape and banana flavored-condoms, but I quickly snatched them off the table and slipped them beneath the cushions under his head. "No, don't sit up yet, keep the bag on your eye. I was just plumping up the pillow. White or black?"

"White, please."

I poured cream in a cup, then pushed down on the coffee press. "I am writing a book, a romance. I don't suppose you read them?"

His eye opened briefly, then closed again. "No. I don't read for pleasure."

I leaned over him and lifted the bag of ice cream to cover his eye better. He must have felt the movement because he suddenly opened his eyes.

And got a good look down my dress to where my boobs glittered in all of their golden glory.

"Sorry," he said in an embarrassed voice, slamming his eyes closed. He grimaced at the resulting pain when his swollen eye protested the cavalier action, and allowed me to replace the bag over it.

"It's OK, they're just boobs. I'm sure you've seen them before."

His good eye cracked open. I smiled and straightened up. "Well, maybe not these particular ones, but others of their ilk. Why don't you read for pleasure? I thought you being a Scotland Yard detective and all, you'd be an avid mystery reader."

His eyelid lazily drifted down again. I went out to the cubbyhole kitchen to dampen a clean dishcloth.

"I'm in the Obscene Publications and Internet Unit."

I stopped wringing out the cloth and cast a worried glance over to the bookcase beside the door, squinting at it and wondering if he could make out the title of the Victorian erotica book I had bought at a used bookstore a couple of days before. For research, of course. Purely for research, nothing more.

Alex's voice continued on in a weary monotone. "I have nothing to do with murders or solving crimes unless they are related to Internet pornography, and I don't read novels because I don't have the time to."

"Internet pornography?" I asked coming back over to the chaise.

"Yes," he said without opening his eye. I folded the cloth and laid it on his cheek, accepting his murmured thanks without comment.

"You mean like those online sex sites and stuff? The ones with the women bumping and grinding to web cams?"

"Some. Our department focuses mainly on the pedophile sites."

"Oh." I nudged his hip with my knee. He scooted over a bit, his good eye open to watch me sit down beside him. "That's a good job to have. I mean—it's not good that it exists, but it's good that you're doing it. I bet you take a lot of satisfaction in getting those slime balls sent to jail."

He pinned me with an emerald-eye gaze. "It's very satisfying, yes."

I couldn't help myself. I reached out to smooth the faint lines between his eyebrows. His eye warily watched my hand withdraw, almost as if he expected a blow. I folded my hands together in my lap to keep from touching him. "Even my husband Matt, who was the biggest workaholic in the continental United States, took time out occasionally to play, although his idea of having fun was sweating on a racquet-ball court. What do you do for fun if you don't read?"

"Your husband?"

I nodded, tightening my grip on my hands. That look of puzzlement he was wearing was just so damn adorable!

"Isabella said you were interested in meeting available men. I assumed that's why you wanted to meet Karl—"

"Ex-husband," I interrupted him, smiling at my own foolish thoughts. His interest in my marital state didn't mean anything—no matter what he claimed, he *was* a detective, and everybody knows detectives detect when they come across something that doesn't add up. "So what do you do?"

"For fun?"

"Yep."

He closed his eye again. "I don't indulge in frivolous pastimes."

"Well, that lets out running around the neighborhood clad in nothing but a pair of frilly knickers and a fright wig, but there must be something you do for entertainment."

"No."

I resisted the urge to peel his eyelid back; his jaw was set so firmly it's a wonder he got that one word out.

"What do you do when you're at home? What do you watch on TV?"

"I don't have one."

"And you don't read for pleasure? *Anything?*"

"No."

"Oh. How about music? You must like some sort of music."

The eye opened. "I don't listen to music, I don't have any hobbies, and I don't care to be interrogated about this any further."

Well, that put me in my place.

"Sorry," I said, and rose to clean up all of the bits of my hair he had cut off earlier. *Prickly, prickly, prickly—that was his early warning system coming into affect*, my inner voice warned. *Don't think about getting too close to this one—*

just when you think he's eating out of your hand, he'll snap your arm off.

"What did you think of Karl?"

I frowned at the wicker wastebasket as I tossed my hair into it, then turned back to assess his expression. His voice had a slightly apologetic tone to it, and was a good deal warmer than the previous sentence he'd spoken. "Why do you ask?"

"You were there to meet him, weren't you? Isabella said she'd asked you there for that purpose. I merely wondered what you thought."

I took a few cautious steps toward Alex. Why on earth had he taken his yummy Rickman voice and turned it into a sterile, emotionless parody? "Karl? I think he's not in the remotest sense of the word perfect."

His good eye opened and watched me as I again seated myself carefully next to him, and reached out to flip the dishcloth over to the cool side. "That's all? He's not perfect?"

I nodded, letting my fingers gently graze the bruised area, then replacing the cloth, lightly tracing a path down his jaw line. His cheeks were a little bristly, but the rough texture of his beard stubble wasn't unpleasant. In fact, it made me a bit goose-bumpily. "You're not perfect either, in case you were wondering."

"I wasn't," he said softly as I followed the line of his jaw to his chin. More bristles, but better than that, his lips were directly above. Alex shifted slightly and pulled the bag of ice cream off his eye, dropping it onto his chest. I took the half-closed lids and darkening eyes to indicate interest, so I brushed my fingers over his lips. They were warm, so very warm, and parted just slightly so I could feel his breath steam softly on my fingertips. I traced the seductive curve of his bottom lip, outlined the soft lines of his upper lip, and with my stomach tensing and my breath caught in my throat, let my finger sweep across the long length of his sensitive mouth.

"You aren't what?" I asked, forgetting what it was we were talking about.

Halfway across his lips he opened his mouth slightly, allowing my finger to slip inside. My stomach twisted into a tight little coil as he sucked my finger in deeper, his tongue a little rough, but hot and wet and wonderful, and doing things I never thought could start little fires all over my body, but damned if it wasn't! The coil inside me tightened even further when he gently bit the pad of my finger, making me shiver with desire, building a pressure inside me that cried out to be satisfied. His lovely green eyes went completely black as I leaned forward, intent on replacing my finger with my mouth. His right hand swept me forward suddenly, pulling me down across his chest, our lips a hairbreadth apart.

"Alix," he said in that sexy, almost hoarse voice that pushed the pressure inside me even